DEBBIE MACOMBER

1225

CHRISTMAS TREE LANE

HARLEQUIN®
entertain, enrich, inspire™

ISBN-13: 978-0-7783-1390-8

1225 CHRISTMAS TREE LANE

Copyright © 2012 by Harlequin Books S.A.

The publisher acknowledges the copyright holder
of the individual works as follows:

1225 CHRISTMAS TREE LANE
Copyright © 2011 by Debbie Macomber

LET IT SNOW
Copyright © 1986 by Debbie Macomber

Recycling programs
for this product may
not exist in your area.

For questions and comments about the quality of this book, please contact us
at CustomerService@Harlequin.com.

www.Harlequin.com

Printed in U.S.A.

Praise for Debbie Macomber's Christmas stories

[*A Cedar Cove Christmas*] is a "sweet humorous romance…
a satisfying, almost tongue-in-cheek retelling
of the Christmas story."
—*Library Journal*

"Macomber once again demonstrates her impressive skills
with characterization and her flair for humor."
—*RT Book Reviews* on *When Christmas Comes*

"*Call Me Mrs. Miracle* is an entertaining holiday story
that will surely touch the heart… Best of all, readers
will rediscover the magic of Christmas."
—*Bookreporter.com*

"No one does Christmas stories better than
Debbie Macomber, and *Call Me Mrs. Miracle* proves that
Macomber should be given the title Mrs. Christmas!"
—*Sharon'sGardenofBookReviews.blogspot.com*

[*When Christmas Comes*] "is a sweetly satisfying,
gently humorous story that celebrates the joy
and love of the holiday season."
—*Booklist*

"Once again author Debbie Macomber is back to offer
readers a delightful seasonal story of friendship and love.
Macomber is a master storyteller and this small volume is
a testament to her lively skills… A warm and loving novel
that is destined to quickly become a Christmas favorite."
—*Times Record News,* Wichita Falls, Texas,
on *The Christmas Basket*

"A fast, frothy fantasy for those looking to
add some romance to their holidays."
—*Publishers Weekly* on *The Snow Bride*

"*Where Angels Go*…should definitely get anyone
in the mood for holiday cheer and warmth."
—*FreshFiction.com*

"It's just not Christmas without a Debbie Macomber story."
—*Armchair Interviews*

October 2012

Dear Friends,

Well, this is it. The very last installment of the Cedar Cove series, originally published as a hardcover in October of 2011. We've also included a bonus title, the novella *Let It Snow*, which was first published in the mid 1980s. I'm sure you'll enjoy both stories.

Did you know that it was you, my readers, who inspired the idea for the long-standing Cedar Cove series? I'd written other groups of connected books, but you told me you didn't want to leave the towns of Promise (the Heart of Texas series) or Hard Luck (Midnight Sons) or Buffalo Valley (the Dakota books). So...I created Cedar Cove. Not once did I dream this series would be the success it has become. One of these books gave me my first #1 *New York Times* position—and a number of the subsequent stories also hit number one!

But wait...there's more. This isn't the end, after all. I recently learned that the Hallmark Channel is interested in creating a television version of Cedar Cove. The pilot will air in January 2013 and, if all goes well, the series will launch in March. Is that exciting or what?

Actually it's fitting that the Cedar Cove series of books should end with a Christmas story. The holidays have always been my favorite time of the year. Just like my family and yours, the families of Cedar Cove will be gathering, remembering Christmases past and looking toward the future. You'll get one last glimpse of all your friends here in town....

Again, thank you for the support you've given these books. I hope the characters will continue to resonate for you as they come to life on the television screen.

Merry Christmas!

Debbie Macomber

P.S. You can reach me at www.debbiemacomber.com or at P.O. Box 1458, Port Orchard, WA 98366.

Also by Debbie Macomber

CONTENTS

1225 CHRISTMAS TREE LANE

To
Paula Eykelhof
my wonderful editor
for more than 25 years

Some of the Residents of Cedar Cove, Washington

Olivia Lockhart Griffin: Family Court judge in Cedar Cove. Mother of **Justine** and **James.** Married to **Jack Griffin,** editor of the *Cedar Cove Chronicle*. They live at 16 Lighthouse Road. **Eric** and **Shelly** are Jack's son and daughter-in-law, who live out of state.

Charlotte Jefferson Rhodes: Mother of **Olivia** and of **Will Jefferson.** Now married to widower **Ben Rhodes.** Ben and Charlotte have recently moved to an assisted-living facility in Cedar Cove.

Justine (Lockhart) Gunderson: Daughter of Olivia. Mother of **Leif** and **Livvy.** Married to **Seth Gunderson.** The Gundersons owned The Lighthouse restaurant, which was destroyed by fire. Justine then opened The Victorian Tea Room. The Gundersons live at 6 Rainier Drive.

James Lockhart: Olivia's son and Justine's younger brother. Lives in San Diego with his family.

Will Jefferson: Olivia's brother, Charlotte's son. Formerly of Atlanta. Divorced, retired and back in Cedar Cove, where he has taken over the local gallery and has just moved into his mother's former home on Eagle Crest Avenue.

Grace Sherman Harding: Olivia's best friend. Librarian. Widow of **Dan Sherman.** Mother of **Maryellen Bowman** and **Kelly Jordan.** Married to **Cliff Harding,** a retired engineer who is now a horse breeder living in Olalla, near Cedar Cove. Grace's previous address is 204 Rosewood Lane (now a rental property).

Cecilia Randall: Married to **Ian,** who is in the navy. The family was most recently stationed in San Diego but is returning to Cedar Cove. They have two children, **Aaron** and **Mia.**

Zachary Cox: Accountant, married to **Rosie.** Father of **Allison** and **Eddie Cox.** The family lives at 311 Pelican Court. Allison is attending university in Seattle, while her boyfriend, **Anson Butler,** has joined the military.

Rachel Peyton (formerly Pendergast): Previously worked at the Get Nailed salon. Married to widower **Bruce Peyton,** who has a daughter, **Jolene.** The Peytons live at 1105 Yakima Street.

Bob and **Peggy Beldon:** Retired. They own the Thyme and Tide B & B at 44 Cranberry Point.

Roy McAfee: Private investigator, retired from the Seattle police force. Three adult children, **Mack, Linnette** and **Gloria Ashton.** Married to **Corrie.** They live at 50 Harbor Street.

Linnette McAfee: Daughter of Roy and Corrie. Lived in Cedar Cove and worked as a physician's assistant in the new medical clinic. Now living in North Dakota.

Mack McAfee: A fireman and paramedic who moved to Cedar Cove and subsequently married **Mary Jo Wyse.** They have a daughter, **Noelle,** and live at 1022 Evergreen Place.

Gloria Ashton: Sheriff's deputy in Cedar Cove. Natural child of Roy and Corrie McAfee. Pregnant by **Dr. Chad Timmons,** who previously worked at the Cedar Cove medical clinic. He and Gloria had an on-again, off-again relationship but are now a couple.

Troy Davis: Cedar Cove sheriff. Widower. Father of **Megan.** Now married to **Faith Beckwith,** his high school girlfriend, who was also widowed. They live at 92 Pacific Boulevard.

Bobby Polgar and Teri Miller Polgar: He is an international chess champion; she was a hair stylist at Get Nailed. They have triplet infant sons. Their home is at 74 Seaside Avenue.

Christie Levitt: Sister of Teri Polgar, living in Cedar Cove. Now married to **James Wilbur,** Bobby Polgar's friend and driver.

Pastor Dave Flemming: Local Methodist minister. Married to **Emily.** They live at 8 Sandpiper Way and have two sons, **Matthew** and **Mark.**

Shirley Bliss: Widow and fabric artist, mother of Tannith **(Tanni)** Bliss. Recently married to artist **Larry Knight.**

Miranda Sullivan: Friend of Shirley's. Also a widow. Now working as an assistant to Will Jefferson in his gallery.

Linc Wyse: Brother of **Mary Jo (Wyse) McAfee.** Formerly of Seattle. Opened a car-repair business in Cedar Cove. Married to **Lori** (who was formerly Lori Bellamy and is from a wealthy area family).

Beth Morehouse: Dog trainer and Christmas tree farm owner. Moved to Cedar Cove three years ago. Divorced from **Kent Morehouse** and mother of two college-age daughters, **Bailey** and **Sophie.** Beth lives at 1225 Christmas Tree Lane.

Ted Reynolds: Cedar Cove veterinarian.

One

"Mom!"

The front door slammed and Beth Morehouse hurried out of the kitchen. Three days before Christmas, and her daughters were home from college—at last! Her foreman, Jeff, had been kind enough to pick them up at the airport while Beth dealt with last-minute chores. She'd been looking forward to seeing them for weeks. Throwing her arms wide, she ran toward Bailey and Sophie. "Merry Christmas, girls."

Squealing with delight, they dropped their bags and rushed into her embrace.

"I can't believe it's snowing. It's so beautiful," Bailey said, holding Beth in a tight hug. At twenty-one, she was the oldest by fourteen months. She resembled her father in so many ways. She was tall like Kent and had his dark brown hair, which she'd tucked under a knitted cap. Her eyes shone with a quiet joy. She was the thoughtful one and that, too, reminded Beth of her ex-husband. Three years after the divorce, she still missed him, although pride would never allow her to admit that. Even her budding relationship with Ted Reynolds, the local veterinarian, paled when she thought about her life with Kent and their history together.

"My turn." Displacing Bailey, Sophie snuggled into Beth's embrace. "The house looks fabulous, Mom. Really Christmassy." This child was more like Beth. A few inches shorter than her sister, Sophie had curly auburn hair and eyes so blue they seemed to reflect a summer sky. Releasing Beth, Sophie added, "And it smells wonderful."

Beth had done her best to make the house as festive and bright as possible for her daughters. She'd spent long hours draping fresh evergreen boughs on the staircase leading to the second-floor bedrooms. Two of the three Christmas trees were loaded with ornaments. The main tree in the family room was still bare, awaiting their arrival so they could decorate it together, which was a family tradition.

A trio of four-foot-tall snowmen stood guard in the hallway near the family room where the Nativity scene was displayed on the fireplace mantel. Decorating had helped take Beth's mind off the fact that her ex-husband would be joining them for Christmas. This would be the first time she'd seen him in three years. Oh, they'd spoken often enough, but every conversation had revolved around their daughters. Nothing else. No questions asked. No comments of a personal nature. Just the girls and only the girls. It'd been strictly business. Until now.

Until Christmas.

They both loved the holidays. It was Kent who'd first suggested they have several Christmas trees. Always fresh ones, which was one reason Beth had been attracted to the Christmas tree farm when she started her new life.

"I've got lunch ready," Beth said, trying to turn her attention away from her ex-husband. He still lived in California, as did the girls. He'd stayed in their hometown of Sacramento, while Bailey and Sophie both attended university in San Diego. According to their daughters, Kent had asked to come for Christmas. She'd known for almost two weeks that he'd made reservations at the Thyme and Tide B and B in Cedar Cove. The news that he'd be in town had initially come as a shock to Beth. He hadn't discussed it with her at all. Instead, he'd had their daughters do his talking for him. That made everything more awkward, because it wasn't as if she could refuse, not with Bailey and Sophie so excited about spending Christmas together as a family. But Kent's plans had left her with a host of unanswered questions. Was this his way of telling Beth he missed her? Was he looking for a reconciliation? Was she? The questions swarmed in her head, but the answers wouldn't be clear until he arrived. At least she'd be better able to judge his reasons. His intentions. And her own...

"Just like it used to be," Bailey finished. Beth had missed whatever she'd said before that, although it wasn't hard to guess.

Just like it used to be. These were magic words, but Beth had recognized long ago that the clock only moved forward. Yet the girls' eagerness, Kent's apparent insistence and her nostalgia for what they'd once shared swept aside her customary reserve.

"Mom?" Bailey said when she didn't respond. "We're talking.... Where are you?"

Beth gave a quick shake of her head. "Woolgathering. Sorry. I haven't had much sleep lately." Exhausted as she was, managing the tree farm and getting ready for Christmas with her daughters—and Kent—she'd hardly slept. She couldn't. Every time she closed her eyes, Kent was there. Kent with his boyish smile and his eyes twinkling with mischief and fun. They'd been happy once and somehow they'd lost that and so much more. Beth had never been able to put her finger on what exactly had gone wrong; she only knew that it had. In the end they'd lived separate lives, going their own ways. Their daughters had kept them together— and then they were off at college, and suddenly it was just Kent and Beth. That was when they discovered they no longer had anything in common.

"You're not sleeping?" Bailey's eyes widened with concern.

Sophie elbowed her sister. "Bailey, think about it. This is the busiest time of year for a Christmas tree farm. Then there's all this decorating. And, if we're really lucky—"

"Mom made date candy?" Bailey cut in.

"And caramel corn?" Sophie asked hopefully, hands folded in prayer.

"Yes to you both. It wouldn't be Christmas without our special treats."

"You're the best mom in the world."

Beth smiled. She'd had less than three hours' sleep, thanks to all the Christmas preparations, her dogs and… her incessant memories of Kent. Traffic at the tree farm had thinned out now that Christmas was only three days away. But families were still stopping by and there was quite a bit to do, including cleanup. Her ten-man crew was down to four and they'd coped just fine without either her or Jeff this morning. While he drove out to the airport, she'd been getting ready for her daughters' arrival. However, as soon as lunch was over, she needed to head back outside.

Beth and the girls had booked a skiing trip between Christmas and New Year's, and after the hectic schedule of the past two months, she was counting on a few relaxing days with her daughters. Their reservations were made and she was eager to go. Ted Reynolds, good friend that he was, had offered to take care of her animals, which reminded her of the one hitch in her perfectly planned holiday escape.

"Before we sit down to eat, I need to tell you we have special guests this Christmas."

"You mean Dad, right?" Bailey led the way into the other room, where there was more greenery and a beautifully arranged table with three place settings.

"Well, yes, your father. But he's not the only one...."

"Mom." Bailey tensed as she spoke. "Don't tell me you have a boyfriend. It's that vet, isn't it?"

"Ten guests, actually," she said, ignoring the comment about Ted, "and they aren't all boys."

"Puppies?" Sophie guessed.

"Puppies," Beth confirmed, not surprised that her daughter had figured it out. "Ten of them."

"Ten?" Sophie cried, aghast.

Without asking, Bailey went straight to the laundry room off the kitchen. "Where did you get ten puppies?" The instant she opened the door, all ten black puppies scampered into the kitchen, scrambling about, skidding across the polished hardwood floor.

"They're adorable." Sharing Beth's love for animals,

both girls were immediately down on the floor, scooping the puppies into their arms. Before long, each held at least two of the Lab-mix puppies, the little creatures intent on licking their faces.

Unable to resist, Beth joined her daughters and gathered the remaining puppies onto her lap. One curled into a tight ball. Another climbed onto her shoulder and began licking her ear. The others squirmed until one wriggled free and chased his tail with determined vigor, completely preoccupied. They really were adorable, which was good because in every other way they were a nuisance.

Sophie held a puppy to her cheek. "Where'd you get them, Mom?"

"They were…a gift," she explained, turning her face away to avoid more wet, slurpy kisses.

"A gift?"

"But why'd you take all ten?" Bailey asked, astonished.

"I didn't have any choice. They showed up on my porch in a basket a week ago." Beth didn't say that discovering these puppies had been the proverbial last straw. They'd literally appeared on her doorstep the same day she'd learned Kent was coming here for Christmas. For an insane moment she'd considered running away, grabbing a plane to Fiji or Bora-Bora. Instead, she'd run over to the Hardings' and ended up spilling her heart out to Grace. Under normal conditions, Beth wasn't one to share her burdens with others. However, this was simply too much—an ex-husband's unexpected visit and the arrival of ten abandoned puppies, all during the busiest season of the year. The Hardings had given her tea and sympathy; Ted had been wonderful, too. Beth was grateful for his willingness to watch her animals but she refused to leave him with these ten additional dogs. So she'd made it her goal to find homes for all of them before Christmas. Which didn't give her a lot of time...

"How could someone just drop off ten puppies?" Bailey asked as she lifted one intrepid little guy off her shoulder and settled him in her lap.

"Who could do that and not be seen?" Sophie added. "I mean, you have people working all over this place."

Beth had certainly asked around. "Jeff saw a woman with a huge basket at my door. He thought he recognized her from his church, but when he asked her, she denied it. Then later, Pete, one of the drivers, claimed he saw a man on my porch with a basket. I talked to five different people and got five different stories. All I know is that I've got to find homes for these puppies before we leave for Whistler." And preferably before Kent arrived, although that was highly unlikely.

"Have you found any yet?" Bailey asked.

"No...but I've put out the word."

"You'll do it, Mom," Sophie said confidently. "I know you will."

"How old are they?" Bailey stroked a soft, floppy ear.

"Ted thinks about two months. Between six and eight weeks, anyway."

"They're irresistible. You won't have trouble finding homes," Sophie said.

Beth wished she had even a fraction of her daughter's faith. In October, she'd found homes for four part-golden-retriever puppies. Coming up with those homes had been hard enough—and now ten more. She hoped the season would help.

She'd offer assistance with training if the new owners wanted it—and she'd push the all-important spay-and-neuter message. Ted had promised to give the owners a break on the price, too.

Working together, Beth and the girls corralled the puppies and got them back inside the laundry room. Then they washed up for lunch. Thankfully the girls' favorites didn't require much effort; the tomato basil soup and toasted cheese sandwiches were on the table within minutes.

"Now I truly feel like we're home," Bailey said, spooning up the thick soup.

Sophie sighed contentedly. "This place is starting to feel more like home all the time."

Beth had moved to Washington State following her divorce. For fifteen years she'd taught business and management classes at an agricultural college outside Sacramento. After she and Kent had split up, Beth felt she needed a change. A big one. An escape. She'd read about this Christmas tree farm for sale while browsing on the internet and had become intrigued. As soon as she'd visited the property and toured the house, she was sold.

Her general knowledge of farm life and crop cultivation had come in handy. She knew just enough about trees not to be intimidated. Besides, Wes Klein, the previous owners' son, had helped the first couple of years. She'd soon picked up everything else she needed to know. She hired the same crew each season and was pleasantly surprised by how smoothly things had gone this year, the first year she was on her own.

In addition to Christmas trees, she sold wreaths and garlands, which were created by three members of her staff who devoted all their time to this endeavor. The Kleins used to have only a handful of orders for holiday wreaths. Beth had turned that into a thriving aspect of the business. Plus, overseas sales of Christmas trees had doubled in the past three years. Beth had always enjoyed the season, but never more than now. She felt she was actively contributing to a lot of families' happiness this Christmas.

The girls cleared the table and put their plates and bowls in the dishwasher.

"I've got to get back outside, but before I go, I need you to tell me what's going on with your father." From the girls' startled expressions Beth realized she should have led into the conversation with a bit more finesse. But subtlety wasn't exactly her strong suit and she was short on time.

"Dad wanted to come for Christmas," Bailey answered, as if that was all the explanation required.

"Did he give you any particular reason?" she asked suspiciously.

Sophie shook her head. "None that he mentioned."

That wasn't too helpful; still, Beth persisted. "But why this year?"

Bailey shrugged. "Don't know. All I can tell you is that he said he missed us and asked if he could join us for Christmas. We couldn't say no. You wouldn't want us to, would you, Mom?"

"Of course not." Beth looked from one daughter to the other. "He didn't say anything more than that? You're sure?"

"Positive." Both girls widened their eyes, expressions innocent as could be.

Convinced there was more to this sudden desire to

be with them—and remembering Grace's suggestion that the girls might be more involved than they were letting on—Beth hesitated. She wanted to probe deeper but really needed to get to work. As it was, she'd lingered with her daughters well into Jeff's lunch hour.

"You'll be okay without me?" Beth asked, abandoning all inquiries for the moment.

"Mom, it isn't like we're six years old!"

"I know, I know, it's just that I hate leaving you so soon after you got here."

"Go," Bailey said, ushering her toward the door. "We'll be fine. We'll unpack our suitcases and put *It's a Wonderful Life* in the DVD player."

"I want to watch it, too," Beth protested. It was their favorite Christmas movie.

"Okay, we'll hold off until tonight. Now go."

Walking out the door, Beth blew them a kiss, the same way she had every time she left for work when they were youngsters.

The second the door closed, Bailey turned to her sister. "Do you think Mom suspects anything?"

"I'm not sure...."

"I told you we needed to get our story straight before we saw her!"

"I didn't think she'd drill us with questions the instant we walked in the door. Just remember, this whole idea was yours," Sophie reminded her.

"But you agreed! Dad's miserable without Mom, and Mom needs Dad whether she's willing to admit it or not."

"Well, she's *not* willing to admit it, not yet," Sophie said. She rinsed out the soup pan and placed it in the dishwasher. "I never really understood why they got divorced," she mused.

"Yeah." Bailey was wiping off the kitchen counter. "It didn't make any sense."

"When they told us I thought they were joking. Some joke, huh?"

"Could there be anyone else involved?" Bailey asked, growing introspective. "Mom mentioned that vet again. Ted something."

"Ted Reynolds. She hasn't dated in ages, but she seems to like him. He could be trouble."

Bailey frowned. "The problem with Mom is that she's living inside an…an emotional cocoon." She nodded, pleased with that description. "She's consumed by this tree farm so she doesn't have to think about Dad or the divorce or anything else."

"Who made you the expert?" Sophie muttered.

Bailey ignored the sarcasm. "I took this really great psychology class, and I recognized what Mom's been doing for the past few years. We've got to shake her up, make her realize the divorce was a terrible mistake."

"It's not just the tree farm, it's those darn puppies," Sophie lamented. "With puppies constantly showing up on Mom's porch, she can focus all her attention on them. She spends a lot of time training her dogs for those canine therapy programs—"

"And being the unofficial rescue facility," Bailey threw in.

Sophie nodded. "And now there's this Ted guy. Getting Mom and Dad together isn't going to be as easy as you think."

"What did you tell Dad?" Bailey asked.

Sophie slouched into a chair and stared at her sister. "Just that it's important to Mom that we all spend Christmas together."

"Did he ask why?"

"Not really. He said he didn't have any fixed plans for Christmas, and if Mom wanted him to come he would."

"What are we going to tell them when they discover we arranged this?"

"What we should've said when they told us they were getting divorced. This is stupid. They should've tried harder."

"They just grew apart, that's all, but if they'd made an effort they could've gotten close again, right?"

"Right."

"Marriage takes work," Bailey said, feeling wise. The research for her recent psych essay on "Family in the New Millennium" had made that very clear to her.

"I just don't want them to be upset with us," Sophie said, worried.

"They can't. It's Christmas. We brought them together…okay, under false pretenses, but they can't be mad because we're only doing what's best for them."

"Amen. Sing it, sister."

"We'll sing it in two-part harmony."

"Dad gets here when?"

"Tomorrow afternoon."

"Perfect." Sophie held up two crossed fingers. "I believe. I believe."

"So do I," Bailey echoed. This was going to be the most wonderful Christmas of their lives and it didn't have a single thing to do with the wrapped packages under the tree. It was because of the gift they intended to give their parents.

And each other.

* * *

The snow had stopped falling, and the grounds were so pristine and lovely, they could've been on a book cover. Or a Christmas card. The evergreens were daubed with snow, giving them a flocked look that was more beautiful than anything Beth could reproduce with the sticky artificial stuff her crew applied to the more elaborately decorated trees in the shop.

"We're back," Bruce Peyton said as he approached Beth. "And this time, we're definitely going home with a tree."

His pregnant wife, Rachel, looked so much better than she had two weeks ago. Beth had learned later that Rachel was hospitalized with food poisoning that same evening. Bruce's teenage daughter, Jolene, was with them today, as she'd been before.

"Are all the best trees taken?" the girl asked, her eyes wide with concern.

She had a point. The trees closer to the house had been thinned out, but there were still a number of excellent spruces and firs in the far lot. "Not to worry," she assured Jolene. "I always save the best for last." She handed the girl a cup of warm cocoa. "If you'd like, I'll have my foreman take you to the back twenty in the ATV and you can see for yourself."

"Really?"

"Really," Beth confirmed. She led them over to Jeff, made introductions and gave him Jolene's request.

The ATVs were built for two, so Jeff took one and Jolene climbed on behind him. Bruce took the second vehicle. Rachel looked at the hard seat, then eyed the dirt road speculatively.

"I think I'll stay here and visit with Beth while you two choose the tree."

"You can't," Jolene said loudly. "You *have* to help pick out the tree. That's the most fun part."

"I'm just not sure I'm up to this."

"Let me take you for a test run," Bruce suggested.

Rachel remained hesitant, then nodded. "Okay, but don't be upset if I decide to stay back."

"I won't," Bruce said.

"I really want you to come with us," Jolene insisted.

"I know, honey. I will next year. I'll come with you and your little sister. Don't forget, it'll be her very first Christmas."

Jolene hugged her quickly. "Okay."

Ten minutes later, Rachel was sitting in the office, drinking a bottle of apple juice as Beth finished her paperwork.

"I doubt they'll be long," Beth told her. "The trees there are gorgeous, especially with this afternoon's snow."

"I hope Bruce and Jolene don't go overboard and choose the biggest tree on the farm."

Beth chuckled. "Jeff knows that people look at a tree and have no idea how large it is until they try to get it in the house. He'll keep them realistic."

"Oh, good. Jolene loves Christmas." Rachel leaned back in her chair. "I consider this our first real Christmas as a family. We were married last year but I was so busy cleaning and moving that it didn't feel very Christmassy."

"There seem to be a lot of firsts for your family," Beth said gently.

"I agree. It hasn't been a smooth transition for us, but everything's come together in the past couple of weeks."

"I'm glad," Beth said. She wasn't entirely sure what Rachel meant. Busy though she'd been, when the Peytons originally came for their tree, Beth couldn't help noticing the tension between Rachel and Jolene. The change in attitude, particularly on Jolene's part, was encouraging.

Twenty minutes later, the two ATVs roared into the yard. As soon as the engine was shut off, Jolene leaped off the back of her father's vehicle and raced toward Rachel.

"We found the most beautiful tree," she said excitedly. "It's just *perfect*."

"Where is it?" Rachel asked, laughing at Jolene's unabashed enthusiasm.

"You should've seen her," Bruce said, joining them. "Jolene was like a rabbit, hopping from one tree to the next."

"Dad, you're embarrassing me," the girl protested, but not too vigorously. In fact, it looked as if a smile was permanently affixed to her face.

"Exactly where is this wonderful, perfect Christmas tree?" Rachel asked again.

"Jeff's going back in the pickup for it now," Bruce explained. He reached into his pocket for his wallet. "While he's doing that, I'll pay for the tree and get out the rope so we can tie it to the top of the car."

"When we take it home, we're all going to decorate it together," Jolene said happily.

"My girls and I do that," Beth told her. "I always decorate several trees, but I leave one undecorated so the four…three of us can do it together once they're home from college."

Jolene looked at her father and Rachel. "Will you wait for me when I'm in college, too?"

"You bet," Rachel said, raising one thumb.

That seemed to satisfy the teenager. "It won't be that long, you know."

"No need to rush it," Bruce commented.

The phone rang, and since Jeff was busy, Beth grabbed it. "Cedar Cove Tree Farm," she said. "Beth speaking."

"Oh, Beth, I'm so glad I caught you."

It was her friend, Grace Harding, the head librarian who'd adopted a golden-retriever mix from the previous batch of puppies. She sounded harried.

"What can I do for you, Grace?" Beth asked.

"We need a small tree."

"How small?"

"One that'll fit in a hotel room. It's for a family who just arrived in town. Friends of ours."

"Sure. I can have Jeff cut one for you and deliver it myself."

"Oh, would you? I know this is last-minute, but these are two special friends who once rented our house on Rosewood Lane. That was years ago—but Ian's in the navy and it looks like they're moving back. They have two children. They're only here for a few days, but I can't bear the thought of them spending Christmas in Cedar Cove without a tree."

"I'm on it," Beth said. "Don't worry, I'll see to everything, including lights and decorations. Shall I bring it to your place?"

"Yes, please. I don't know how to thank you."

"You already have," Beth said. Replacing the phone she looked at Bruce. "Now, I don't suppose I could interest you in adopting a puppy?"

"A puppy?" Jolene perked right up. "Could we, Dad? Rachel? *Could* we?"

Bruce shrugged uncomfortably. "I don't think so, sweetheart. With the baby coming and everything…"

"What kind of puppy?" Rachel asked, reaching for Bruce's hand.

"They're a Labrador mix. They're all black and extremely cute. You could have the pick of the litter."

Jolene clasped her hands and turned pleading eyes to her father.

Bruce held Rachel's gaze and after a moment nodded. "But remember, Jolene, you're responsible for training and taking care of the puppy."

"I will, Dad, I promise. I've always wanted a dog! I want a girl and I'm going to name her Poppy."

"Poppy's a good name," Rachel said.

"I can help with the training," Beth offered, leading all three of them to the laundry room. It didn't take Jolene long to choose the puppy she wanted.

One down, nine to go.

Two

Earlier in the month, Grace had been pleasantly surprised to get a phone call from Cecilia and Ian Randall, who were stationed in San Diego. They phoned again once they got into town.

"Would it be possible for Ian and me to stop by and visit?" Cecilia asked.

"Cecilia, of course! How are you? I hoped I'd get a chance to see you and Ian and the kids." Grace had a hundred questions. The young couple had always been close to her heart, and she was thrilled at the prospect of having them back in the area.

"Remember I told you the navy transferred Ian back to Bremerton?" Cecilia said. "He's going to be working in the shipyard instead of on the aircraft carrier. Cedar Cove feels like home to us, so we're really happy about coming back."

"That's wonderful!" The Randalls reminded Grace of when she and her first husband, Dan, had purchased their house almost forty years ago. They'd been young, too, with a child and another on the way. Maryellen was a toddler and Grace had been pregnant with Kelly, and

204 Rosewood Lane had been their first real home. In fact, Grace had lived in that house most of her adult life. She'd raised her children there, buried her husband and learned to deal with life as a widow all on Rosewood Lane. The place held a great deal of sentimental value for her and she hadn't been able to let it go, even after marrying Cliff Harding. So she'd decided to rent it out.

The Randalls had been ideal tenants, but the navy had transferred them all too soon. Over the years, Grace had seen a number of renters come and go. Faith Beckwith had resided there for a while; she'd had a difficult time with break-ins perpetrated by the tenants preceding her. That was long past now and the culprits were behind bars, thanks to Sheriff Davis. The most recent renters had left, and the house was sitting empty.

"I think I mentioned that Ian has leave over Christmas. We flew out here yesterday. We came to see my dad and look for housing." She paused. "Dad lives in a small apartment, so we're staying at the Comfort Inn."

Grace had assumed as much, based on their previous conversation. And other than the Beldons' B and B, the Comfort Inn was the only hotel in downtown Cedar Cove.

"Do you have a car?" she asked.

"A rental."

"Come over today if you can and we'll chat."

"What time?"

"Two," she suggested. "Olivia is planning to stop by around then, and I know she'd love to see you."

"Judge Lockhart...I mean, Judge Griffin?"

"Yes."

"I'd love to see her, too. Ian and I owe her so much."

Indeed they did owe a debt of gratitude to Olivia, as

did many others in the community. Despite her decades as an attorney and then a family court judge, Olivia had never become jaded or cynical. She looked at each case individually. Over the years she'd made some controversial judgments. In Ian and Cecilia's case, she'd denied their divorce. That decision had caused quite a stir in the courtroom and around town. She'd used a technicality, urging the couple to try harder and not to give up on each other so soon.

As it happened, Jack Griffin, the new *Chronicle* editor, had been visiting the court that day and had written an article about her decision, which had greatly embarrassed poor Olivia. Nevertheless, his inflammatory piece had been the start of their relationship. And look where that had led! Grace couldn't hold back a smile.

"We'll be there at two," Cecilia said.

"Be sure to bring the kids," Grace told her. "Cliff is boarding a pony over the holidays. She's very gentle, and the owner said we can give rides to anyone we want."

"Oh! Aaron and Mia will love it. See you at two."

Grace finished addressing the last of her Christmas cards and walked down to the mailbox to send them off, knowing they'd be late this year. She wondered how she'd gotten so far behind.

Cliff helped her prepare by setting out a plate of cookies, although Grace suspected he ate as many as he put on the plate. The cocoa was warming on the stove when a car rolled into the driveway.

Beau, her puppy and guard dog, barked, warning them of impending visitors. "Is it the Randalls or Olivia?" Grace asked.

Cliff peered out the kitchen window. "Looks like

Olivia." He reached for his coat. "I'll be outside with Pixie, saddling her up for the Randall kids."

"Thanks." Grace dried her hands and hurried to the door. Olivia immediately handed her a fruitcake wrapped in aluminum foil.

"From Mom," she announced, stooping to pet Beau. "She baked them while she was living with Jack and me, and wanted to be sure you got one."

Grace wasn't a fruitcake fan—except for Charlotte's, which included green tomato mincemeat and pecans. She put it on the counter next to an evergreen spray in a narrow vase.

"That's so thoughtful. How's Charlotte doing?" Grace was well aware that Charlotte and Ben's recent move into the assisted-living complex hadn't been easy.

"She has good days and bad days." Olivia removed her gloves, stuffing them in her pocket, then slipped off her coat and draped it across the back of a kitchen chair. "On Tuesday, Mom phoned and told me she'd made a big mistake and wanted to return to the house."

"But Will's living there now."

"I didn't remind Mom of that. I figured out what was wrong. It's Christmas and she misses all the things that represent the holidays to her. She associates them with the house."

"Poor Charlotte."

"It *is* hard to make such a huge move at this point in her life."

As Beau settled on the rug by the kitchen door, Grace poured them each a cup of coffee. She carried the mugs to the table, then pulled out a chair. "So what did you do?"

"I found the crèche she'd tucked away in the basement and brought it over to their apartment, along with a small Christmas tree and a few other decorations. Then we sat and chatted over tea for a while. After about an hour, Mom said she'd had a change of heart and the assisted-living complex would suit her just fine."

"That's a relief." Grace knew this had been as difficult for Will and Olivia as it was for their mother and Ben. On the whole, though, the new arrangement seemed to be working out.

"I had a call earlier today," Grace said.

"Oh?" Olivia sipped her coffee.

"Remember I mentioned that Ian and Cecilia Randall were coming to town? In fact, Beth was by just a short while ago to drop off a tree for them."

"So they're here?"

"Yes. Since Ian's been transferred to the Bremerton shipyard, they came to spend Christmas with Cecilia's father, and look for a place to live. They're staying at the Comfort Inn."

"When did they get in?"

"Yesterday. Cecilia phoned and they'll be stopping by—" She paused to glance at the kitchen clock. "Anytime now," she finished.

"Why the Christmas tree?" Olivia asked.

"You know as well as I do that Bobby Merrick isn't going to have a Christmas tree for those kids. I explained the situation to Beth and she brought over the cutest tree you can imagine. It's in a pot and won't take up much space. They should be able to set it in a corner of the hotel room without a problem. She even threw in lights and a few ornaments." Grace appreciated all the effort Beth had put into this spur-of-the-moment idea.

"She owes you big-time after you decided to keep Beau," Olivia said.

On hearing his name, Beau scampered from his place by the door to Grace's feet. When she picked him up and held him in her lap, Beau licked her hand, then settled down to snooze, content to be close to his mistress.

"I'm the one who owes Beth," Grace said, brushing her hand along Beau's soft fur. She'd resisted her affection for Beau as long as she could, but his sweet temperament had eventually won her over.

"I heard Beth has ten more puppies to find homes for now."

"Nine," Grace was pleased to tell her. "Beth is elated. Bruce and Rachel Peyton let Jolene have a puppy for Christmas. She's named her Poppy."

"I hope everything's okay," Olivia said, frowning slightly. "I don't want to see them in my courtroom."

"The situation seems to have resolved itself. When I spoke to Rachel, she said all three of them were in counseling and making great strides." Then Grace added, "I'll be grateful when Rachel returns to the salon. My nails are a mess without her."

"Grace!"

"Well, it's true."

They heard a car door slam in the distance. Beau's head came up and he leaped down from his resting place on Grace's lap. Barking, he ran to the front door, tail wagging furiously.

She followed him and opened the door to Cecilia Randall.

"Merry Christmas," Cecilia said, giving her a bright red poinsettia.

Cecilia didn't seem to have changed since the last

time Grace had seen her. True, her dark hair was shorter now, stylishly cut, but she was as slim and elegant as ever.

Cecilia broke into a big grin. "You look exactly the same as I remember."

"I was just thinking the same thing about you." Grace set the plant on a small table near the entry. As she closed the door she glanced over at the barn. Ian and the two children were already talking to Cliff, who'd led the pony into the yard. Cliff had Pixie saddled and was introducing her to the children. Grace would serve them cookies and hot chocolate later when they came in. "Olivia's here."

"Oh, good! I was hoping for a chance to see her." As Cecilia moved into the kitchen, Grace hung up her scarf and wool coat.

"Hello, hello," Olivia said. Standing, the two women exchanged hugs.

"Sit, please," Grace said. She took out another mug and filled it with coffee.

There was a lot of laughter and smiling as they caught up with one another, but then Cecilia grew serious. She turned toward Olivia. "I was out to see Allison this morning." She bowed her head slightly. "Do... do you ever visit your son's grave?" she asked in a small voice.

"Yes," Olivia admitted softly. "On Jordan's birthday, Justine and I put flowers by his headstone."

"Ian and I went this morning and cleaned off her grave. The kids brought her a poinsettia."

"It's still difficult, isn't it?" Olivia said, reaching across the table to squeeze Cecilia's hand.

Grace leaned over to grab a tissue and passed it to the young woman.

"Do you still cry?" Cecilia asked, unmistakable pain in her voice. The loss of her infant daughter was an anguish that might fade but would never disappear. Grace knew that from her own experience, losing Dan.

"Yes," Olivia said. "We don't forget our children. Ever. We can't. There's been a gaping hole in my heart—in my life—ever since we lost Jordan. He was only thirteen...." She cleared her throat. "I've chosen to fill that hole with love."

"I have, too," Cecilia whispered. "Love for Ian and our other children. Both Aaron and Mia know they had an older sister. On Allison's birthday last year, Aaron wanted to bake her a cake."

"Did you?"

Cecilia nodded. "It never felt right to leave Allison when Ian was transferred. I'm so glad we're moving back."

"We're glad, too," Grace told her. Then because she was afraid they'd all end up weeping, she changed the subject. "So, you're looking for a house...."

"Oh, yes." Cecilia wiped the tears from her eyes and straightened. "Ian and I want to talk to you about the house on Rosewood Lane."

Grace smiled happily. "Well, as I said, my last renters left when their lease expired, and the house is empty. Cliff and I would be delighted to rent it to you."

Olivia checked her watch. "Sorry to rush off, but Justine needs me to babysit this afternoon."

"Of course." Grace stood, too, and hugged her friend. "If I don't see Charlotte, make sure you thank her for the fruitcake."

"Will do."

"See you Christmas Eve at Noelle's birthday party, right after church." She briefly explained, for Cecilia's benefit, who Noelle was and that she'd been born here at the ranch a year earlier.

"Yes, see you then," Olivia confirmed. She put on her coat and gloves and wished Cecilia a merry Christmas. Grace walked her out, returning to find Cecilia by the back door, looking at her children, who were taking turns on the pony. "About the house," Cecilia began, moving back to the kitchen table. "Ian and I—"

A polite knock sounded at the door, but before Grace could reach it, Ian Randall came inside. "Hello, Grace," he said warmly. "Cliff said I should go on in. He's taking the kids into the barn to feed the horses." Giving an obligatory bark, Beau trotted over to him and Ian crouched down to stroke the sleek, soft head.

"They're going to love that," Cecilia said. "Aaron is such an animal person." She might as well have said, *And so is Ian.*

"Would he like a puppy for Christmas?" Grace rushed to ask, knowing how desperate Beth was to find good homes.

"He'd love one," Cecilia replied, "but with the move, a puppy—"

"He can pick one out. They're at a tree farm owned by Beth Morehouse, a friend of ours. If you get a puppy, Cliff and I can keep him here with Beau until you're back in Cedar Cove."

Cecilia and Ian exchanged a glance. "That's too much to ask."

"Not at all. And it would be a huge help to Beth.

Someone abandoned ten puppies on her porch and she needs good homes for them before Christmas."

"Aaron's responsible, and he'd love it," Cecilia prompted. "Besides, we'd be rescuing a puppy. What do you think?" She looked at her husband, obviously attracted to the idea.

Ian shrugged. "A puppy for Aaron would be a great gift…if you're positive you don't mind keeping him for a few weeks."

"We wouldn't mind in the least," Grace assured him.

"Okay, that's settled. We'll go and see your friend, pick out a puppy." Ian pulled out a chair and sat down next to his wife. "Did Cecilia mention the house on Rosewood Lane?"

"We'd just started to talk about it," Grace said. "I told her it's available and we'd love to rent it to you again."

Ian shook his head.

"You don't want it?" This surprised Grace because she remembered how fond Cecilia had been of the place and all the small homey changes she'd made. "My mistake. I'm sorry," she said with some embarrassment.

"Actually, Cecilia and I were wondering," Ian said, clasping his wife's hand, "if you and Cliff would consider selling us the house."

"Selling," Grace repeated. "Oh…I hadn't thought of that."

"I brought it up to Cliff," Ian continued, "and he said the decision was yours."

"Well…yes, I suppose it is," Grace murmured. Her immediate reaction was not to sell. Her emotional attachment to the house on Rosewood Lane remained strong. "Can I think about it and get back to you sometime in the next couple of days?"

"Of course," Ian said.

The back door opened again and Cliff came in with the two children. Aaron was instantly on the floor, playing with Beau, and Mia ran to tell her mother all about riding Pixie.

The rest of the visit passed in a blur for Grace, preoccupied as she was with Ian's request. She served cocoa and cookies and presented the Randalls with the small Christmas tree, which thrilled the kids, but she was hardly aware of anything that was said. The young family left soon afterward.

Grace and Cliff waved them off and returned to the house.

"From the look on your face, Ian must have said something about wanting to buy the house." Cliff walked over to the coffeepot and refilled his mug. He leaned against the counter as he waited for her reply.

"He did."

"And?"

"I...don't know if I can give it up."

"Then tell them it's only available to rent," he said matter-of-factly.

"But...this is exactly the type of family I'd want to sell the house to." Grace found she couldn't keep still. She walked over to the refrigerator and opened it for no reason. Closing it, she circled the kitchen table.

"I understand." Cliff came up behind her, placing his hands on her shoulders. "It's a big decision."

Grace exhaled slowly. "It is...but I think it's time," she said with sudden resolve. "My old life was on Rosewood Lane. My new life is here with you—and Beau."

Lying on the braided carpet beneath the kitchen table, Beau raised his head and barked once. Apparently, he was in full agreement.

Three

Two down and eight puppies to go.

Saturday morning, the day before Christmas Eve, Aaron Randall—as well as his parents and little sister—had stopped by and picked out a puppy. Grace, bless her, had agreed to keep tiny Poko until the Randalls returned to Cedar Cove in the second week of January. He was with her now, as it would've been too difficult to look after the puppy in the hotel room.

The Randalls' rental car pulled out of the driveway just as another vehicle turned in.

Kent. Obviously driving a rental, too. It was a bright blue sedan, not his usual style at all.

It couldn't be anyone else. He'd phoned shortly after he'd arrived at Thyme and Tide, and said he was on his way over.

Despite herself, Beth felt another wave of excitement. She hadn't slept all night, trying to make sense of his unexpected need to connect as a family again. Granted, he saw their daughters more often than she did, since both attended college in California. But all four of them together at Christmas... It had been a long time. Even

.

if, as she suspected, Bailey and Sophie were involved in this, Kent didn't have to go along with it. But he had....

Still, she wondered if she was reading more into the situation than it warranted; all the same, she considered scenarios of what this Christmas would be like. Then there was Ted. He was a close friend, and while they'd shared little more than a few chaste kisses, the relationship looked promising. She felt it and thought he did, too.

Beth remembered Christmases when the girls were young. She remembered laughing with Kent, the two of them shushing each other as they stayed up half the night assembling tricycles and later bicycles and then fell into bed exhausted. In an hour or two, Bailey and Sophie would be jumping up and down on the mattress, shrieking that Santa had come.

One Christmas Eve they'd gone for a sleigh ride in freshly fallen snow, snuggling under a blanket, keeping one another warm. Kent had stolen a few hot kisses while the girls giggled and hid their eyes, complaining that it was "yucky" to see their parents kiss.

Beth smiled. They'd had some really good years together. Somewhere along the way, though, their lives had changed. No, their marriage had. They'd grown apart. It wasn't any big disagreement, no betrayal or unforeseen revelation. Instead, an accumulation of small slights and annoyances had eventually grown from a small distance into a huge crevasse. One that had deepened and widened over the years until they'd been unable to reach across it....

Was it possible? Did Kent regret the divorce? Beth had more than a few regrets herself. They'd both been so stubborn, so unreasonable, so eager to prove they didn't need each other anymore.

Perhaps if they'd been the kind of people who yelled and stomped around the house, everything might have gone differently. Instead, once the subject of divorce had been broached, they'd been so darned polite. Attorneys said there was no such thing as a "friendly" divorce, but that hadn't been Beth's experience. Theirs had been not only friendly but accommodating and fair. But maybe that was just on the surface. Maybe going ahead with the divorce was *unfair*—to both of them.

She'd gotten busy at the college and Kent had his engineering company. They'd been like those ships in the old cliché, passing in the night, each drifting in a different direction. She had her life and he had his.

Kent claimed he found her friends stuffy and boring, and stopped attending social functions with her. Beth decided *his* friends were snobs. He didn't seem to mind that she stayed home when he had an event, and after a while she wondered if he'd met someone else. It wouldn't have surprised her. Although he'd never admitted it… They were so remote at that point, spending almost no time together. Oh, they slept in the same bed but rarely touched, rarely communicated about anything other than routine or functional things. Like who was picking up milk or paying the electricity bill.

She was the one who'd suggested divorce. At first Kent had seemed shocked. But he'd recovered quickly enough. He'd simply said that if she wanted a divorce, he wouldn't stop her…and he hadn't.

They'd divided everything as equitably as possible, sold the house and parted ways. It'd all been so civilized, so straightforward, as if twenty-three years as husband and wife meant nothing.

When the final decree came through, Beth decided to leave the academic world. She'd been seeking a geographical cure, she supposed, considering it now. The Christmas tree farm had been the solution she'd been looking for. She had her dogs and a menagerie of other pets, including two canaries, a guinea pig and now the puppies. Eight puppies. She also fed a number of feral cats. And she'd made new friends and found new purpose....

Kent—and, yes, it was Kent, as she'd expected— parked the car and turned off the engine. Beth pretended she was busy. Too busy to even glance in his direction. But despite herself, she was excited. Happy.

All she'd ever wanted from him was some indication that he still loved her, that he still cared. His insistence on spending Christmas with her and the girls, no matter how it had come about, was the first time either of them had made a move toward the other. Could this be the start of a reconciliation?

Her heart rate accelerated and she brushed her hair behind both ears. She wished now that she'd worn something other than her ever-present jeans. Dressing up a bit would've been a subtle way of letting Kent know how pleased she was that he'd extended an olive branch. She had on a long-sleeved shirt beneath her red V-neck sweater, which would have gone nicely with her black wool pants. Oh, how she wished she'd put on her black wool pants.

The car door closed, and Kent stood there, looking at her.

"Hello," she said, surprised by how shaky her voice

sounded. "Welcome to Christmas Tree Lane—and Cedar Cove Tree Farm."

He zipped up his jacket and grinned. "The house is fabulous. The girls were right."

"Thank you." The porch railing was covered with swags of evergreen and twinkling white lights. More lights hung from the roofline, glittering brightly in the dull gray winter morning.

The passenger car door opened and Beth saw that Kent hadn't come alone. A lovely, young—much younger than Beth—woman climbed out. She was tall, lithe and stylishly dressed in a full-length black coat and long, high-heeled black boots. She towered an inch or two above Kent, who stood at nearly six feet. Her blond, shoulder-length hair was perfect.... Actually, everything about her seemed perfect in an urban, sophisticated way that contrasted painfully with Beth's farm clothes, disheveled hair and work-roughened hands.

Beth blinked and her heart almost stopped as reality hit her. *Kent had brought another woman.* They were together. A couple. He was seeing someone else now. This little fantasy she'd built around a reconciliation was only that—wishful thinking.

It took her a moment to recover and realize that every assumption she'd made was completely and totally off-base. Kent hadn't come to spend Christmas with her and the girls. His sole purpose was to show off this... this model.

Nothing had changed. Nothing ever would.

"Hello." Beth greeted the other woman with a forced smile and an extended hand. "I'm Beth Morehouse. The ex-wife."

"I know," the woman said in a sultry voice that was sweet enough to caramelize sugar. "I'm Danielle."

Just Danielle? No last name? Like Cher or Madonna or Beyoncé?

"Welcome to *my* Christmas tree farm," she said, placing emphasis on her ownership.

The screen door flew open and Bailey raced onto the porch. "Dad!"

Sophie was directly behind her sister. They darted down the stairs like young fawns in their rush to hug Kent.

Her ex-husband opened his arms, and his daughters launched themselves into his wide embrace.

"How are my girls?" he asked, his voice warm with affection.

"Missing you, Daddy," Sophie murmured.

"Who's that?" Bailey asked starkly, frowning at Danielle. Apparently, she was as shocked as Beth.

"This is Danielle Martin," he said, sliding his arms around each of their waists.

Oh, so there was a last name.

"What's *she* doing here?" Sophie demanded.

"Sophie," Beth snapped, appalled at her daughter's lack of manners.

"Danielle's a friend from work who traveled with me," he said by way of introduction.

"Why don't we all step inside, out of the cold," Beth suggested, and marched into the house, assuming everyone else would follow.

The girls had obviously been playing with the puppies when Kent arrived because the second the door opened they swarmed onto the porch, eager as jailbirds to make an escape. Four were already out the door and racing down the porch steps.

"Don't just stand there," Beth cried to her daughters. "Help me."

Laughing, Sophie and Bailey hurried in one direction while Beth went in the other. Even Kent got involved in the chase. The only one who didn't move was Danielle. With her arms crossed, she remained immobile, as if moving a single inch would have dire consequences.

Once the puppies were all inside the house, Beth brought Kent and Danielle in. Danielle perched on the arm of a recliner with her feet off the carpet. She seemed to fear that all the puppies would rush toward her at one time.

Beth called out instructions. "Get the puppies into the laundry room," she told the girls. "I'll give them some treats." This was not the way she'd planned to greet Kent, with puppies creating havoc.

In the momentary quiet of the laundry room, Beth pressed one hand to her chest, which felt as though it was knotted with pain. She would not, *could* not, yield to the icy tide of disappointment or to the surprising burst of white-hot anger. Not now. Not here. She'd rather be dipped in Christmas-tree sap and rolled in holly leaves before she made a fool of herself in front of the girls.

With a deep breath, Beth squared her shoulders and opened a bag of canine treats just as the girls herded in the last three pups. Whether it was the rustle of the bag or the distinctive aroma, Beth didn't care, only that they all came on the run. On another calming breath, she promised to deal with her emotions later as she distributed the miniature bone-shaped biscuits.

She slowly and deliberately wiped her hands on her jeans while arranging her features in her best hostess smile. Returning to the living room, she motioned Sophie and Bailey to the couch and nodded at her guests. "Now, where were we?"

The girls exchanged a puzzled look and obeyed. At Beth's question, they fixed their gazes on their father.

"Are all those dogs...yours?" Danielle asked incredulously.

"No, no. I'm finding homes for them."

"Where are *your* dogs?" Kent asked. "Do you still have Lucy and Bixby?"

"Of course. They're in the heated kennel in the back."

"It's huge. You should see it, Dad," Sophie said, growing more animated as she spoke. "Mom's got six dogs of her own, and she helps with the Reading with Rover program at the library and...and she trains dogs and she just got a puppy herself." She was out of breath by the time she completed her list.

"He's been sickly so she keeps him upstairs," Bailey added.

"In your *bedroom?*" Danielle's eyes widened with what appeared to be horror.

"You started to tell us about Danielle," Bailey reminded her father, turning away from the other woman.

"Well, yes." Kent looked at Danielle. "She's a... friend."

"A good friend," Danielle murmured. "A *very* good friend."

"I can't believe this." Bailey paced their bedroom with her hands locked behind her back. "This is all wrong! Nothing is working out like we planned."

"When did Dad meet Danielle?" Sophie, the practical one, asked. "And where?"

"Why are you asking me? I don't know any more than you do."

Sitting on the edge of the bed with her hands in her hair—as if trying to pull out an answer—Sophie said, "Well, she wasn't there when we visited him at Thanksgiving. And he didn't say a word about her to me, but I thought he might've mentioned it to you."

"I wish." Bailey threw a scowl at her sister. "If he had, we never would've invited him for Christmas. That's for sure. Besides, I'd have told you. What's Dad thinking? Or *is* he thinking? Anyone with half a brain can see she's all wrong for him."

"She can't be much older than we are."

"Did you see how she reacted to the puppies?" Bailey cried. "Like they were diseased or something. Sitting with her feet in the air, as if they'd mistake her leg for a tree trunk. Too bad they didn't."

Sophie groaned. "And did you hear how she talked to me? Like I'm ten years old. For a minute I thought she was going to pinch my cheek and tell me how cute I was."

"Dad and Danielle? It's a joke," Bailey muttered. "A terrible joke."

"That's what you said about the divorce—until it happened."

"I know. I just don't want to believe this...whatever it is." But she'd seen the way Danielle had looked at their father. Clearly, he didn't have a clue. This woman was set on getting a big diamond ring from him. Bailey was bound and determined that wasn't going to happen. Not on her watch. If ever their father had needed

help, it was now. They had to do something before he
made the second-biggest mistake of his life. The first
had been going through with the divorce.

"Well, you'd better come up with an idea fast, or
you'll be spending next Thanksgiving with Dad and
your new stepmother. Just you and Danielle and Dad.
'Cause I'm not going. I'll be here with Mom."

"Don't say that," Bailey moaned. "Besides, you'll
have to come."

"Nope. I don't like Danielle."

"Me, neither."

"There's got to be something we can do," Sophie
said.

"What?" Bailey asked in frustration, which was immediately followed by discouragement. "We can't let
this happen. We just can't."

"I agree. Think, Bailey. You always come up with
good plans."

"I'm trying, I'm trying."

Sophie kicked off her shoes and sat cross-legged on
the bed. "First, we have to figure out what Danielle
wants. No woman that young and perfect-looking would
ever date our dad."

Bailey nodded. As harsh as it sounded, Sophie wasn't
saying anything she hadn't already considered.

"We could introduce her to a younger man."

"Who?" Bailey asked.

"Jeff is cute."

"Mom's foreman? He's married. I don't want to be
responsible for breaking up a marriage in order to get
our parents back together."

"Yeah, that's bad," Sophie agreed. "Okay, who else

is there? It's got to be somebody young. I mean, Dad's way over forty."

"So is Mom."

"Oh, Mom," Sophie said miserably, flopping back onto the bed. "She knew. She was so stoic when she introduced herself to Danielle, I wanted to scream."

Bailey had been too shocked to tear her eyes from her father. When she did look at her mother, she couldn't bear the return of the polite frozen smile. From the moment she and Sophie had mentioned that their father would be coming for Christmas, they'd both noticed a change in her.

In the beginning, when she'd heard the news, Beth had seemed confused and a bit panicky. Over dinner the night before, she'd peppered them with questions about their father. She was interested, all right. Interested and intrigued and, after a while, Bailey had sensed a definite excitement. She'd seemed happy, and for the first time since the divorce, they'd seen a brightness in her eyes.

It was exactly the reaction Bailey and Sophie had been looking for. Over the past three years, Mom had put on a great act. To all outward appearances, she was content; she certainly claimed to be. Her new life suited her just fine, she said. What had frightened the girls into taking action was the fact that their mother had started to casually drop Ted Reynolds's name into their conversations.

Beth's eagerness about seeing their dad convinced both Bailey and Sophie that all this talk about contentment was false. They'd been up half the night whispering in the dark, so sure they were right—and now this.

"Have you got any ideas yet?" Sophie sounded worried.

"Where's Mom?"

"Where she always goes when she's upset. She's with her dogs."

"With her dogs," Bailey echoed. The kennel was a place of comfort for Beth, a place of solace. The thought of her mom sitting on the ground with her precious animals gathered around her made Bailey want to weep.

"Where did Dad and Danielle go for lunch?"

"I don't know...."

He'd invited Bailey and Sophie to join them, but of course they'd declined.

"We should've gone with him," Bailey said.

"No way." Sophie shook her head. "I am not socializing with *her.*"

Bailey reviewed various options that began occurring to her. Yes, it would work. She hopped onto the bed and tucked her legs underneath her.

Sophie stared at her. "What are you thinking?"

"We need to show Dad that Danielle's completely wrong for him."

"Well, duh. Just how are we going to do that?"

"There *are* ways." Bailey gave a conspiratorial smile.

Immediately, Sophie straightened. "You think we can do it?"

"I don't just think, I know. Watch out, Danielle. You're in for it now."

Four

Judge Olivia Griffin pulled into the parking lot at the Pancake Palace. She'd ordered two coconut cream pies for their Christmas Eve dinner at Justine's. After the meal, they'd attend church services, then head over to Noelle's birthday party. Picking up the pies was on the list of errands she needed to run before collecting Mom and Ben that evening.

The restaurant was packed, which surprised her. She hadn't expected it to be this busy on Christmas Eve Day. But she should have, she mused, as she hunted for a parking space at the back of the lot. Based on last year's experience, her daughter had warned her. With a firm conviction that family came first, Justine had decided to close the Tea Room for Christmas Eve as well as Christmas Day. Her staff was thrilled with the unexpected gift of this extra time off.

Inside the restaurant, Olivia stood in line at the counter waiting her turn. Wave upon wave of happy voices washed through the room. Looking around, she noticed the painted windows, decorated with a variety of holiday scenes. Holly on one window, a snowman on another. She gazed across the room and saw the Randall family in a booth with Cecilia's father, Bobby Merrick. Holding fistfuls of crayons, the two Randall children were bent over their place mats, solving puzzles, connecting the dots or just coloring.

Remembering her conversation with Cecilia the day before, Olivia couldn't help releasing a sigh. The young mother had asked about Jordan, Olivia's son and Justine's twin brother.

It seemed to Olivia that her entire life was divided by that summer. Life before Jordan died and life afterward. Her world had imploded that summer afternoon. No sooner had they buried their son than Stan, her husband, announced that he wanted a divorce. Within a matter of months, she'd lost her son *and* her marriage.

Watching Cecilia and Ian Randall now, sitting close together, so attuned to each other, so much in love, she didn't regret denying their divorce. How could she? She would've given anything if someone had done the same for her and Stan. The pain of losing their son had been so horrific that, instead of bringing them together, it had driven a wedge between them.

When Stan remarried only months after their divorce, Olivia's friends had speculated that he'd been involved with Marge long before Jordan's death. It'd been easy to believe, especially then. Her mother, who was reluctant to say anything bad about anyone, felt Stan had acted irrationally in leaving his family.

Irrationally? Their son was dead. How could either of them remain rational? The grief had killed them, too.

It was all a moot point. Stan had married Marge, and some years later they'd divorced, as well. For a time it seemed that he wanted to get back together with Olivia

and had done his best to thwart her budding romance
with Jack Griffin. By then, however, Olivia had fallen
for Jack, and her sights were set on the future instead
of resurrecting the past. It was far too late for her and
Stan. When it became apparent that she wasn't interested, he'd found someone else. Justine had told her
that Susan, the new woman in his life, was living with
him now. Olivia assumed he wasn't willing to try marriage a third time.

Yesterday, Cecilia had asked if she still cried over
Jordan. Did a mother ever stop weeping over a lost
child? Olivia doubted it. While going through cancer
treatments a couple of years ago, Olivia had become
desperately ill with an infection. From what others told
her later, she knew she'd been close to death. It was
while her fever raged that Jordan had come to her. For
the briefest of moments she'd seen him as he was that
summer, a skinny thirteen-year-old, full of life, eager
to prove himself. He'd been a happy boy, smart and
witty. Even now when she heard his favorite song by
the group Air Supply, tears would prick her eyes. When
she thought of her son, she remembered his ready smile,
his ease with people, a natural charm that never failed
to endear him to others.

Once again, Olivia wondered what would have become of her son had he lived. He had a variety of inter-
ests. He'd been good at math and loved to take things
apart, then put them back together. He might have been
an engineer. Then, too, he was often the go-between
when Justine and James argued, helping his siblings
settle their differences. Perhaps he would've followed
in her footsteps and become an attorney.

Olivia felt a thickening in her throat and blinked

back tears. This was silly. Christmas was supposed to be joyous, festive. Now wasn't the time to reminisce about Jordan.

Cecilia glanced up and, seeing Olivia, she smiled. Their eyes connected—mother to mother. Heart to heart. Cecilia knew Olivia was remembering Jordan. And Olivia knew Cecilia was remembering the infant daughter she'd held so briefly in her arms.

Cecilia nodded and rested her head against Ian's shoulder. For an instant Ian looked surprised, and then Olivia saw him reach for his wife's hand and give it a gentle squeeze.

Tammy, the hostess, touched Olivia's arm. "I have your pies, Judge Griffin."

"Oh…oh, sorry, I got distracted." Olivia pulled out her wallet, paid for the pies and carried them out to the car without looking back.

Olivia had just opened the driver's-side door when her cell phone chirped. She dug it out of her purse, saw it was her husband and pushed the talk button.

"Hello, sweetheart," she said.

"Where are you?" he asked, sounding rushed.

"The Pancake Palace, why?"

"Eric and Shelly arrived with the boys."

"I didn't think they were due until five." Her stepson and his family were hours early. They'd driven from Reno to spend Christmas Eve with Jack and Olivia at Justine's, and Christmas Day with Shelly's family. "Can you feed them lunch or do you want me to come home?" she asked.

"Lunch isn't a problem. I'm calling because I need to know if Beth Morehouse has any of those puppies left."

"I'm sure she does."

"Great. Eric was saying he wanted to get Tedd and Todd each a dog after the first of the year, and he was hoping to find a couple of Labs. I told him about Beth's situation and he's interested."

"Oh, Jack, Beth would be so grateful!"

"That's what I thought. I'll give her a call and take Eric and the boys out to her place later this afternoon. Do you want to meet us there?"

"If I have time…"

"Okay. Love you."

"Love you, too." She ended the call and dropped her cell back in her purse. Beth would be thrilled to find homes for two more puppies.

Olivia's next stop was the Sanford assisted-living complex, where her mother and stepfather had recently moved. The snow had been cleared from the parking lot and the sidewalk swept and salted. Hugging her coat around her, she hunched her shoulders against the wind and hurried inside.

A large, beautifully decorated Christmas tree sparkling with lights and classic ornaments graced the entry. Red bows were attached to a set of twin chandeliers. Six fresh wreaths festooned the second-floor railing and left a lingering scent of pine. The complex had a homey, welcoming appeal.

Olivia saw Ben first. He was in the card room set off to the side of the main room. He was apparently playing either pinochle or bridge, his two favorite games. Olivia knew Charlotte was waiting for her upstairs. Her mother insisted on reviewing their Christmas-dinner menu, although Olivia had already prepared most of the dishes in advance. Tonight and tomorrow were for family. She had no intention of spending Christmas Day in the kitchen, although she planned to put the turkey in the oven sometime Christmas morning.

The menu was the same one they had almost every year, many of the recipes directly from the cookbook Charlotte had compiled for Justine. Last Christmas, Justine had made copies of her grandmother Charlotte's favorites for the extended family and it was a much-loved treasure.

Olivia headed for the elevator without interrupting Ben's game and went up to the third floor. Charlotte and Ben's small apartment was at the end of the hall. The door was propped open, a sign to all who came that they were welcome.

"Come in, come in," Charlotte said, putting aside her knitting and getting up. She was definitely moving more slowly, struggling a bit. Harry had arranged himself on the back of the recliner, his tail hanging straight down.

Olivia kissed her mother's cheek and urged her to sit again. She herself sat down in Ben's recliner. An end table served as a catchall between the two chairs, and Olivia saw not only Charlotte's knitting but Ben's current crossword. Dutifully, she took out a pad and pen. "You wanted to talk about Christmas dinner."

"Oh, yes. I do hope you intend to serve that wonderful artichoke appetizer."

"Got it," Olivia assured her. It was done and ready to go in the oven. The artichoke and caramelized onion filling was baked in a flaky dough. Everyone loved it. In fact, Olivia had made two because they were sure to disappear quickly.

"The potato casserole?"

"Wouldn't be Christmas without it," Olivia told her. "Ben likes it with bacon crumbled on top."

"I can do that." Olivia made a notation on her pad to add bacon to please Ben.

"Did Jack make his special cookies?"

Generally speaking, Jack in the kitchen was a laughing matter but he had managed to prepare his favorite cookies—chocolate-dipped crackers sandwiched with peanut butter. They were a hit every Christmas. The cookie had been his own invention, and considering Jack's pride in the recipe, anyone would think it had won him a Cooking Channel top-chef award.

"The cookies are ready, as well."

"And what did the kitchen look like afterward?" Charlotte asked with a knowing gleam in her eye.

"A disaster. I helped with the cleanup."

"You're a good wife."

Her mother had set a good example.

"Justine wanted to serve beef Wellington, so I thought we'd do a turkey tomorrow."

"You can't go wrong with that," Charlotte said.

"No, you can't," Olivia agreed. There'd be stuffing and plenty of gravy, too. Her mother would work with her and add her personal assortment of herbs and spices to create the distinct taste everyone loved. Although Olivia had watched carefully and taken notes, hers never turned out quite the same.

"Anything else?"

Olivia hesitated. With her mother, everything was homemade, from the dinner rolls to the desserts, of which there was always a wide variety. Pecan pie, fruitcake, rum cake, apple strudel and more.

"I bought a couple of coconut cream pies from the Pancake Palace." Half expecting her mother to berate her for taking the easy road, Olivia held her breath.

"Oh, that's wonderful."

Wonderful? Olivia could hardly believe it. Her tensed shoulders sagged with relief.

"Everyone knows the Pancake Palace makes the best pies in town."

Olivia understood how difficult it was for her mother to deal with change. It wasn't easy for anyone, but the older people got, the harder it was. In her eighties now, Charlotte had coped with the transition from home to the assisted-living complex pretty well. She'd given up the house where she'd lived so many years of her life and surrendered much of her independence. Olivia was exceptionally proud of Charlotte and Ben. Naturally, there'd been doubts along the way, but all in all, the move had been a success.

"Anything else you'd like on the menu?" Olivia asked.

"My homemade applesauce."

"Of course, with the sweet pickles from last summer."

Charlotte rested her hands in her lap. "Those will be the last sweet pickles I put up," she said and, after a short pause, resumed her knitting.

Olivia opened her mouth to reassure her mother that there'd be more pickles and more summers, then realized this was Charlotte's way of telling her she was willing to give up that part of her life. No longer would she maintain a large garden or make applesauce and sauerkraut. The time had come to set all those endeavors aside.

A sharp pang of loss stabbed Olivia, but then she brightened. None of those activities, those special times, were really lost. With a little planning and foresight, they could continue into the next generation, and the one after that, too.

"Justine was talking about your pickle recipe a little while ago," Olivia said, and gently patted her mother's knee. "It wouldn't surprise me if she decided to put up sweet pickles next summer."

Her mother nodded approvingly. "I'll help if she needs advice."

"I know you will." A shift had taken place in their family. It hadn't been apparent at first and the irony of it was that Charlotte had recognized it before anyone else. Olivia felt a burst of joy. The recipes, the special family times, the laughter and the pleasures of being together would remain intact. Each generation would take what was produced and what was passed on by the one before, and then share it with the next. Eventually other traditions would be added, too.

"I'll be by to pick you and Ben up at five," she said. Reaching for her purse, Olivia stood.

"When are James and his family coming?" her mother asked as her fingers expertly wove the yarn around the needle. Socks again. Charlotte must have knit more than a hundred pairs over the years. These, no doubt, were for one of the great-grandchildren.

"James, Selina and the children will be there in plenty of time, don't worry." Olivia didn't have the heart to explain that they'd arrived the night before. Charlotte had spoken to her grandson on the phone but she'd obviously forgotten.

Unfortunately, these lapses happened more and more often. Her mother could recall the recipe for sweet pickles from memory, but a brief conversation the day before completely eluded her. They'd have a more definitive answer to Charlotte's memory problems when they met with the specialist in January. Until then, all they could do was wait.

"I love you, Olivia," her mother said softly as Olivia started out the door.

The comment struck her as odd. Her mother rarely said those words. She smiled. "I know, Mom, and I love you, too." She came back and bent over to kiss her mother's cheek. "I'll see you in a few hours."

For an instant Charlotte regarded her blankly and Olivia knew that her mother had no idea why her daughter would be returning so soon.

Five

Five puppies now had homes. Five to go.

It'd been love at first sight. Jack Griffin had come by with his son, Eric, and Eric's family. The grandsons had each chosen a puppy. They'd fallen to their knees and eight puppies had raced into their arms. It had taken quite a long time for the boys to make their decisions. In the end, they'd selected two males; in fact, they'd already given their puppies names, albeit not very original ones: Baron and Duke. Five were left, since Eddie Cox had picked one up for his parents—three females and two males. Ted had volunteered to watch over whatever puppies didn't have homes when Beth and the girls drove to Whistler, but she hated to burden him with extra animals.

Instead of returning to the house after she'd seen off the Griffins and their puppies, Beth wandered into the back of the yard where she had the heated kennel. She opened the gate and let her dogs run in among the trees. They were happy to exercise and she enjoyed playing with them, enjoyed their boundless energy.

Her whole family had been pet lovers. From her earliest memories, they'd always had a dog. Kent loved animals, too, which was one of the reasons she'd been attracted to him all those years ago…and now. At one time he'd considered entering veterinary college, but the application process was complex and difficult, with only a few candidates accepted each year. He'd tried two years running and was declined both times. Although bitterly disappointed, he'd decided to change his course of study to engineering. In the end, that career choice had suited him well.

Thinking of Kent, Beth was forced to confront his news head-on. He was involved with someone else. Danielle had made a point of telling everyone what "good" friends they were. Although Kent had called her merely a friend, it was obvious that Danielle intended it to be so much more.

After three years, this shouldn't come as such a shock—only it did. Her heart felt weighted down by grief and disappointment. Yet she was the one who'd set him free. Not once had she made an effort to turn the tide of the divorce proceedings. Perhaps this was one of those classic scenarios; she didn't want him but she didn't want anyone else to have him, either.

Still, she had to ask herself: Did she want her ex-husband back? She couldn't answer that, not with certainty, and in any event the decision had been taken out of her hands. This sense of loss and confusion was probably typical of ex-wives, she reasoned. It must be.

"Mom?" Bailey was calling her.

Pulling herself out of her musing, she shouted and waved. "Over here."

"I saw the Griffins leave and you didn't come back in the house."

Beth didn't feel much like company at the moment. "I thought I'd let the dogs run a bit first," she said.

Sophie joined her sister. It'd started to snow again, thick flakes that drifted lazily down. The wind chilled her through her thick jacket. Because she spent so much time outdoors, she'd learned to ignore the cold. But this particular chill seemed to come from the inside out....

"Are you upset about Dad and Danielle?" Sophie asked, still putting on her gloves. She didn't look at Beth, as though she wanted to hide her own reaction to Kent's "friend."

"You mean because your father has someone else in his life? Oh, heavens, no." She wondered how effective her lie had been.

"We don't like Danielle," Bailey announced for the two of them.

"You have to admit she's beautiful."

Both girls rolled their eyes. "Mom, she's plastic. I can't imagine what Dad sees in her. Besides, she treats us like we're still in diapers."

"Give her a chance," Beth urged. She didn't know why she was championing the other woman when she agreed with everything her daughters said.

"Tell us again, how did you and Dad meet?" Bailey asked.

Instead of answering their question, she asked one of her own. "Did you know that at one time your father wanted to be a veterinarian?"

"Dad?"

"Get out of here!"

"We met in college," Beth said. "You remember that." They'd heard the story a hundred times. It didn't make sense to repeat it now. "Are you sure you want to hear this?"

Their response was immediate and enthusiastic. "Yes!"

"Okay. We met on campus. A friend-of-a-friend situation. My roommate was dating your father, and I was dating another guy named Steve. I liked your father a whole lot more than Steve, but he was with Melanie and I couldn't very well make a play for him. We dated as a foursome quite a bit and then one day Melanie told me she liked Steve better than Kent and I confessed that I liked Kent better than Steve."

"And the two of you wanted to switch dates," Sophie finished for her.

"That is so cool," Bailey said.

"Well, it would've been if the guys felt the same way about us, but they didn't. Steve claimed he wanted to marry me, but I wasn't interested. Kent, on the other hand, only had eyes for Melanie."

"Oh, brother. Clearly, Dad's needed direction in the girlfriend department for a long time."

"We worked it out. Melanie broke up with Kent and I took the initiative and phoned to console him. What he wanted was for me to convince Melanie to take him back…." She paused and kicked at a pile of snow. "I guess I was always the second choice with your father."

"Oh, Mom, that isn't true!"

Beth smiled, letting her daughters know she wasn't serious. Well, maybe she was, not that it mattered.

"Whatever happened to Melanie? Did she marry Steve?"

"No. She left college in our junior year and dated a guy from France. Eventually she followed him there.

We lost contact after a while. I haven't heard from her in years."

Princess raced to Beth's side. Panting, the collie dropped a stick at her feet. "You want to play fetch, do you?" she asked, and bent to pet her thick fur. Princess was a rescue someone had brought her. Her friend had found the collie on the side of the road near the freeway. With some effort she was able to get the large dog into the car. Rather than take her to the animal shelter, Beth's friend had brought her to Beth. Half-starved, Princess was in bad shape, and Beth had nourished her back to health. She'd tried to find her owner, but the dog had no identification. Now Princess was deeply attached to Beth and was one of the dogs in the Reading with Rover program Grace had instigated at the library.

"Dad still loves you," Bailey insisted.

"Of course he does," Beth said, and meant it. "We were married for twenty-three years. I'm the mother of his children. While we might have opposing opinions on certain issues, when it comes to you girls, we're in total agreement."

"Bailey means he *really* loves you."

Beth threw her arms around her daughters and brought them close. "Listen, you two. I know this is difficult. Maybe you believed that your father's visit to Cedar Cove meant more than he intended it to mean. Maybe you believed he was making a statement about reconciliation." Well, he'd made a statement, all right. He wanted to introduce their daughters to his "friend." "The reason your father's here is because he wanted us all to meet Danielle. He wants us to welcome her into the family."

"I can't do it." Sophie's chin rose defiantly.

"Me, neither."

For that matter, it wasn't going to be any easier for Beth. Nevertheless, she was determined to do her best.

"They'll be coming back here, and I want us all to make an effort, okay?"

Bailey sighed expressively and, after a moment, said, "I'll try...I guess."

"Will Dad be here when we decorate the tree?"

Beth had assumed not. He was with Danielle and it would be awkward to include the other woman. "I...I don't know, but I don't think so."

"Dad used to enjoy that," Sophie said.

Beth had, too. It was their special family tradition. They'd always waited until Christmas Eve to decorate the tree, which went back to her German roots. Her grandparents hadn't put up a tree until the night before Christmas, a tradition that had come from the old country.

"Shouldn't we at least ask Dad about decorating the tree with us?"

"I suppose..." Beth said without much enthusiasm. He would probably assume the invitation included Danielle.

The girls returned to the house, and Beth stayed outside, letting the dogs run until they were tired. She gave them each a healthy snack, then they retreated to their kennel and she went back inside.

Beth had never intended to own six dogs—make that seven with the puppy upstairs. But then she'd never intended to have her children barely a year apart, either. Kent was still in his last year of engineering school and she was working as a teaching assistant to help support them when she discovered she was pregnant with Bailey. Sophie hadn't been a planned pregnancy, either, and she'd arrived a mere fourteen months after her sister.

Beth had gotten pregnant with Bailey at Christmastime. Christmas Eve, to be exact. Hard to prove, perhaps, but she was sure of it. She'd *felt* it, felt they'd made a baby that night. Beth wondered if Kent remembered and suspected that, after all these years, he'd put it out of his mind.

They could only afford a small tree that year and had waited until Christmas Eve to decorate it. Beth had said it was tradition, and while it hadn't been *his* family's tradition, he'd been a good sport about it. With little money for ornaments, Beth had made their own. Kent had done his part, stringing popcorn and cranberries while she sewed gingerbread men from pieces of felt, decorating them with eyes and a row of tiny buttons down the front. Each was unique, individual. She still had several of the original ones and others, too, that she'd crafted through the years. She kept them carefully packed away in boxes.

It'd snowed that Christmas Eve, too, but their tiny basement apartment was warm and cozy. As a surprise, Kent had purchased two miniature bottles of rum to make hot drinks. After decorating the tree, they sat in front of the woodstove, their only source of heat, and with Beth on Kent's lap and the cat curled up on the ottoman, they'd toasted the holidays. They'd started kissing and then one thing led to another and three weeks later the stick was blue.

That was Bailey.

How excited Kent had been to have a daughter. When they learned Beth was pregnant a second time, he'd hoped for another girl and had gotten his wish.

The early years of their marriage were financially tight. They'd met every crisis, refusing to let their money problems come between them. They were a unit, a couple, determined to beat the odds. And when it was smooth sailing financially, her marriage had fallen apart.

Somewhere, while the girls were in their early teen years, they'd lost the glue that held them together.

Well, good grief, there was no need to analyze the past at this late date. What was done was done. She smiled despite her mood. If ever there was a profound statement, that was it. *What's done is done. Accept it.* Beth found herself humming a Christmas carol as she headed back to the house.

Bailey was on her cell phone in the kitchen. When she saw Beth, she abruptly ended the conversation.

"That was Dad," she explained. "He said he wants to be here when we decorate the tree."

Beth's chest tightened. "Is he... Did he say he was bringing Danielle?"

"I don't know. I didn't ask."

"Where did he take her to lunch yesterday?" she asked conversationally as she considered the situation. Danielle didn't appear to be the sensitive sort who'd recognize that her presence might be uncomfortable for Beth and the girls. Beth decided she needed to brace herself for the inevitable.

"The Lighthouse restaurant, I think."

"Oh." Of course Kent would take Danielle to one of the most expensive places in town.

"What are you making for dinner, Mom?" Bailey asked.

Sophie sent her a pleading look. "*Please* let it be your lasagna."

Beth laughed. "Of course." She'd better add two extra settings to the table.

"With Grandma Carlucci's marinara sauce?"

"Would I use anything else?" The recipe came from Kent's maternal grandmother, who was Italian. Because the dish demanded a lot of time and effort she only served it on special occasions. It was one of Kent's favorites, too. She'd actually made it for him, thinking... well, what she'd thought was irrelevant.

"Did your father tell you when he plans to come over?" she asked, trying to hide how anxious this news made her.

"He's on his way now."

"Okay," she said, rubbing her palms together. "Why don't you girls help me carry down the ornaments and we can have everything ready for when your dad gets here."

"Can we bring Roscoe downstairs?" Bailey pleaded.

"Sure, but you'll need to keep a careful eye on him. He's still a bit weak."

Roscoe was Beau's—the Hardings' puppy's—brother, and the sickliest of the litter. Ted hadn't held out much hope for his survival, but Beth had given the undernourished puppy plenty of love and attention, bottle-feeding him and carefully administering his medication. At three months he seemed to have turned the corner and she thought he'd survive.

"Can we bring Princess in the house, too?" Sophie asked.

"Of course." Her dogs spent more time inside than out. For the next few minutes Beth and her daughters carried down boxes from the storage area upstairs. Princess watched from her place by the sofa. Roscoe was in his bed with his chin resting on his paws, still too weak to move about much, although he seemed to enjoy the activity around him. "Did you and Dad ever have birds?" Bailey asked, standing near the canaries' cage.

Beth unsuccessfully hid a smile.

"What's so funny?"

"I did have a canary named Tweetie shortly after we were married, but we had to give her away."

"But why? Dad loves animals, too!"

"Yes, I know, but both your father and I were gone during the day. We had to keep the apartment heated for Tweetie, and after the first heating bill, your father insisted I find her a wealthier owner."

"Did you hate giving her up?"

"A little. She went to an aunt of mine, who had her for years." She smiled again. "Your father promised me there'd be other birds when we could afford them."

"But you never got another canary until you came to Cedar Cove."

"And now you've got two."

"So they could keep each other company," Beth said. Kent had long ago forgotten his promise and, frankly, so had she. Then one day last year she saw the canaries in a feed store and impulsively purchased them.

They heard a car drive up to the house.

"Dad's back," Bailey said, looking out the living room window.

"Is… Did Danielle come with him?" Beth asked, trying to make the best of this.

Sophie joined her sister and glared out the window.

"Yup. Danielle's with Dad," Bailey said in a stark voice.

Beth didn't know why she'd expected anything else.

Six

"Is that Allison?" Rosie Cox called from the kitchen.

Zach glanced out the window and, sure enough, his daughter's car had just pulled into the drive. "Yes," he called back. She'd gone to pick up her boyfriend, Anson Butler, at the airport, since he'd be spending the holidays with them. Rosie had been cooking and decorating for days in preparation for Christmas. Zach had gotten roped into helping, not that he minded.

Eddie, their son, who was home from college, came out of his bedroom. He'd spent most of the afternoon there, which was unusual. Eddie was tall and lanky, and he'd shot past Zach's six feet by two or three inches. Eddie must be working on some project in his room, but when he heard the commotion in the hallway, he hurried out, earbuds plugged into his ears and his iPod playing. He yanked one plug free. "What did you say?"

"Your sister and Anson are here."

"Cool."

Zach already had the front door open. The decorative lights on the roof flashed on and off, their colors reflecting in the layer of fresh snow. Anson waved. He'd flown in from Washington, D.C., that afternoon.

Anson had entered the army at eighteen and currently worked in Military Intelligence at the Pentagon. Zach was proud of Anson's achievements, although there'd been a time he was convinced the young man was a felon. Zach had done everything he could to keep his daughter away from Anson.

Fortunately, as Zach had discovered, he'd been wrong about his daughter's boyfriend. Anson hadn't been born with many advantages, but he'd risen above those difficulties, thanks in part, Zach believed, to his daughter. The two of them had met in high school, and they'd maintained their relationship all these years.

At this stage, Zach would welcome Anson as his son-in-law. Rosie cautioned him not to rush their daughter into an engagement, and she was right. Allison and Anson were still young and, as Rosie said, these things had to develop on their own. Parents shouldn't involve themselves one way or the other.

Zach opened the screen door for his daughter and Anson, who set down his bag as he stepped inside and extended his hand. "Mr. Cox, thank you for having me." His handshake was firm and solid.

"My pleasure."

Rosie came forward and hugged Anson. "Merry Christmas!"

"You're bedding down with me," Eddie said, leading Anson down the hallway to his room. "You can have the top bunk."

While Eddie showed Anson where he'd be sleeping, Allison followed her mother into the kitchen. "The traffic was a nightmare," she said. "I can't believe this many people are out on the roads on Christmas Eve."

"Everyone has places to go," Zach said, tagging behind his wife and daughter. "Hey, it smells good in here. What's cooking?"

"Honestly, Zach, I've baked ham every Christmas Eve since we were married. You'd think after twenty-four years you'd remember that."

"Right. Ham." Now that he thought about it, they did seem to have ham every year. Rosie used the bone for a black bean soup she served on New Year's Day, which was some Southern tradition she'd read about and adopted. It was supposed to guarantee good luck for the upcoming year. He doubted anyone believed that, but he liked black bean soup and so did Rosie.

By New Year's, the kids would be heading back to school, and he and Rosie would be alone again. Zach had to admit he missed his children. Without them, the house seemed too quiet.

"What can I do?" Allison asked, reaching for an apron.

Zach smiled at his daughter's eagerness to help. She was an intelligent, considerate young woman, and one day she'd make a fine attorney. In her first year of law school, Allison had gotten top grades. Zach was proud of her.

"Dinner won't be ready for a while, but if you want to make the salad you can."

"Sure." She went over to the refrigerator, collecting the lettuce, tomatoes and other vegetables.

Normally, Zach would've sat down in front of the television at this point. He and Rosie both enjoyed football and had spent many a lazy Sunday afternoon watching the Seattle Seahawks. At first she hadn't understood much about football, but she was a fast learner. Before long, she knew the players' names and positions and understood the game. Spending Sunday afternoons with his wife was *fun*.

Anson joined him at the breakfast bar, pulling out a stool and sitting down.

"So how does it feel to be back home?" Zach asked him. Anson wore jeans and an army sweatshirt, and his hair was shorn. Very different from his high school days when his hair straggled to his shoulders and he wore a long black raincoat. The difference between then and now was striking.

"I talked to my mother," Anson said. He looked down as if to hide his reaction.

"You're welcome to invite her for dinner, if you'd like," Rosie offered.

Zach wasn't keen to spend Christmas Eve with Cherry Butler, but he certainly wouldn't refuse to entertain her.

"Thanks, Mrs. Cox, but Mom has other plans. She's got a new…friend." Anson's tongue seemed to trip over the word. "She's sure it's love this time and wants to be with him."

"You'll have a chance to see her while you're on leave," Rosie said reassuringly.

"I probably will."

Zach noticed that Anson didn't sound all that confident.

Rosie started into the dining room and paused in the doorway—underneath the mistletoe. Zach couldn't have planned this better had he tried. He'd hung it there earlier and now, taking advantage of the opportunity, he slipped out of his chair and hurried toward his wife.

Rosie gave him an odd look as if she didn't understand what he was doing.

"You're standing under the mistletoe," he told her.

Surprised, Rosie immediately looked up.

Taking her in his arms, he kissed her deeply, and with an exaggerated flourish bent her backward over his arm. He might be middle-aged, but he wasn't dead yet and he loved his wife.

Anson and Allison hooted and cheered, but he didn't need any encouragement.

"Zach." Rosie was breathless by the time he released her.

So was he.

She planted her hand over her heart as though to slow its beat.

Zach winked at his son, who'd just joined them.

"I remember when we never used to see you and Mom kiss," Eddie reminded them.

Disbelief on his face, Anson looked from Allison to Eddie.

"My parents were divorced for a while," Allison explained. "I'm sure I told you."

"You did, but…it's hard to believe, seeing them now."

Eddie pulled out a stool on Anson's other side and propped his elbows on the counter. "It wasn't a good year for our family, but it all turned out okay in the end."

Anson shook his head incredulously.

"It was a long time ago," Eddie said.

"Not *that* long," Rosie countered.

"What happened?" Anson asked. "I mean, if you don't mind talking about it."

"Basically the divorce just didn't work out for us," Zach teased, his eyes meeting Rosie's. That had been a difficult period in their marriage, but, as Eddie had said, it'd all turned out in the end, due in large part to...

"The judge... Well, she..." Rosie looked at her husband. "You tell them."

"It was Judge Lockhart. That was her name back then. She's Judge Griffin now. I think she could see that the divorce was a mistake for us, but she didn't have any grounds for denying it the way she did with another couple we heard about."

"Actually, I don't think either of us would have accepted a denial. At the time, we were pretty much at loggerheads."

That was putting it mildly, Zach thought, but kept quiet. No point in mentioning it.

"Mom and Dad wanted joint custody of Allison and me," Eddie said. "If Judge Olivia okayed their parenting plan, it meant Allison and I would've had to change houses every few days. Three days with Dad, four days with Mom—that sort of thing."

"They would've stayed in the same school district," Rosie added. She closed the refrigerator and leaned against the kitchen counter, facing the three of them, all sitting at the breakfast bar. "Zach got an apartment a few miles from the house."

"Judge Olivia told Mom and Dad they weren't the ones who needed a stable life," Allison went on to tell him. "Eddie and I were. The judge didn't want us changing residences every few days, so she gave us the family home. Mom and Dad had to move in and out."

"In other words," Eddie said, "when Dad was with us, Mom stayed at his apartment, and vice versa."

"Zach and I weren't too keen on this plan," Rosie inserted.

Anson grinned. "But apparently it worked."

Zach had to agree. "I remember the night Allison and Eddie brought us together, arranging for us to have a romantic dinner here at the house."

"Our parents needed our help," Eddie said, smiling at his sister. "Actually, that was Allison's idea and it was a good one."

"It was indeed." Zach reached across the counter to take Rosie's hand. He raised it to his lips and kissed her fingers. "And I'm very grateful."

"I am, too," Rosie whispered.

"We owe the judge a big debt of thanks," Allison said.

"And I owe *you* one," Anson said in a low voice, his gaze connecting with hers. "You always had faith in me."

"Oh, Anson, I had my moments. I so badly wanted to believe you didn't have anything to do with the fire that burned down the Lighthouse restaurant."

"The evidence *was* damning," he said, frowning slightly. "I couldn't blame you for doubting me."

"When I learned you'd been at the restaurant that night, and then later, when your mother told me you'd started a number of small fires when you were a kid, my faith wavered."

"Mine would have, too." Again Anson came to her defense. "I looked guilty as sin. I can't blame you, Allie."

"Luckily you saw the man who really started the fire and were able to identify him."

Zach had played a role in determining that Warren

Saget, a local builder, was the arsonist. Teaming up with
Sheriff Troy Davis, Zach had convinced Anson to come
forward and speak to the authorities.

"If it wasn't for your dad, I might still be on the run,"
Anson said. "Your family's been a lifeline to me," he
continued. "Mrs. Cox, Rosie, you've been more of a
mother to me than my own. I know Cherry loves me in
her way. She never counted on being a single mother,
and she didn't have the greatest role model herself. She
does the best she can."

Zach admired Anson for defending his mother. He
didn't question that she loved her son. Unfortunately,
Cherry's life had been a long series of low-paying jobs
and living with ne'er-do-wells who used and abused
her. Anson had been instructed to refer to these men
as "uncle," none of them ever being a father figure of
any kind. His father had left Cherry as soon as he discovered she was pregnant. Turned out he already had
a wife and family.

"Are we going to play bingo?" Eddie asked, straightening. "It's tradition, you know." He nudged Anson as
he said that, and Anson elbowed him back.

"Why don't we set it up while Allison and your
mother finish getting dinner ready," Zach suggested.
He slid off the stool and headed into the living room.
He didn't recall how Christmas Eve bingo had begun,
but the kids couldn't have been more than eight and ten.
He thought Rosie's parents might've started it and that
Rosie had carried it on, since she was big on traditions.

In the living room, Zach took out the game. He
handed the cards to Anson to arrange, while Eddie
gathered up the small prizes and placed them on the
coffee table.

"If you have a few minutes I'd like to speak to you privately," Anson said, sitting next to Zach on the sofa.

Eddie picked up on the "private" part right away and excused himself, mumbling that he needed to make a phone call.

Anson waited until Eddie had left the room. "What I said earlier about you and Mrs. Cox being more of a family to me than my own? I meant that."

"We feel the same way about you, Anson. I'm proud of what you've accomplished."

Anson smiled, as if Zach's words had pleased him. "I never applied myself in school. I didn't really have to. Everything came easily to me, so I got through without trying. I had no real plans, no aspirations. Then I met Allison and she encouraged me to do better—to *be* better. I would've done anything to make her happy."

Zach remembered how he'd separated the two as teenagers. Anson had given his word and broken it, and as a result Zach had refused to allow Anson and Allison to date or even talk to each other. On Valentine's Day, Anson had come to the door and handed Zach a card for Allison. At that moment Zach had begun to see a real sense of honor in the boy.

"I loved Allison when I was seventeen, and I love her now," Anson went on. "It hasn't been easy to maintain a long-distance relationship with me living in D.C. and her going to school here in Seattle."

Zach nodded; he understood the challenges of such a relationship.

"I want you to know I've dated other women, but it's Allison I love."

His daughter had gone out with other young men

through the years, but she felt the same way about Anson.

"I believe this conversation is leading up to something," Zach said.

"I'd like to ask your permission to marry Allison," Anson said quickly.

Zach leaned back on the sofa. He'd known this was coming, but hadn't thought it would be so soon. "Allison still has a year of law school left."

"I know. We've talked about that and she's applied to law schools in the Washington, D.C., area."

Zach arched his brows. "She has, has she?" Apparently, this had been an ongoing discussion between them. "So Allison's already accepted your proposal?"

"No, sir," Anson said. Then he nodded. "Well, yes. I realize speaking to you about this is just a formality, but it's important to me."

Zach sent him an encouraging smile.

"Allison wanted me to give her the ring when she picked me up at the airport. I told her I wanted to talk to you and Mrs. Cox first."

Zach could bet his daughter hadn't been keen on that. He approved, though. He liked Anson's old-fashioned sense of protocol and his respect for both Allison and her family.

"Rosie!" Zach called his wife. "Could you come here for a minute? Allison, you, too."

"Sure."

Allison came into the other room, holding her mother's hand.

"It seems that Anson here would like our permission to marry our daughter."

Rosie turned to look at Allison. "But you haven't finished school yet and...you're both so young."

"They've taken both matters into account and still want to get married. Allison will continue her schooling in D.C."

"Oh."

"What do you think?" Zach asked Rosie.

"Well...yes, of course. I would welcome Anson into the family with open arms."

"Oh, thank you, Mom." Allison kissed her mother's cheek and then hurried across the room to her father.

"Hold on a minute," Zach said, stopping her. "I haven't given my consent."

"Daddy!"

Wearing a huge grin, Zach stood and hugged his daughter, and then Anson. "I couldn't imagine a son-in-law I'd rather have. You both have our blessing." Zach was confident in the strength of this relationship, despite their age. They'd proven their commitment to each other. He'd miss his daughter, but the family was close and they'd see her frequently.

"What's going on in here?" Eddie asked, returning to the living room.

"Anson and I are engaged."

"Cool," Eddie said.

"We'd like a June wedding, and then I'll move to Washington, D.C., to be with Anson."

Eddie shook his head. "I don't know about Mom and Dad having an empty nest."

"Hey, it hasn't been a problem so far," Zach told him.

"But it could be." Eddie seemed intent on making his case. "Allison's going to be on the other side of the country, and I'll be away at school."

Rosie frowned and looked at Zach. He shrugged, unsure what his son was getting at.

"Mom," Eddie said. "You need someone to mother. And, Dad, who are you going to boss around? Everyone knows Mom won't put up with that for long."

Allison laughed, but Zach was less amused.

"Now, just a minute, young man—"

Eddie interrupted him. "I've come up with the perfect solution."

"You have?"

Eddie nodded. He turned away for a moment and stepped into the hallway, then came back carrying a basket—with a puppy curled up inside, fast asleep.

"Merry Christmas, Mom and Dad."

"A puppy!" Rosie said, lifting the sleeping pup from his warm bed and holding him close. "He's adorable!"

"What a great idea." Zach grinned, delighted at the prospect of taking a dog for long country rambles. He could already picture the three of them—Rosie, the puppy and him—sitting by the fire....

"Actually, you gave me the idea, Dad. A while back you said you missed having a dog around the house. I'm a starving college student and I couldn't afford to buy you guys a big gift. When we went to get the Christmas tree I heard one of the workers say that Beth Morehouse had a houseful of puppies she needed to find good homes for. So...voilà."

"Now, we'll need to come up with a name," he said.

"I've already named him, okay? I had to call him something. I know you like 1940s and '50s movies, so... meet Bogart. Or Humphrey if you prefer."

"Bogie!" Allison said. "That's it."

"Bogie." Rosie smiled. "This is quite the Christmas," she said, cradling the puppy in her arms. "Not only do we gain a son, but we add a dog to the family, as well."

Seven

"I'll start making the hot chocolate," Beth said, turning away from her daughters. A few minutes in the kitchen would help her prepare to deal with her ex and his…friend. Kent kept insisting Danielle was "just a friend," but Beth felt there was more to it. Really, why would he bring "just a friend" to a traditional family occasion?

Although she had no idea what Kent was thinking, Beth couldn't imagine him actually spending the rest of his life with this woman. It was a mistake. Even her daughters could see that. Kent wouldn't appreciate hearing her opinion, so Beth was determined to keep it to herself—although that was a struggle.

From inside the kitchen Beth heard Sophie greeting Kent and Danielle at the front door and ushering them into the family room. The Christmas tree was still bare, surrounded by the boxes they'd carried down.

"Mom's in the kitchen."

This came from Bailey. Kent must have asked where she was. A moment later, he joined her. "Listen, I'd appreciate it if we—"

"Is there anything I can do?" Danielle asked in the sweetest of voices.

"No, thanks. I've got everything under control," she told the other woman. Her eyes connected with Kent's. She wanted to berate him for bringing Danielle to a family function; instead, she bit her tongue and tried to disguise her feelings, although she suspected she'd failed.

She realized she'd need to get used to the fact that Kent was his own man now and made his own decisions. Beth forced a smile and continued stirring the chocolate.

"Dad," Bailey called. "Come and help."

Kent hesitated and it looked as if there was something else he wanted to say. With obvious reluctance, he returned to the family room, Danielle on his heels.

Beth took as long as she dared in the kitchen. Fortunately, Grace phoned while she was there, which kept her occupied for another five minutes. Beth peered into the living room when she'd hung up. From her vantage point, she could see that the girls had opened the boxes of old ornaments and were reminiscing with their father. Danielle sat on the sofa, her expression bored. Eventually she reached for her cell phone and started texting.

"Mom!" Sophie shouted. "Where are you?"

"Coming!" Beth loaded the serving tray with pretty holiday mugs. She'd decorated the top of each mug of cocoa with whipped topping and chocolate sprinkles, which was how Kent and the girls had always liked it. "Here we go," she said, hoping she sounded cheerful. Surely there was a reward in heaven for first wives who were nice to their exes' new girlfriends.

"Remember this one?" Sophie said, and held up a

snowman she'd made with a wood-burning kit when she was around ten.

"What I remember is the blister you got on your finger because you weren't careful," Kent teased his daughter.

"I was so proud of this silly snowman. I was sure I'd make a career out of wood-burning."

Danielle gave a saccharine smile. "It's…lovely." The words rang empty as her phone chirped and she returned to texting.

"It's terrible," Sophie said. "In fact, it's downright ugly."

"Well, maybe," Danielle agreed, putting her cell back in her sweater pocket, "but you were just a kid. I'm surprised you kept it, though. If it was me I would've tossed it years ago."

Beth opened her mouth to defend her daughter, then closed it. No need to get into a useless argument.

"If you think it's ugly, why would you put it on the tree?" Danielle asked. "I mean, you're right, it really isn't very attractive." She stood and retrieved an ornament from the box. "There are some darling ones here." She held up one of the felt gingerbread men Beth had sewn the first Christmas she and Kent were married. "Now this is kind of amateurish, but it's…nice. By comparison."

"We put up the wooden snowman," Beth said, carefully handing Danielle her cocoa, "because Sophie made it herself. The decorated tree in the living room is for show. This one is for family, for memories of Christmases past."

"Sort of like that Charles Dickens book," Danielle said. "The one with the ghosts. And Tiny Tim."

"Something like that," Beth murmured as she brought Kent his hot cocoa.

"Do you have one without any chocolate sprinkles?" Danielle asked.

"Sure." Beth retrieved the cup and went back to the kitchen. She dumped the whipped cream in the sink and added a fresh dollop minus the chocolate sprinkles.

"Mom sewed those for her and Dad's first Christmas," Bailey was telling Danielle when Beth came back.

"The hot chocolate is even better than I remember." Kent spoke quickly, breaking into his daughter's reminiscence.

"I make good hot chocolate, too," Danielle said. "I'm an excellent cook. I want you to try my macaroni and cheese."

"Uh, sure." Kent looked decidedly uncomfortable.

Danielle beamed. "I have a special cooking trick. You start with the boxed kind and then you just add stuff. My secret is to put ketchup in the water when I cook the noodles."

"I'll have to try that myself," Beth said politely, trying not to cringe. Difficult as it was, she turned her mind away from Kent and his...friend. She hated to admit this, but she was jealous of Danielle.

Danielle sneezed once, loudly. So loudly, in fact, that it startled Beth and Princess, too. The sneeze sounded like a moose in heat—or what Beth imagined that would sound like.

"Oh, sorry," Danielle said, clearly embarrassed.

"Bless you," Sophie said.

Bailey handed Danielle a tissue.

"Thank you." She noisily blew her nose. "It's that

dog," she said, pointing an accusing finger at Princess. "I'm allergic to dogs."

"Oh, you should've said something earlier." Beth immediately collected Princess and took her to the kennel outside. Even with Princess out of the room, there was still Roscoe, sleeping beside the fireplace. While Beth kept a tidy house, there was bound to be dog hair everywhere. It was the perfect excuse to send Kent and Danielle on their merry way.

"Beth."

Kent met her on the back porch as she returned from the kennel. He kept his hands in his pockets, his arms held close to his body to ward off the cold. He followed Beth inside, to the laundry room. One of the five remaining puppies jumped up, balancing his paws against her calf. Beth automatically reached down and brought him into her arms, resting her cheek against his soft head.

"Listen," Kent said. "I hadn't planned to bring Danielle with me. It's just that—"

"Don't worry about it."

She carefully put the puppy back on the floor. She attempted to brush off his apology because her heart was doing crazy things. With the two of them in such a small space, the atmosphere was intimate, and with both doors closed it was private. All she needed to do was lean forward ever so slightly and their lips would meet…

Where did *that* idea come from? She couldn't give in to the impulse. But it seemed so natural to kiss Kent, to press her mouth to his. Beth immediately opened the door leading into the house.

Unfortunately, she forgot about the puppies. An open

door was an opportunity and they took it. They shot out of the room as though fleeing a burning building.

Beth rushed after them and Kent did, too. He trapped one by falling to his knees and had him back inside the laundry room seconds later. Beth wasn't nearly as lucky. Seizing their opportunity, the other four dashed in different directions.

Beth knew the instant one of the puppies made it into the family room because Danielle let out a squeal. "Get that dog," she cried, apparently to one or both of the girls. Her command was followed by another moose-in-heat sneeze.

Beth hurried into the room. "I'm so sorry," she said, and she was. She'd had no intention of freeing the puppies when she'd opened the door. The truth was she'd completely forgotten they were there.

Bailey grabbed one puppy and Sophie another. Beth scooped up the third. The last one made a beeline for the Christmas tree and got tangled in the bottom garland.

"Get those dogs out of here," Danielle shouted between sneezes. "Oh, good grief, there's another one. What is this place—a puppy mill?"

"My mother would *never*—"

"It's all right," Beth said, cutting Bailey off. "Danielle is understandably upset. I apologize, Danielle. I opened the door without realizing—"

"You did that on purpose!"

"Danielle," Kent said, his voice calm and reasonable, unlike hers. "It was an honest mistake."

The other woman sank down on the sofa and held a wad of tissues to her nose before she sneezed three times in quick succession.

"I'm afraid there's dog hair all over the house," Beth said. "Maybe it would be best if—"

Danielle held up one hand, stopping her. The other clasped a tissue to her face. "I have allergy medication. We will not be leaving on my account." This last part was said in a muffled voice that nonetheless conveyed steadfast determination.

Kent sat next to Danielle, who sneezed again.

It wasn't funny; still, Beth couldn't help it—she had to smother a giggle. Kent caught her eye and knew instantly that she was having trouble hiding her amusement, and that was when Beth lost it. She started laughing and tried desperately to hide her laughter by coughing.

"What's so funny?" Danielle demanded.

"Nothing," Kent said promptly, getting to his feet. "I think, uh, Beth might have swallowed wrong."

"This…isn't funny."

"No, it isn't," Kent said. He bent down and untangled the last puppy from the garland on the tree and brought him back to the laundry room.

In the meantime Beth carried Roscoe upstairs and out of harm's way. Making it through tonight would require a Christmas miracle.

The phone rang as she came down the stairs. Call display told her it was Bob Beldon. They exchanged Christmas greetings, then he said, "I heard you're looking for homes for some puppies."

"Yes, I am."

"Great. Well, I'm interested in taking one."

They chatted for a few more minutes and she'd just replaced the receiver when the phone rang a second time.

"Your mother gets more phone calls than a bookie," Beth heard Danielle comment.

Teri Polgar was inquiring about a puppy for her sister, Christie.

A moment later, another call. This time it was Ted. "How's it going?" he asked.

"About as well as could be expected." She'd mentioned casually that her ex-husband was coming to Cedar Cove for Christmas. Lowering her voice, she said, "Except that Kent arrived with a...friend."

"A friend?" Ted sounded perplexed. "I was asking about the puppies."

"Oh...the puppies." She wanted to roll her eyes. Of course he'd be phoning about the puppies. "Five down and five to go, although I just heard from someone who's a possibility. And if Bob Beldon takes one too, that'll leave three."

"Listen, I know someone else who could be interested. Gloria Ashton—for her parents," he said. "Would it be all right if I stopped by later to say merry Christmas?"

"Sure. That would be nice." Ted was exactly the balm she needed. And, if he came over, Kent would see that she hadn't been twiddling her thumbs for the past three years.

She missed Kent. She missed their life together and it was killing her that he'd found someone else. The divorce wasn't the end, she realized now; his remarriage would be. If he married Danielle—and the other woman had certainly staked her claim on him—it would mean their life together was over. Really over.

"Who just called?" Bailey asked.

"Bob Beldon. And then Teri Polgar. And Ted."

"Bob from the B and B?" Kent looked up at her. "Did he want to speak to me?"

"No, no, he was inquiring about a puppy."

"Oh, dear," Danielle murmured and, for good measure, sneezed again.

Beth had assumed she would've taken one of her allergy pills by now.

"What did Ted want?" Sophie asked.

"He'll be visiting later."

Bailey and Sophie seemed gratified by this bit of news. "That's wonderful," Sophie said as Bailey nodded. "He's a real sweetheart."

"Oh?" Kent asked, turning to his daughters for an explanation.

"Yeah, he reminds me of the vet in those James Herriot books you read us when we were little," Bailey told her father.

Ted? James Herriot? What were her girls up to? Beth sent Bailey a disapproving frown, which her daughter chose to ignore.

They resumed trimming the tree, and when they'd finished, it didn't look half-bad. With its mismatched ornaments collected over the years, it had its own homespun charm. There was the wooden snowman Sophie had made at the age of ten. And a photo of Bailey in the first grade, framed in Popsicle sticks. Another that resembled a pincushion, which Sophie had made when she was in the third grade. Beth's gingerbread men. And a few that she and the girls had constructed through the years with varying degrees of artistic skill.

They stepped back and, hardly aware she was doing it, Beth stood next to Kent. Delighted with their tree, she glanced up at him and smiled. He smiled back and their eyes met. Beth had to force herself to look away; when she did, she saw Danielle watching them both.

The other woman's eyes narrowed, and Beth could tell that Danielle wasn't pleased. Without making an issue of it, Beth moved away from Kent.

Searching for something to do, Beth picked up the empty cocoa mugs and carried them into the kitchen. She was busy placing them in the dishwasher when Danielle joined her.

"I know what you're doing," Danielle said without preamble. She rested her hip against the kitchen counter, crossed her arms and glared at Beth.

"Putting dirty dishes in the dishwasher?" Beth asked.

"You don't like it that Kent brought me here."

Beth straightened and leaned against the counter, too, crossing her own arms. "And what gives you that impression?"

"I saw the way you looked at him just now."

"Really? And how was that?"

"You're jealous."

"Am I?" Beth asked, striving to sound anything but jealous.

"You want him back."

Beth laughed. "In case you've forgotten, I had him for twenty-three years."

"And you miss him."

Beth faked a short laugh. "I don't know what you think you saw, but let me assure you, you're mistaken."

"No, I'm not," Danielle insisted.

Beth looked into the other room to make sure Kent and the girls couldn't overhear this rather unpleasant conversation. "Well, then, let's agree to disagree," she suggested in a low voice, hoping to avoid a pointless exchange.

"You want him."

Beth disregarded the comment, turned her back on Danielle and continued loading the dishwasher.

"You can deny you're jealous all you want, but if you listen to only one thing, listen to this," Danielle said tightly. "He told me about the divorce and how you wanted out of the marriage. You blew it and now you regret it."

This was too much. If Danielle thought she was helping… Well, she wasn't. "Listen," Beth said, pronouncing each word distinctly. "If you want Kent, he's all yours. You're welcome to him." With that she slammed the dishwasher closed and turned to see Kent standing in the doorway.

Eight

The scent of cinnamon and allspice filled Peggy Beldon's kitchen as she arranged the decorated sugar cookies on colorful plates lining the counter.

The plates of cookies, toffee and hand-rolled chocolates were her and Bob's gift to their friends each year. Peggy enjoyed baking and never more than at Christmas. She began wrapping the plates in red cellophane and tying the ends with a ribbon. She and Bob delivered the plates on Christmas Eve, usually late in the afternoon.

Thyme and Tide, their bed-and-breakfast, did fairly well this time of year and she was grateful that despite a weak economy they continued to be busy. They already had several reservations for the winter months and the summer looked promising.

Currently they had two guests, who seemed to be a couple, although they had their own rooms. Beth Morehouse's ex and…Diana? No, Danielle. It wasn't unusual to have guests over the Christmas holidays, although Peggy would've preferred to close, but as Bob said, they couldn't turn down business. Christmas or not, they had rooms to rent. She could guarantee that the Christmas morning buffet would be something Kent Morehouse and his friend would long remember.

Humming a Christmas carol to herself, Peggy glanced out the kitchen window and saw her husband pull into the driveway. He'd run a few errands for her. A couple of minutes later, she glanced outside again, wondering why he hadn't come in.

Just then the door opened. Bob knocked the snow off his boots as he entered the house, a big grin on his face. By nature her husband was an upbeat, happy person, always sociable, which was one reason their B and B was successful. Peggy tended to remain in the background, creating the meals, while Bob provided the warm welcome and the entertainment.

"What took so long?" she asked, pausing to kiss him and take the bags out of his hands.

"You should see the grocery store. There wasn't a cart to be had."

"Christmas Eve…what did you expect?"

"Everyone seems to leave the shopping until the last minute—even my wife." He kissed her cheek but not before Peggy saw him swipe a cookie.

Bob reached for a date bar and she returned his sheepish smile with an approving grin. She had plenty to spare and, after his trek to the store, Bob deserved a reward.

"Do you have one for Roy and Corrie?" Bob asked, surveying the kitchen counter and the row of finished plates.

"Of course."

"Troy and Faith Davis?"

"Bob, you know I do. What makes you ask?"

"Just wanted to be sure. I saw Faith shopping and Corrie was coming into the store as I was leaving." Bob poured himself a cup of coffee and sat on the kitchen stool, watching as Peggy put the final touches on the gifts, adding small handmade cards. These cards were another gift. Each included a personal note thanking the recipients for their friendship.

"I'm so thankful to Roy," she said fervently. "Who knows what would've happened if he hadn't been willing to take us on as clients." The private investigator had stepped in at a crucial time in their lives.

"Troy Davis, too," Bob reminded her.

"Oh, yes."

The memory of those painful days took over her thoughts for a moment. A stranger had arrived late one night in the middle of a storm, rain-drenched and seeking a room. Bob hadn't recognized the man but had sensed…something. He'd had a bad feeling about him. Peggy, however, couldn't turn someone away in the middle of a downpour. In retrospect, she wished she'd listened to her husband, because the next morning the man was dead.

"I know what you're thinking," Bob said, sipping his coffee.

"So now you're a mind reader, too?" she asked with a smile. Her husband did possess multiple talents—including acting and singing—but she had serious doubts regarding his psychic abilities.

"After all these years I can read you like a *People* magazine," he joked right back. "It's about Max Russell, isn't it?"

She could pretend otherwise but didn't. "Yes. I was

remembering the night he showed up and how you didn't want to give him a room."

"That night was a turning point for me," Bob admitted. "The start of healing. I was finally able to lay what happened in 'Nam to rest."

Bob and his best friend from high school, Dan Sherman—who'd married Grace—had enlisted in the army together under the buddy program. Following basic training they'd been sent to Vietnam. Max had been part of their unit.

The war changed all three men. An incident involving the deaths of innocent civilians had haunted them.

For years Dan Sherman had struggled with depression. When he was in that state of mind, he'd block out family and friends, isolating himself from the world.

After the war Bob had turned to alcohol for solace. Their marriage suffered, and more than once Peggy decided to leave him, taking their son and daughter. Each time Bob convinced her he'd give up drinking and be the husband she deserved. He'd tried, but with limited success. After a few weeks of sobriety Bob would return to the bottle. He hit bottom after losing a promising job, and that was when he went into rehab. Thankfully, he came out a different person. He hadn't had a drink since that day more than twenty years ago. Or was it twenty-five? She no longer kept count of the years. Each day was a victory, each day a blessing.

"I mailed Hannah a Christmas card," Peggy confessed. Even now, knowing what she did about the young woman, Peggy had a soft spot for her despite the grief she'd caused them both.

Hannah was the dead man's daughter and, in fact, had been responsible for his murder.

"Did she write back?"

"No." Peggy knew it was highly unlikely that Hannah would acknowledge the card. That was fine. Perhaps it was for the best.

"You really came to care for her, didn't you?"

"Well, yes, but..." Peggy had mixed feelings about the woman. Hannah had attempted to steer blame for the murder toward Bob, and that was unforgivable in Peggy's eyes. Still, the poor girl had lived a hard life with a father tortured by the past. Max took his self-hatred out on Hannah and her mother. Hannah's mind became as twisted as her father's, and as far as she was concerned, he deserved to die.

She'd tried to kill him once before and, to Hannah's horror, her beloved mother had died instead. Her father had survived the car accident, which made Hannah's hatred of him even greater. She had deeply loved her mother and to lose her when she'd so carefully planned to kill Max had nearly destroyed her. Hannah redoubled her efforts to make her father pay.

Again Bob's instincts had been on target. From the first he hadn't trusted Max's daughter, who'd shown up at their home after her father's death. Although he wasn't able to identify exactly what he disliked about Hannah, he'd made his feelings clear. Hannah had avoided him as much as possible. It wasn't until much later that they understood why.

"I'll be forever grateful those days are gone," Bob murmured, still sipping his coffee.

"Me, too," Peggy agreed. "You're free now. The past is over and the future is bright."

"I'm a lucky man," Bob said.

Nevertheless, those memories were all too vivid, all too real.

"Hey, why so melancholy?" Bob said, tipping up her chin with his index finger. "We have a lot to celebrate. Hollie and Marc will be here this afternoon and we'll have a real family Christmas."

Peggy instantly brightened. Their children were coming for the holidays and spending a few days. To have both of them there was a rare treat. Their family had healed in the past few years.

Hollie and Marc had grown up in the volatile atmosphere created by their father's problems with alcohol. As much as possible, Peggy had shielded them. It'd taken her years of Al Anon meetings to straighten out her own thinking. Without realizing what she was doing, Peggy had enabled Bob in his drinking. Once she'd stepped aside and allowed him to deal with the consequences of his actions, he was forced to admit that he had a problem.

Those years of struggle had taken a heavy toll. It was only since the move to Cedar Cove that Hollie and Marc were willing to have a relationship with their father. Both were professionals, married but without children. Peggy envied her friends their grandchildren but, so far, her own kids had shown no interest in starting families. Peggy had accepted the situation and was content to lavish affection on her friends' grandchildren, especially those of her best friend, Corrie McAfee.

"We'd better head out with those gift plates soon, don't you think?" Peggy said. She wanted to be home when the children arrived with their spouses.

"Anytime now."

"Everything's just about ready," she said, and finished the last of the gift cards with a flourish.

Bob put his cup in the sink and walked into the large family room, where they'd set up the Christmas tree. "I have an early present for you."

"Oh?" she asked, her curiosity piqued.

He looked pleased with himself. "Actually, your gift's in the garage."

"Bob," Peggy breathed. They'd discussed buying her a new vehicle, but she'd assumed she'd be making the choice. "You bought me a car?"

Bob laughed. "Sorry. That's a natural assumption but no, it isn't a car. I hope you aren't disappointed."

"Of course not, but I am somewhat curious as to why this can't wait until morning."

"Well... This is the type of gift we'd generally talk about in advance."

She couldn't imagine what he was talking about. "Give me a clue."

"Remember the other day when we were at the library?"

"Of course...but what's that got to do with anything?" Peggy couldn't recall anything special taking place. They'd dropped off books and picked up others. Both were big readers and loyal library patrons.

"Remember the children reading to the dogs?"

"Well, yes, Grace told me about the program. It seems to be doing well."

"Largely thanks to Beth Morehouse, the woman who owns the Christmas tree farm."

"Where we bought our tree," she said, certain Bob would clarify everything in a moment. Her husband had a flair for drama, which was one reason he volunteered at the local theater. Over the years Bob had appeared in a number of productions, everything from musicals to *Death of a Salesman*. It was his creative outlet the same way gardening and cooking were hers.

"I'm sure there's a point to all this," she said, urging him to explain.

"There is."

"Wonderful. Might I suggest you get back to my Christmas gift that's currently being stored in the garage?"

"You'll see."

"I'm waiting with bated breath," she returned, smiling.

"Stay here."

"Okay," Peggy said. "Do you want me to close my eyes?"

Bob paused at the back door and nodded. "Good idea. Close your eyes."

Peggy sat at the kitchen table with one hand on her coffee mug and the other in her lap and squeezed her eyes shut. She wondered if her gift was what had kept Bob in the garage so long after he'd driven home. After a couple of minutes she heard him come in.

"Can I open my eyes yet?"

"Just a second."

Her husband's footsteps echoed as he moved toward the Christmas tree. "All right," he called out. "You can open your eyes now."

Peggy did, and then blinked. Beneath the tree, surrounded by wrapped gifts, sat a basket, one she kept in the garage and often took into the garden. Bedded down inside was…a puppy. A small black puppy.

Peggy didn't know if she should laugh or cry. "You got me a *puppy?*"

"I was thinking we could use a dog," Bob said.

"But a puppy?" she said, unsure of her feelings.

"Look at her, Peggy, she's so cute. I couldn't resist. We need a dog, and Beth Morehouse has a litter of ten she needs to find homes for."

"So *that* was the connection with Beth and the library. You volunteered," she said. "Obviously."

"Well, yes…"

"You'll train her?"

"If you want, but she's your dog. You're happy about this, aren't you?"

The puppy raised her head and regarded Peggy with large doleful eyes.

"What do you want to name her?" Bob asked, lifting the tiny squirming creature out of the basket and bringing her to Peggy.

The puppy immediately made herself at home in Peggy's arms. "Let's name her…Millie."

"Millie, it is," Bob said. "Merry Christmas, sweetheart."

"Merry Christmas, darling. And Merry Christmas, Millie."

Millie barked, adding her own greetings.

Nine

"Let's go for a sleigh ride," Bailey said excitedly, as if this was the most brilliant idea of the century. "Can we, Mom?" She clasped both hands. "I mean, now that Gloria and Chad have picked up the puppy…"

"Ah…" Beth hesitated as a sense of dread filled her. Every minute with Kent and Danielle felt more awkward than the one before.

"Mom, we should. Dad's never seen the Christmas tree farm." Sophie was as animated as her sister.

"You want to, don't you, Dad?" Bailey asked, hurrying to her father's side and slipping her arm through his.

"That way Danielle can breathe some fresh air and not have to worry about sneezing," Sophie said in a solicitous voice.

Beth didn't dare look at her ex-husband. She had to believe he was as miserable as she was. This entire family Christmas was a disaster. She'd seen the expression on his face when she'd so vehemently declared Danielle was welcome to him. Shock and pain had flashed in his eyes so quickly she wasn't even sure she'd read his feelings correctly. Everything inside her cried out to take the words back, swear that none of it was true. But she couldn't do that. Not with Danielle standing right there.

"Danielle probably isn't up to this," Kent said with an unmistakable lack of enthusiasm.

Beth figured the other woman would willingly return to the Thyme and Tide. She couldn't be enjoying the afternoon any more than Beth was. The only ones who seemed to derive any pleasure from this fiasco were Bailey and Sophie, who were apparently oblivious to the tension in the room.

"A sleigh ride *might* be fun," Danielle said with a halfhearted shrug.

Bailey and Sophie leaped up and down and clapped their hands. Their behavior reminded Beth of when they were youngsters and were told they could stay up past their bedtime.

"I didn't know you had a sleigh," Kent said as he reached for his coat and gloves. His scarf, Beth noticed, was one she'd knit him years earlier for Christmas. It warmed her to know that he still wore it. Did he think of her every time he put it on?

"The sleigh, which is pretty old, is in one of the outbuildings," she said. "It came with the property. We don't use it much."

"A sleigh ride is perfect after a snowfall, though. Right, Mom?" Sophie asked.

Perfect wasn't exactly the word she'd use.

"You don't have any horses." Kent seemed to be looking for excuses to get out of this. Beth didn't blame him; she'd rather avoid a cozy ride herself. She'd had about all the togetherness she could handle.

"Mom's neighbors. The Nelsons," Bailey explained. "They have horses and said we can borrow them anytime we want." Without waiting for the go-ahead, Bailey picked up the phone and grabbed the personal directory Beth kept in a kitchen drawer.

"We'll have a great time," Sophie told Kent.

"The Nelsons said no problem." Bailey replaced the receiver, her eyes shining with glee.

"I'll go get a few blankets," Beth muttered, eager to make an escape. She rushed up the stairs and into her bedroom. Slumping on the edge of her bed, she brought her hands to her heated face. She wasn't sure how much longer she'd be able to pull this off.

"Get a grip," she ordered herself. She walked into the master bath and splashed cold water on her cheeks. Her reflection in the mirror revealed that her face was flushed. She looked feverish. This wasn't due to illness, though, but acute embarrassment.

"Mom," Sophie called her from the foot of the stairs. "The Nelsons said they'd bring over the horses."

Beth came out of her bedroom. "Okay," she called down. "I'll be there in a minute." Collecting warm blankets from the hall closet, she returned to the main floor.

By the time she got her hat, coat and gloves, Kent and the girls had opened the doors to the storage shed where the sleigh was kept. The large white uncovered sleigh had two red velvet benches, one of them for the driver.

John Nelson, who lived next door, walked over, leading two large geldings. Kent introduced himself. Danielle was still in the house, refreshing her makeup or so Beth assumed.

"When you're finished, would you mind if we took the sleigh out for a ride?" John asked.

"Of course not," Beth told him. She glanced up at

the sky. "I can't imagine we'll be out long. When we're finished, I'll take the sleigh over to your place."

"I appreciate it, Beth. You're a good neighbor."

"So are you."

The harnesses were in the storage shed, and John helped Beth hitch the two horses to the sleigh.

Danielle had come out of the house but remained on the porch until that was done. John left, and the girls climbed on board the sleigh to arrange the blankets.

Danielle looked uncertain, as if she wasn't sure a sleigh ride was something she wanted, after all. "It's cold out here." She squinted at the sky. "And it looks like it's going to snow. Plus, I'm expecting a phone call."

"Snow! Isn't that *wonderful?*" Bailey sounded as if snow was the most magical thing that could possibly happen.

"I'm not used to the cold."

"Then you need to sit between us," Sophie said. "Bailey and I will keep you snug and warm."

Kent helped Danielle into the sleigh, and Bailey and Sophie immediately covered her lap with blankets and wrapped an extra one about her shoulders. By the time they'd finished, all that showed was Danielle's pinched face.

Not until Beth climbed into the worn front seat did she realize that the only place left for Kent to sit was next to her. He seemed to realize that at the same time she did. They stared at each other until Kent got into the sleigh. They sat as far apart on the bench as humanly possible.

"Would you like me to take the reins?" he asked, refusing to look at her.

"If you'd like." She handed them over, knowing he was capable of managing the horses and sleigh.

They started off with a jolt and Danielle let out a cry of alarm. After the initial jerk, the ride went smoothly. The horses' hooves made muted clopping sounds as the sleigh glided over the snowy road.

"You going to be my navigator?" Kent asked.

"Sure."

Kent had moved toward the middle of the seat and she did, too, for fear of falling off if the sleigh hit bumpy ground.

Kent seemed willing to overlook her earlier comment. She was grateful and wished she could take back the lie. "Go left at the fork in the road," she told him, pointing in that direction.

"How many acres do you have here?" he asked, sounding genuinely interested. The trees had been trimmed and shaped until they were the perfect size for Christmas. Now they glistened with bright, fresh snow.

"Forty acres in total, but only twenty are planted in trees. I'm planting another five acres each year and replacing the ones we've cut."

Kent held the reins loosely. "I assumed most families bought artificial trees these days."

"Certainly that's the trend, but there are still plenty of people who prefer a fresh tree, especially if they can chop it down themselves. It makes for wonderful memories. And after Christmas, people cut them up for compost, so ecologically speaking, you could argue that they're superior."

"That's good."

"In addition, a lot of my trees are shipped overseas."

"Really."

She chatted easily, explaining what she'd learned in the past three seasons and her hopes for the future. After a while, she paused, embarrassed that she'd talked for so long. "I apologize. I didn't mean to drone on like that."

He gave her a quick smile. "You really love it here, don't you?"

"It's a very different lifestyle from California, but I needed a change. I was in a horrible rut." The instant the words were out, she regretted being so honest. "I didn't mean that the way it sounded. What I said earlier, it…isn't— I wish…"

"Don't worry about it," he murmured.

Kent had always been ready to forgive and forget; she admired that about him. She was the one who held on to hurts far longer than she should.

"We should sing Christmas carols," Bailey suggested, and then broke into "Silent Night." Sophie joined in and so did Kent. Beth added her own voice. The last one to sing was Danielle. Unfortunately, she was off-key and sounded terrible.

Beth chanced a look at Kent and found him glancing at her at the same time. They broke into giggles, which they did their best to hide.

The group's enthusiasm faded after two or three songs, and their voices gradually dwindled away.

"Remember our first Christmas?" Kent asked, keeping his voice low.

"I thought about it…recently. It was a magical time for us, wasn't it?" He met her eyes for several seconds until she forced herself to look down. The intensity of the attraction she felt confused her. Disconcerted her. Oh, dear. It was happening again and this time Danielle was with them.

As the sleigh glided through the snow, she pointed to another turn in the road, one that cut through the property.

"Right or left?"

"Left." She was so caught up in the moment that she'd said *left* when she meant *right*.

Kent turned right. "Sorry," he said, sounding flustered. "You said left, didn't you?"

"No, this is fine," she told him. She clenched her gloved hands in her lap, grateful that the wind and cold were a convenient excuse for the color splotching her face.

"Oh, look," Sophie cried. "It's snowing again."

Thick, fat flakes drifted lazily from a slate-gray sky.

"It'll probably melt by morning," Danielle said, "and everything will be mud and slush."

"But for now it's beautiful," Beth countered. This was the coldest winter on record in the Pacific Northwest. The weatherperson broadcasting from the Seattle TV station had been effusive about the unusual amount of snow in the area, especially this early in the winter.

"I'm cold," Danielle complained. "And I can't move my arms."

"Let me help you," Bailey said.

"Ouch! You're pulling the blankets tighter. I feel like a sausage."

"I thought you said you were cold."

"I am, but I want to breathe, too," Danielle snapped. "Take this ridiculous thing off me."

"Girls," Beth said, twisting around. Danielle was right; she did resemble a sausage. "Make her comfortable."

"Can we go back to the house soon?" Danielle pleaded.

"I'll head over there now," Kent told her. He glanced at Beth and grinned boyishly. "Okay, navigator, which way?"

"Recalculating, recalculating," she said, using the tinny voice of her car's navigational system.

Kent laughed and turned the sleigh around when he came to a place where that was possible.

"Do you ever think back to those early years?" he asked with his attention focused on the road ahead. "When we were first married…"

The snow was coming down thicker and faster, making for limited visibility.

"I…try not to, but yes, I do." She hadn't wanted to admit that, but it seemed senseless to deny the truth. "You?"

"Sometimes." He paused. "What happened to us, Beth?"

"I…wish I knew."

"Me, too."

"Are we there yet?" Danielle asked plaintively.

A question hovered on the end of Beth's tongue but she refused to ask it. If Kent was looking for a second wife who was completely her opposite, he'd found that woman in Danielle. She and Beth were about as dissimilar as any two women could be. Perhaps that was what he wanted. The thought depressed her…. Unless he was telling the truth and Danielle really *was* just a friend. But in that case, why did she stick to Kent like glue? Why had he even brought her to Cedar Cove?

"Mom?" Bailey asked. "My birthday's in September—when did you get pregnant with me?"

"Bailey!" Beth was shocked that her daughter would ask such a question, especially in front of Danielle.

"Christmas Eve," Kent answered.

"Really? Wow. You're sure?"

"Yup."

"So tonight's more of a celebration than I realized."

"What about me?" Sophie wanted to know.

"Easter," Beth said. "It was an early Easter that year. We were at your parents'. Remember, Kent?"

His eyes widened as the memory drifted back. He caught her eye and they both struggled to contain their amusement. They'd slept in the guest bedroom, which was just down the hall from his parents' room. Their bed squeaked...so they'd rolled onto the floor and Kent's foot had become tangled in the lamp cord and the lamp came crashing down on him. On hearing the crash, his mother had knocked on the door to make sure everything was all right. It'd been a comedy of errors.

"What's so funny?" Danielle demanded.

Beth felt guilty for being so rude as to exclude everyone else from their private conversation. "I apologize, Danielle," she said, turning around. "Kent and I were... just remembering something that happened years ago."

"I was the result," Sophie announced proudly.

"Can we talk about something different?" Danielle said, clearly not amused.

"Of course," Beth assured her.

"I always wanted a brother," Bailey said. "An older brother."

"You got your sister instead."

"Yeah. And not only that, she's younger."

"I never had a sister," Danielle said. "And *my* brother

was younger and a real nuisance. He used to spy on me and my friends."

"Sophie used to spy on me."

"Did not."

"Did, too."

"Girls," Beth said, annoyed by their behavior. "You're out of grade school. Please act like it."

They broke into peals of laughter.

"What?" Beth turned again to see what her daughters were laughing about now.

"Mom, you're so predictable. That's exactly what we told Danielle you'd say."

Kent pulled the sleigh over to the shed and handed the reins to Beth while he jumped down. He helped Sophie out first, then Danielle and Bailey.

"I'll take the sled over to the Nelsons'," Beth said, but before she could set off, Kent leaped back into place beside her.

"I'll go with you."

"That isn't necessary," she told him, thinking he'd want to be inside with the others.

"Yes, it is. You aren't going to argue with me, are you?"

"I…no."

"Good, because it would be very tempting to stop you the way I used to once upon a time."

Beth swallowed hard. She'd forgotten. In the early days of their marriage, anytime she disagreed with him, Kent would take her in his arms and kiss her.

Ten

"Honey, can you get the door?" Corrie called from the back bedroom. She swore that if Roy didn't get his hearing checked soon, she'd start ignoring every word he said. That would give him a little demonstration of what she put up with every day.

"Okay," he yelled from the living room.

With an exasperated sigh Corrie went back to her wrapping paper and ribbon. She was almost finished with Noelle's birthday gift, the one they'd take to Grace Harding's party. She still needed to arrange the last of the Christmas presents under the tree before their children arrived for dinner, which would be followed by Christmas Eve church services. After that, they'd go to Noelle's first-birthday celebration at the Hardings'. Gloria, Roy and Corrie's eldest daughter, would be coming tonight. Corrie hoped Gloria would bring Chad Timmons.

She couldn't help worrying about Gloria, who was single, pregnant and determined to manage on her own. What disturbed Corrie most was the fact that there was no reason for Gloria to be so stubborn. Chad loved her;

Corrie was convinced of that. She'd invited him to dinner and hoped Gloria wouldn't be upset with her. Oh, she hadn't made a secret of it, but she hadn't talked it over with Gloria, either.

Mack and Mary Jo would be with them and of course little Noelle, too. She'd been born on Christmas Eve one year ago, at the Harding ranch; Mack had delivered her. Corrie had a lovely birthday cake ready for her adopted granddaughter, not to mention a pile of gifts. Corrie couldn't wait to watch Noelle open them. There was nothing like a baby to bring excitement and joy back to Christmas.

"Corrie," Roy shouted. "It's the Beldons."

"I'll be right there," she shouted back as she finished tying the ribbon on the gift she'd just wrapped.

Corrie had been expecting Peggy and Bob to stop by at some point that afternoon. It was tradition. Every Christmas Eve the Beldons came over with a plate of Peggy's homemade cookies and specialty candies.

"Merry Christmas," Corrie said, hurrying into the room and opening her arms. She hugged Bob and then, after taking the plate from Peggy, embraced her, too.

"I hope we aren't interrupting your day."

"Nonsense," Corrie told her. "You know you're welcome anytime."

"Especially when you come bearing gifts," Roy joked.

"Sit down, please. I've got eggnog and coffee, whichever you prefer."

"We can only stay a few minutes," Bob said, claiming the corner of the sofa. "Hollie and Marc are driving over from Spokane."

"Wonderful! I'm glad they can make it." Corrie

hadn't met the Beldons' daughter and son, but she'd heard lots about them. She and Peggy often met for lunch and had a strong friendship.

"It'll be good to have them here for Christmas."

"We'll have a full house ourselves," Roy said. "Mack and Mary Jo are coming for dinner tonight and they'll be here on Christmas Day, as well."

"Gloria will be here tonight, too, and she'll attend church services with us," Corrie added.

"And Christmas Day?" Peggy asked.

Corrie shrugged. "She didn't say. I imagine she'll come for dinner, unless…"

"Unless?"

"Unless she plans to spend it with Chad."

"Ah, yes. How are things going between her and Chad?"

"Fine, I think. Gloria hasn't said much, but she seems happier these days, less…confused. I know they're seeing each other regularly. If they have any wedding plans, however, they haven't shared them with us."

"Chad put the crib together," Roy said. "I volunteered and so did Mack, but Gloria said Chad would do it."

"That sounds positive," Peggy murmured.

"I just wish those two would get married," Corrie responded. "I know the world's different these days. So many young women choose to be single mothers, but it's hard work."

"A baby needs a father," Roy inserted. "I wanted to tell Gloria that, but Corrie wouldn't let me."

"When has that stopped you in the past?" Corrie retorted as she headed into the kitchen to get their drinks. It still annoyed her that her husband had gone against her wishes and informed Chad of Gloria's pregnancy.

After she and Chad had broken up, Gloria had wanted to keep the information from him.

The irony of her daughter's situation astonished her. This was history repeating itself. Well, almost...

Years ago, in college, Corrie had discovered she was pregnant after Roy had ended their relationship. Instead of letting him know, she'd returned home and given her daughter up for adoption. Not until they'd reunited a couple of years later did Roy learn about his baby. And not for more than three decades did they actually meet her. Her husband had been determined that the same thing not happen to Chad Timmons.

Peggy helped her prepare the coffee. Roy and Bob had both requested eggnog, which Corrie poured into festive glasses decorated with green holly leaves and red berries. They'd once belonged to her mother and Corrie reserved them for this special season and for special friends.

"What have you heard from Linnette?" Peggy asked when they were all seated again.

"She and Pete will be in North Dakota over Christmas."

"Was it just a year ago that Pete drove her to Cedar Cove for Christmas?" Roy asked, shaking his head.

Corrie felt the same way. So much had taken place this past year.... During the holidays, Linnette, their younger daughter, had brought home a man she'd met, a farmer named Pete Mason. They'd liked him, but at the time Peggy hadn't thought the relationship was going anywhere. Pete farmed with his brothers near Buffalo Valley, where Linnette had recently accepted a position as a physician assistant. Although Linnette hadn't been in Buffalo Valley long, she seemed genuinely happy for the first time since Cal Washburn had broken her heart. Soon after that, she'd packed up her car and set off with no destination in mind. Peggy had worried endlessly, sure this was a formula for disaster. Then Linnette had phoned from this small prairie town where she'd ended up and sounded…content. She'd sounded more like herself than she had in a very long while.

Corrie hated that her younger daughter lived so far from the family. But she loved Linnette enough to realize she had to make her own decisions. Pete had fallen in love with her first and initially Corrie feared Linnette might have married on the rebound. Those concerns had been laid to rest. On Corrie's recent trip to Buffalo Valley, after the birth of Linnette and Pete's son, she had all the reassurance she'd ever need. It was abundantly clear that Linnette loved her husband and the life she'd created in this small North Dakota community.

"We had quite a Christmas last year," Roy commented, chuckling. "Mack had just been hired by the fire department and he was at the Hardings' to deliver Mary Jo's baby."

Bob grinned. "What I remember was Mary Jo's three brothers racing around town looking for her."

"And not a one of them had any sense of direction."

"Hey, be fair. They'd never been on this side of the sound before."

"And now Linc lives here, too."

"And married to the Bellamy girl."

"They are the sweetest couple," Peggy said with the hint of a sigh. "I saw them in the grocery store the other day. It was positively romantic just seeing the two of them together. We spoke for a few minutes and apparently Linc and Lori are spending Christmas with her family."

"Well," Bob said, "that's an improvement. Bellamy was trying to ruin Linc's business. Until you and Troy intervened…"

Roy shrugged off Bob's comment. "I'm glad they reconciled with Lori's family, but I don't know why Bellamy couldn't just accept the fact that they're married. End of story."

"It wasn't the only wedding this past year, either," Bob said. "Faith and Troy tied the knot, and of course so did Mack and Mary Jo."

"I do love a wedding," Corrie said. To her way of thinking, there should be one more, and preferably soon. She'd feel so much better about Gloria's situation if she was married to Chad.

"Well…" Bob lowered his empty glass. "I hate to cut this short, but we've got a few other stops to make."

Corrie and Roy walked their friends to the front door and thanked them again.

"This is one small way of repaying you for all you've done for us," Peggy said.

"How can you say that?" Corrie asked. Their friendship had been one of her biggest blessings since moving to Cedar Cove. "You've done so much for *us*."

"You kept me out of prison," Bob reminded them, referring to the death at the B and B. "Believe me, I'll be forever grateful for that."

"Ancient history," Roy insisted, standing on the front porch. He wrapped his arm around Corrie's shoulders.

"Ancient history to you, perhaps," Bob said, "but it's something I'll never forget."

They got into their vehicle, and Corrie and Roy returned to the warmth of the house.

"I really didn't do that much," Roy protested. "Bob was so obviously innocent...."

"Are you complaining about the cookies and candy they brought?" she asked, half-joking.

"No way!"

"Then enjoy and quit your muttering."

He laughed. "You're right. Have you tasted that English toffee yet? It's good stuff."

"Don't tell me how good it is, I'm resisting."

"Why?"

Corrie rolled her eyes. "Because it's hard enough not to overindulge during the holidays without you telling me how good everything tastes."

"Fine. Leaves more for me."

Sighing, Corrie brought the tray into the kitchen and covered it with a towel. Out of sight, out of mind. She returned to the back bedroom and resumed wrapping gifts.

Fifteen minutes later, Roy poked his head in. "You about done?"

"Yup. I'm putting the final touches on the last package. Why?"

"Anything here for Gloria?"

"Of course."

"Well, she just parked outside the house."

"Oh." Corrie felt a bit flustered.

"She isn't alone."

"Did Chad come with her?" Corrie couldn't hide the excitement in her voice.

Roy nodded. "Only they don't seem to be in any big

hurry to come inside. They've been sitting in the car chatting for the past ten minutes."

Corrie arched her eyebrows. "Can you tell if they're arguing?" She certainly hoped not!

"I didn't want it to be obvious that I saw them."

"Good point." Still, one might think that Roy, a private investigator, would know how to watch without being seen.

"Besides, this is *their* business."

Another good point, although that hadn't troubled him earlier when he'd gone to see Chad, which she restrained herself from mentioning.

The doorbell chimed.

"I'll get it," Roy said.

Corrie made her way into the kitchen and brewed a fresh pot of coffee. She heard Roy greet their daughter and Chad, and she quickly joined them.

"I know we're early," Gloria said. She held hands with Chad—a positive sign. "Chad thought we should all talk before everyone came for dinner tonight."

"Sure," Roy said, sitting down in his recliner.

Gloria and Chad took the sofa, huddled close to each other.

Corrie slid onto her favorite chair, her heart in her throat.

A tense silence pervaded the room as both she and Roy waited for whatever announcement was about to be made.

Gloria looked at Chad as if she wanted him to do the talking.

"Gloria and I wanted you to know we decided to get married," he blurted out. "She agreed to marry me a couple of weeks ago but we wanted to keep it to ourselves until Christmas, and—"

Corrie was instantly on her feet. "That's wonderful news!" she said, interrupting him and clasping her hands together. Her mind was whirling. While she hoped it would be soon, for the baby's sake, she'd love a June wedding. That would give her enough time to plan. She'd get started first thing after Christmas. They'd need someplace special for the reception and, of course, there were the invitations, which they'd want to send out immediately. They'd have to find a dress; at this stage of her pregnancy, Gloria probably wouldn't fit into Corrie's wedding gown, which was a shame.

"When's the happy date?" Roy asked.

"Actually…we're already married," Chad said.

Corrie blinked, assuming she'd misunderstood. "Already married?" she repeated. That wasn't possible!

"When?" Roy asked, following the first question with a second. "Where?"

Again it was Chad who explained. "I'm afraid I'm responsible. Gloria said she'd marry me but we couldn't agree on a date."

"I wanted to wait until after the baby's born and have a summer wedding," she told them.

Corrie nodded, understanding.

"And I wanted us to be married *before* the baby's born," Chad said.

Ah, yes, Corrie thought, seeing the problem.

"So we decided to simply go ahead and get married right away and then, this summer, have another ceremony and a reception."

"Makes sense to me," Roy said, obviously pleased by this unexpected turn of events.

"Why didn't you let us know?" Corrie asked, feeling a twinge of hurt despite her happiness. Even if it was a quick affair, she would've liked to be there.

"I agree we should have asked you to attend," Gloria said. "But if you were there and Chad's parents weren't, they would've felt cheated. So we just did it. We applied for the license and were married a couple of days later."

"By whom?"

"Judge Griffin," Chad said. "At the courthouse. Mack and Mary Jo stood up with us." He paused. "I don't blame you for being upset."

"We're not upset," Roy told him, and Corrie nodded.

"As Gloria mentioned, we plan to have another ceremony later, with friends and family from both sides."

"This way we *all* get what we want," Corrie said happily. A marriage and a baby—another grandchild for her and Roy—and a wedding.

Roy stood, extending his hand to Chad. "Welcome to the family."

"Thank you." The two men shook hands.

Corrie hugged her daughter and Chad. She'd spend the next few months getting ready for the wedding and reception, and the thought filled her with anticipation.

"Mom and Dad, there's another reason we stopped by early."

"Oh?" Corrie murmured.

"You're not pregnant with twins, are you?" Roy asked, half-joking.

"No. We wanted to get your okay before we had one of your gifts delivered."

"All right…." Roy glanced at Corrie, clearly wondering if she knew what this was about; she shook her head, as confused as he was.

"Did you hear someone left ten puppies on Beth Morehouse's porch?"

"We did," Corrie confirmed. "In fact, Bob was just telling us he got one of those pups for Peggy."

"And we chose one for you," Gloria said.

Their daughter had gotten them a puppy?

Corrie stared at her.

"Not long ago, Dad talked about a Labrador he had while he was growing up and he got a nostalgic look in his eyes. I heard about these puppies from Ted Reynolds, and Chad and I went to Beth's house today to pick one up."

"If you don't want the dog," Chad said, moving toward the edge of the sofa, "Gloria and I will take her. She's cute as a bug and has personality to boot."

"Where is she now?" Corrie asked.

"At my place," Gloria replied. "We thought we'd bring her over tomorrow."

"A puppy." Roy wore a silly grin, as if the prospect delighted him. "What about a name?" he asked.

"I know—Asta. That's the dog in the *Thin Man* movies, remember?" Corrie suggested.

"Perfect for a detective's dog." Roy smiled. "Even if the original Asta was a boy."

"Asta it is," Corrie said, adding, "We need a puppy in the house again."

This was going to be the most wonderful Christmas in recent memory. Weddings, grandchildren—and now a puppy.

Eleven

"Come in out of the cold," Danielle said as Kent and Beth returned to the house after delivering the sleigh to the Nelsons'. It might have been Beth's imagination, but she suspected Danielle had been standing by the door waiting for them. She had her cell phone in her hand again.

She immediately ran up to Kent and spoke urgently in his ear. Kent looked decidedly uncomfortable as she hugged him, but put his arms lightly around her. Beth saw Danielle's hug as a claim of ownership. Unable to watch, she stepped around the embracing couple and hurried into the kitchen, grateful for the escape.

Bailey and Sophie were standing in a corner of the family room, whispering heatedly.

"Girls?" Beth said, wondering what they were up to. They didn't seem to be arguing, but clearly had different opinions on something or other. "Is everything all right?" she asked.

Bailey turned around so quickly, she nearly stumbled. "Ah...sure. Why wouldn't it be?"

Sophie narrowed her eyes as Danielle and Kent stepped into the room.

"It was a…lovely afternoon, but it's time I…we left," Danielle said, and then inclined her head as if to say the decision was final.

"You're *leaving?*" Bailey cried in apparent shock.

"You're not staying for dinner?" Sophie sounded equally shocked.

"I thought you came to Cedar Cove so you could spend Christmas with us," Bailey reminded her father.

Frankly, Beth was just as glad to see them go. She didn't understand exactly what had happened between her and Kent in the sleigh, but whatever it was had made her feel confused and a bit panicky. She'd actually *wanted* him to kiss her. Her ex-husband had brought another woman to spend Christmas with the family, and yet Beth could hardly stop herself from leaning into him.…

"Kent will be back on Christmas Day," Danielle said to the girls, as if they were small children in need of reassurance. "Christmas Eve is a time for family and—"

"Our father *is* family," Bailey protested as she curled her hands into tight fists. She seemed to be on the verge of tears.

Sophie cast a pleading glance at her father. "Daddy?" she implored.

Kent hesitated.

Danielle tugged him over to the door. "I need to go. Don't worry, your father will be back in the morning." She turned to him, hissing, "The girls need to spend time with their mother, too."

"I'll stay," Kent said decisively. "That is, if you're

sure it's what you want." The question was directed at Beth.

Holding her breath, she realized she didn't have a choice. Which meant that her Christmas Eve dinner would be shared with Kent and…Danielle. What she wouldn't give for a peaceful evening alone with her daughters. Instead, she was forced to watch her husband—er, *ex*-husband—with another woman.

"Mom?" Bailey whispered.

"Of course you should stay," Beth said, just a little too brightly.

"Mom's making lasagna," Sophie said, and then added, apparently to enlighten Danielle, "It's a family tradition. The recipe comes from Grandma Carlucci."

Danielle pursed her lips in a pout, then squared her shoulders, coming to some decision. "In that case, I insist on helping."

The last thing Beth wanted was this woman in *her* kitchen. "All I need to do is get the lasagna in the oven," she said. "It's already put together—just needs to bake."

"Well, then, I'll make a salad," Danielle said.

"Mom always makes Caesar salad and garlic bread," Bailey told her.

"I can make a Caesar salad." Danielle pushed up the sleeves of her sweater and grabbed an apron off the countertop, staking out her territory.

Beth felt as though the other woman had declared war. Fine. In that case, she was prepared to surrender without a fight. This was Christmas, and if Danielle wanted to plant her flag in Beth's kitchen, she was welcome to it. Only Beth wouldn't be there.

"Are you sure you don't mind making the salad?" she asked.

"I offered, didn't I?" Danielle placed one hand on her hip.

"Okay, then, there's no reason for me to stay. I'll use the time to deliver one of the puppies." She'd drive the Randalls' puppy over to Grace Harding's place.

Danielle cast her a triumphant look, as if to say she'd taken great satisfaction in maneuvering Beth out of her own kitchen.

Sophie smiled; Beth could tell this was precisely what she'd hoped would happen. "Dad, you should go with Mom."

"Kent!" Danielle said sharply. "I might…you know, need you."

"Dad," Bailey challenged, "do you want Mom driving on treacherous roads *alone?* What if she had an accident?"

Beth tried to remember whether her daughter had ever taken drama. If so, she'd had a good teacher. The kid was ready for Broadway.

"It's fine, Kent," Beth assured him, trying to hide her laughter and not quite succeeding. "I've driven these roads alone any number of times."

"But not when there's *snow* on the ground," Sophie wailed, as if she'd attended the same drama class.

"Your mother knows what she's doing," Danielle tossed in casually. "She'll be perfectly fine *by herself.*" The last two words were given heavy emphasis.

Again Bailey and Sophie turned to their father with wide eyes even Scrooge couldn't have ignored.

"Dad? Are you really going to let Mom go out all on her own?"

"Would you ever forgive yourself if anything happened to the mother of your children?" Sophie wailed.

Unwilling to be part of this ridiculous conversation any longer, Beth grabbed her coat, gloves and scarf and headed for the back door. She was outside and halfway to the car with the puppy in its carrier when Kent jogged up behind her.

"Hey, wait up," he called.

"Kent, really, this isn't necessary."

"According to our daughters, it is."

Beth rolled her eyes. "I don't remember you being manipulated quite this easily when we were married." She opened the rear passenger door and placed the puppy's carrier inside.

Kent climbed into the front passenger seat and waited until Beth joined him before he responded. "Did you ever stop to think I might actually *want* to accompany you?"

She hadn't. For the life of her, Beth couldn't manage a single word. In fact, it was all she could do to breathe. All at once the interior of her SUV seemed to shrink until it felt as if the two of them were trapped inside a box the size of a milk crate. Her mouth went dry and she concentrated on driving rather than the man she'd loved and married and...left. Oh, how she wished she could turn back the clock.

Risking a look at Kent, she wondered if he was thinking the same thing.

The silence that stretched between them threatened to snap.

"I..." She started to say something—although what, she wasn't sure.

"I was—"

They both spoke at the same time.

"You first," she said.

"No, you."

She laughed. "Please, you go first."

"Well," he murmured after a few awkward seconds, "I was just thinking back to all the animals you rescued while we were married. Remember Ugly Arnie?"

Like she'd ever forget the injured raccoon she'd found at their back door. "How could I forget him?"

"Vicious, ungrateful—"

"Kent, he was in pain! As I recall, you aren't exactly Prince Charming when you aren't feeling well."

"Prince Charming? So is that how you remember me when…I was feeling good?"

She doubted that he expected an answer, but she gave him one, anyway. "You had your moments."

"So did you."

"Thank you." They could play nice, she realized. It hadn't always been this silent battle of wills.

"I kind of thought you'd remarry," he said, frowning as he spoke.

"Really?" She, on the other hand, hadn't even considered the possibility that Kent might marry someone else—well, other than in some vague, abstract way. Certainly not someone like Danielle. Beth was astonished that Kent would find this hard, brusque woman appealing. Yes, superficially Danielle was attractive— okay, gorgeous—but she seemed to lack all the qualities Beth had expected him to value.

"If you did remarry, I assumed you'd choose a vet."

"Oh, my goodness…" Without thinking, Beth eased her foot off the brake and the car swerved on the icy road and went sideways. "Hold on," she cried.

Kent braced his arms against the dashboard until

the car came to a complete stop on the side of the road. "You okay?" he demanded.

"I'm fine...what about you?"

"My heart is somewhere in my throat," he said, "but other than that I'll survive. What just happened? I didn't see anything in the road."

"It's Ted."

"Ted? Who's Ted?"

"The local vet... He said he'd stop by this afternoon and I need to be there."

"Give him a call," Kent muttered, as if it was of little concern.

"I will." She reached across for her handbag and grabbed her cell, pushing the button that would connect her with him.

"You have him on speed dial?" Kent asked with raised eyebrows.

Beth ignored the question and waited impatiently for Ted to answer. After four long rings, the phone went to voice mail. She exhaled loudly, then carefully put the car in Reverse and turned around.

"Where are you going now?" Kent asked.

She would've thought the answer was obvious. "To Ted's place. He's probably with an animal, so he couldn't get the phone."

"You could've left a message."

He was right, she could have, but that seemed rather unfriendly. Besides, she wanted to explain. "His place isn't far from here," she said, instead of responding to his comment.

The silence returned.

Again it was Kent who broke it. "Do you see a lot of this Tim fellow?"

"Ted," she corrected. "About once or twice a week, I guess." She downplayed the veterinarian's role in her life, which had taken on more significance in the past three or four months. There'd been a shift in their relationship, beginning in late September, when he'd come over after caring for a sick goat nearby. He'd stayed for a glass of wine, followed by a leisurely dinner.

A week later they'd met in town, and Ted had insisted he owed her dinner. That was how it had started, almost innocently. Recently, however, it'd become more. Ted had kissed her, and that had been a turning point. Lately, Ted had taken to dropping in during the evenings, and Beth looked forward to his visits.

"Any particular reason Ted was coming to the house?" Kent asked nonchalantly.

"Nothing formal, if that's what you mean. To wish us a merry Christmas. And I want him to meet the girls. He has a line on someone who wants a puppy, too."

"So it's serious? Between you and him?"

"We have a lot in common," she said, well aware that she hadn't really answered the question.

Ted's driveway came into view, and she signaled, then drove down the long gravel road that led to his home and his veterinary clinic.

Ted was in the yard clearing snow. When he saw her car, he smiled and waved, then leaned his shovel against a tree.

Beth parked and turned off the engine, slipping out of the car.

Walking over to meet her, Ted grinned from ear to ear. "Good to see you, Beth," he said. He didn't kiss her, no doubt because he'd noticed there was a man with her.

Beth tried to see the veterinarian as Kent might.

Ted was a few years older, a big man with large, strong hands and an easy smile. He had a receding hairline, visible despite his wool hat. His gentle nature comforted animals—and people.

"Kent Morehouse," Kent said, stepping forward, his hand extended.

Ted pulled off his glove to shake hands but his gaze immediately shot to Beth.

"Kent is my ex-husband. He's here to spend Christmas with the girls," Beth said, feeling uncomfortable saying anything more.

"Oh, yes. You mentioned that Kent was planning to visit," Ted commented.

"I was just driving to the Hardings' to drop off a puppy when I recalled that you were coming over today," she said quickly.

"Well, seeing that you've got visitors, perhaps I shouldn't—"

"No, please, I want you to," Beth said, eager to reassure him. "In fact, I was hoping you'd stay for dinner."

"Dinner?" Kent repeated, frowning.

"Yes, dinner," she said pointedly. "I'm making lasagna. A family recipe."

"My grandmother was Italian," Kent added in a meaningful voice, essentially explaining that this was *his* family's recipe.

"Kent's, uh, friend is with the girls, preparing a Caesar salad and garlic bread."

"That sounds wonderful."

"It will be," Beth said. "*Please* say you'll join us."

Ignoring Kent, Ted stared at her for a long moment. "You're sure?"

"I'm positive."

Ted nodded decisively. "Then I accept. Thank you. What time would you like me there?"

Beth was about to suggest as soon as possible, but before she could, Kent spoke.

"I believe Beth mentioned something about dinner being ready around five."

"Yes, five. We're eating early so we won't be late for church," she murmured.

"Can I bring anything? Wine? Dessert?"

"I've got everything covered, but thanks." She wanted to visit longer, but Kent had already walked back to the car and stood with the door open, waiting for her.

"I'll see you soon," Ted promised. "And I've got a couple bottles of a nice red. To go with the lasagna."

"Thank you," she whispered, and hoped Ted understood how much she appreciated his willingness to show, once again, what a good friend he was. As good a friend as Danielle....

Twelve

Justine Gunderson busied herself in the kitchen, enjoying an afternoon free from the responsibility of managing the Victorian Tea Room. She'd given the staff an extra day off so they could celebrate Christmas Eve with their own families.

The holiday season at the tearoom had been hectic, with a number of special high teas. Her favorite had been Tea with Santa. The children had been so excited, and Santa, a theater friend of Bob Beldon's, had played the role with verve and charm.

In a few years Livvy would be able to go, but for now the toddler, at nearly eighteen months, was too young for Santa in his frightening red suit.

The back door opened, and her husband entered the house. Seth was a blond Swede who towered well over six feet. Just seeing him made Justine's heart react with a surge of love. She'd never expected to marry, let alone have a family of her own. In fact, she'd gone out of her way to avoid serious relationships...until she'd worked on her ten-year high school reunion. That was when she'd run into Seth Gunderson, who was also on the reunion committee.

She'd known Seth nearly her entire life. He'd been her twin brother's best friend. As irrational as it sounded, after the accident that claimed Jordan's life, Justine had wanted to blame Seth. If he'd been with her brother at the lake that day, Jordan might not have died. Seth would have noticed that her brother hadn't surfaced after diving off the floating dock. He would've gone after him. If only Seth had been there....

But he hadn't. It'd been Justine who'd held her brother's lifeless body on the dock until the paramedics showed up.

That fateful summer afternoon had forever changed her world.

Seth smiled at her as he stripped off his coat.

She smiled back and felt, as she so often had in the past, that Jordan would have approved of her marrying Seth Gunderson. Through the years, at various times, Justine had sensed her twin's presence. During those indescribable moments of connection, she hadn't felt the horrific loss of her brother; instead, she'd felt his blessing. Jordan seemed to be standing right beside her, smiling and happy, teasing her the way he'd once done, full of life and boyish humor.

The first time it'd happened was shortly after she'd given birth to Leif. Still in the hospital, exhausted and woozy from the drugs, she'd closed her eyes. Suddenly, Jordan was there before her, and he wore the biggest, goofiest grin she'd ever seen. He was telling her how happy he was for her and Seth; she was sure of it. She could almost hear him saying how excited he was that they'd decided to name their son after him: Leif Jordan Gunderson.

"Daddy, Daddy." Leif shot across the room, dropping his handheld computer game on the way, with Penny barking at his heels. "Santa's coming tonight!"

"He sure is." Lifting the boy high above his head, Seth nuzzled Leif's tummy while the little boy squealed in delight.

Hearing her brother, Livvy toddled out, clutching her teddy bear under her left arm, pressing its face against her side. Livvy and that silly bear were inseparable. She'd be getting her first doll from Santa this Christmas. Justine sincerely hoped Livvy would enjoy the doll as much as she did her teddy bear.

"How's my girl?" Seth asked, setting Leif down and reaching for his daughter. He planted a noisy kiss on her cheek. She, too, squealed with delight.

"Hey, don't I get one of those kisses?" Justine teased.

"You bet." He came to her in the kitchen and slipped his arms around her from behind, planting his hands over her still-flat stomach. "How long have you been working in here?"

"A while." The family cookbook her grandmother, Charlotte Jefferson Rhodes, had compiled, lay open in front of her. Various ingredients, organized according to the recipes, were spread along the counter.

"Seems to me you were in the kitchen when I left for work this morning. Are you sure you're up to this?"

"Stop worrying, okay?" Hosting the family for Christmas Eve dinner required a lot of extra preparation, but Justine never turned away from a challenge.

"Did you bake those homemade rolls I like so much?" Seth asked, eyeing the covered breadbasket.

"I did that first thing this morning."

Seth grinned. "I hope you doubled the batch."

"I did."

"That's my girl."

Justine reached up and kissed him. "I promise you can have as many as you want."

"How are you feeling?" Seth asked.

"I feel wonderful. I always do when I'm pregnant."

Seth closed his eyes. "I don't know how we let this happen," he said as he feathered kisses down the side of her neck.

Justine giggled and put her arms around her husband's neck. "You'd think by now we'd know how babies are made."

"If it was up to you, we'd live in a shoe and have a dozen children."

"Three suits me just fine," she assured him, although she'd be the first to admit she loved being a mother. She could hardly believe that at one time she'd been willing to give all of this up without even knowing what she'd be missing.

The pregnancy would be this year's Christmas surprise for her family. Keeping it secret had been far more difficult than she'd expected. At least a dozen times she'd been tempted to tell her mother and her grandmother. Both would be thrilled.

"Can I help with anything?" Seth asked.

"You could check Livvy's diaper," she said.

Seth swept his daughter into his arms and carried her to her room. When he returned a few minutes later, Livvy's head lolled against his shoulder.

"Did you have a chance to get the mail?" he asked.

"Not yet."

"I'll do it." Seth set Livvy down on the carpet. She leaned her head against the sofa cushion. She'd woken late that morning and hadn't been interested in a nap. Now her eyes drooped as her thumb found its way into her mouth.

Justine had sucked her thumb, too; so had Jordan. After washing her hands, Justine picked up her sweet baby girl and brought her back to her crib. She gently placed her inside and covered her with the blanket Charlotte had knit for her.

Seth came into their daughter's bedroom as she sat beside the crib, watching Livvy's deep, even breaths.

He stood beside her. "It's difficult to fathom how much love we can have for children, isn't it?" he whispered.

"Impossible to believe until we become parents ourselves," she whispered back.

They left the bedroom and Seth closed the door.

"Anything interesting in the mail?" Justine asked as he sat down, flipping through the envelopes. She poured her husband a cup of tea and joined him at the kitchen table.

"The usual Christmas cards—and one rather interesting letter."

"Oh? Who from?"

Seth leafed through the holiday cards until he came across a plain, business-size white envelope. He glanced at it again, then handed it to her.

Justine saw that the envelope held her name—and only hers. The return address made her catch her breath. After taking a moment to compose herself, she raised her eyes to meet Seth's. "It's stamped prison mail. The postmark is Shelton, Washington—that's where the state prison is. One of them, anyway."

"I noticed that, too."

"There's only one person who could be writing me from there." The paper seemed to grow hot in her hands.

"Warren Saget," Seth muttered.

Justine dropped the letter on the table and avoided looking at it.

"Aren't you going to open it?" her husband asked.

"I...I don't know." She'd once had a deep affection for Warren, a successful local builder, although he was old enough to be her father. They'd dated for a while. He'd liked having a tall, beautiful woman on his arm, and she'd liked the fact that he was rich and powerful and made no physical demands on her.

He couldn't. That was their little secret. With Warren she was safe from emotional—and physical—entanglements. Safe, until she'd agreed to work on the class reunion project and Seth had shown up. Justine hadn't wanted to become involved with Seth, yet he was all she thought about. Warren had offered her a huge diamond engagement ring. He was willing to do anything not to lose her. But even that diamond hadn't enticed her. All she wanted, all she *needed,* was Seth.

"I wonder if Warren has any idea of everything he did for us," Seth commented.

Her husband's words jarred Justine from her reverie. "You mean what he did *to* us, don't you?" Warren had tried to destroy them.

"But in the end that's what saved our marriage."

"You're right," she said slowly. "Ironic, isn't it?"

"We were killing ourselves with the restaurant, working all hours of the day and night...."

"You don't need to remind me," Justine said, shaking her head at the memory. It'd been a difficult period in their marriage. They'd been working impossibly long hours with no time as a couple or a family.

The restaurant had been Seth's dream. For nearly ten years he'd saved his money from fishing the crab-rich Alaskan waters. He'd lived on a sailboat in the marina while in town, and spent every waking moment studying restaurant management. He'd dreamed of one day opening an elegant seafood restaurant in Cedar Cove. Together they'd made his dream come true, and the Lighthouse had been the success he'd always planned.

But Seth had worked far too hard. Justine shared his dream, and they'd redoubled their efforts until it all became too much. By then Leif had been born, which meant Justine was torn between being with her son and working at the restaurant.

Their marriage had started to show the stress of too many demands and too few hours. For the first time Seth and Justine had been at odds.

Then, one night, the restaurant had burned down. All their dreams, all their hard work, their blood, sweat and tears, had gone up in smoke.

Even now, memories of that night were surreal. After being contacted by the authorities, they'd rushed to the scene and walked around in a stupor, shocked and bereft. It wasn't long before the fire inspector declared it'd been arson.

Someone had purposely set their restaurant on fire. The police had what they called "a person of interest," a high school kid who'd worked there briefly before Seth let him go. Anson Butler had a history of being in trouble and had started fires when he was younger.

Someone had seen him inside the restaurant that night.
Then Anson disappeared.... Meanwhile, Justine and
Seth were left to pick up the charred remains of their
life. The stress on their marriage brought them close
to the breaking point.

It didn't help that Warren took every opportunity to
talk about how good things had been between them.
Justine didn't believe it, not for a minute; still, it was
comforting to have someone pay her that kind of attention.

Not working and depressed, Seth had struggled emo-
tionally. He'd given up fishing in Alaska, and she was
grateful. She wanted her husband with her. Leif needed
him. So did she.

It was during this time that she'd come up with the
idea of building a tearoom and giving it the ambience
of England's Victorian era. The plans were already in
motion when Seth was approached by a family friend
who owned a boatyard and offered him a job in sales.
Seth took it and turned out to be a natural.

Later, thanks to Sheriff Troy Davis, Warren Saget
was arrested, tried and convicted of arson. Currently,
he was serving time in prison.

Justine poked at the envelope with her finger. She expected to feel *something*. Some emotion. Regret. Anger.
Something. Instead, she felt nothing. Only a sadness
that Warren could have been this vindictive, this desperate. He'd never forgiven her for leaving him and he'd
wanted to punish Seth for stealing away the one woman
who understood him, understood his needs.

"Are you going to read it?" Seth asked.

"Do you want me to?"

He thought about it, then nodded.

Personally, Justine would be content to toss the letter. Yet a part of her wanted to know what Warren had to say. Taking a deep breath, she opened the envelope and pulled out a single sheet of paper. She read it, then crumpled it in one hand.

"What did he say?"

"Just that he'll be up for parole in a few years and wondered if I'd be waiting for him when he's released."

"You're joking!"

"The man is delusional," she groaned. Even now, Warren seemed to be living in a dreamworld. He'd convinced himself that she was pining for him, anticipating his release. Needless to say, she had no interest in the man who'd done his best to ruin her and Seth's lives.

Taking the letter, she threw it inside the recycling bin, among the unwanted flyers and empty cereal boxes.

Seth grinned, and she grinned in reply. "Merry Christmas, my dear husband."

"Merry Christmas, my darling wife."

Thirteen

"What are we going to do?" Sophie whispered to her older sister. "Nothing's turning out like we planned."

"You're telling me?" Bailey muttered back. Dinner was on the table. The lasagna, with the salad next to it, sat in the center. Wooden serving utensils leaned against the side of the large salad bowl. The bread was out of the oven, and the warm pungent scent of butter and garlic wafted through the house.

Peering out the swinging kitchen door into the formal dining room, Bailey saw that the situation was even worse than she'd realized. Mom was in one corner of the room, deep in conversation with Ted Reynolds. Danielle and Dad stood on the opposite side. Danielle appeared to be talking Kent's ears off, no doubt regaling him with horror stories of the time she'd spent alone with his daughters. She was clutching her cell phone—again. While Kent and Beth were away, she'd made repeated calls but hadn't connected, growing more and more frustrated. Her impatience with Bailey and Sophie had increased just as quickly.

Okay, so that part of their plan had worked perfectly.

Danielle had been stuck with the two of them, and she hadn't liked it one bit. She'd been outsmarted by Beth and wasn't in any mood to be friendly with Bailey and Sophie. Besides, she was distracted, frequently calling and texting some unknown person.

Not long after their parents left, Bailey and Sophie had learned that Danielle knew next to nothing about making a Caesar salad. She assumed all salad dressing came out of a bottle. When Bailey informed her their mother made her own, Danielle snarled that she could make her own, too, only she needed a recipe. Tearing through Beth's cookbooks, she finally came up with one but was disgusted by half the ingredients. No way was she using anchovies! In the end, she'd opted for the bottled Italian dressing she'd found in the fridge.

"Your mother makes her own dressing. Oh, yeah, I can tell!" Danielle had brandished the half-full bottle. "That's the most ridiculous thing I've ever heard," she'd raged. "You're just saying that so I'll feel inferior." Danielle fumed until Kent returned. Her cell phone was in her hands constantly, and her thumbs worked at sending text messages. Bailey and Sophie had several whispered conversations about it, wondering who she was trying so hard to reach.

Danielle had cornered Kent in the dining room, her mouth moving at warp speed. It didn't look as if Dad had an opportunity to say much of anything.

Bailey refused to believe he was dumb enough to actually fall for Danielle. It contradicted everything she knew about her father.

The instant their parents had walked in the house, Bailey sensed something was wrong. She'd quickly discovered the cause. Mom had invited Ted Reynolds to dinner. Oh, great. Based on what she'd heard from Beth, Bailey had suspected for a month or two that Ted was interested in their mother. The invitation had probably been a defensive move on Beth's part; unfortunately, it'd sent the wrong message to Dad.

Now Bailey and Sophie were battling on two fronts. They certainly could've done without this additional complication.

"Look at them," Sophie muttered as the sisters peeked out the door. Mom was still talking to Ted, with her back to Dad, who also had his back to her. If that wasn't bad enough, Danielle chattered at their father like a noisy crow. Her parents couldn't even look at each other. Communication, what little there was of it, had come to a complete standstill.

"This isn't going to work." Bailey felt like dumping the so-called Caesar salad over her parents' heads. "We need to figure out what to do next."

Sophie nodded. "We've got to think of something fast."

"This divorce should never have happened," Bailey moaned—not for the first time. If she or Sophie had guessed their parents were planning to split up, the girls would've stepped in much earlier. Now the situation was much more difficult, and there were other people involved. Now she and her sister were stuck cleaning up the mess.

Bailey shrugged. She brought the salad plates into the dining room and said, "Dinner's ready if you'd like to sit down." She did her best to sound cheerful and festive.

They took the chairs closest to where they stood. That put Danielle beside their father, and Ted and their mother across from them, leaving the two end chairs for Bailey and Sophie.

"Mom made the lasagna," Bailey said, although everyone already knew that. Before she could mention Danielle's role in their dinner, the other woman broke in.

"And I made the salad and the bread, which I'm sure you'll find delicious."

Both men smiled, apparently impressed with the woman who'd managed to spread garlic butter on a sliced baguette. From their admiring gazes, one would think Danielle was qualified to open her own restaurant.

Bailey wanted to point out that the lasagna had required a great deal more expertise than buttering bread. She opened her mouth, but before she could utter a word, she caught her mother's look. Funny how much Mom could communicate in a single glance. Bailey snapped her mouth shut.

Beth served generous slices of lasagna. The salad and bread were passed around the table to sighs of appreciation. Ted poured the wine he'd brought with him. After filling the glasses, he looked around the table. "A toast?"

They all raised their goblets, but before Ted could speak, their father beat him to it. "To a wonderful meal shared with family and friends."

"Hear, hear," Ted added. They all touched the rims of their glasses, then tasted the wine.

"This is excellent," Beth said, praising Ted's choice.

"Very good," Kent agreed.

Wine, Bailey mused. That was it. A common link— her parents were both interested in wine. Well, so was Ted, but she was going to ignore that.

"It's a pinot noir," Ted was saying, "from Oregon."

"Ted and I discovered it a couple of weeks ago at a fundraising event," Beth said. "I generally prefer the rich, deep reds, so this one took me by surprise."

Oh, yes, life was full of surprises, Bailey thought. Some of them weren't pleasant, either—her mother and father being a prime example.

Dinner became less awkward as they enjoyed the wine and the meal. Conversation revolved around the holidays. Beth talked about the ski trip to Whistler, and the girls chimed in, excited at the prospect of an entire week on the slopes. In the past it had been a family trip, with their father included.

As soon as everyone had finished, Bailey and Sophie jumped up, eager for an excuse to leave.

Bailey carried two dinner plates into the kitchen and set them in the sink. Sophie followed with two more.

"Why didn't you *do* something?" her sister hissed. "Getting Mom and Dad back together was your idea."

"That doesn't mean I have to do everything, does it?" she returned in a heated whisper. A few suggestions from her younger sister certainly would've helped.

Back in the dining room, Bailey could see that Danielle was texting on her cell phone again, keeping it hidden below the table, although everyone knew what she was doing.

"I'm afraid we'll have to leave early," Kent said reluctantly. "Unfortunately, Danielle isn't feeling well."

"Can I get you anything?" Beth asked, sounding concerned.

Bailey wanted to suggest a broom, but her little joke was unlikely to be appreciated, so she said nothing.

"I apologize," Danielle murmured, pressing her fingertips to her temple. "I have a terrible headache that won't go away."

A headache? That was the weakest excuse in the book. A regular ol' headache? Couldn't she be a bit more imaginative? Perhaps a sprained thumb from all that texting?

"So you won't be able to come to church services with us?" Sophie asked with such a lack of sincerity it was embarrassing.

"I think I should get Danielle back to the bed-and-breakfast," their father said.

Mom didn't waste any time retrieving their coats. Standing at the front door, their dad loitered a moment, as if he wanted to say something else. "It was a lovely day," he finally said.

"Thank you," Beth said simply.

"Kent?" Danielle insisted.

"When will I see you again?" Kent asked, directing the question to Beth. His eyes held hers.

"Ah…"

"Mom." Bailey jabbed her elbow into her mother's side.

"Tomorrow?" Beth suggested, poking her right back. "Christmas morning. You and Danielle are welcome to join us."

Danielle shook her head. "I doubt—"

Kent cut her off. "What time?"

"Anytime you want, Dad," Bailey threw in. "Early, though. You should be here when we open gifts."

"I have a *really* bad headache," Danielle reminded him.

"Why don't we wait until morning and see how Danielle feels," Beth said.

Their mother was being far too congenial. In fact, she was ruining everything. Bailey had hoped it would be just the four of them. If her parents could be together, remember Christmases past and enjoy each other's company, then maybe they'd finally figure things out....

Their father shook Ted's hand. Why did everyone have to be so darned polite? The two men locked eyes for an instant. Bailey hoped her father was staking claim to Beth, but she couldn't read his expression.

"Bailey and I'll do dishes," Sophie offered.

Bailey stared at Sophie. What was her sister doing? The last thing they needed was to give their mother time alone with the local vet. She was half-smitten with him already. *Smitten.* That was an old-fashioned word, one their grandmother might have used, but Bailey had always been fond of it.

She followed her sister into the kitchen. "Why'd you do that?" she cried.

"I thought you wanted to discuss ideas about getting Mom and Dad together."

"By leaving her alone with *Ted?*"

"Oh...yeah. I guess I didn't think about that."

"No kidding! Well, you keep an eye on them," commanded Bailey. "If they get too close, tell me." Sophie obediently pushed the door open a crack and looked out. Bailey started loading the dishwasher. Thankfully, their mother had emptied it earlier, so all Bailey had to do was put the rinsed dishes inside.

"You ready to go back out?" she asked five minutes later.

Sophie shook her head. "No," she said flatly. "Go ahead without me."

"No." It was important to Bailey that they present a united front.

Her sister took her time transferring the leftover salad to another bowl and wrapping up the bread, which Bailey noticed had barely been touched. She didn't want to be catty but Danielle had been a little too generous with the garlic. Their father hadn't tasted more than a bite or two. And Bailey was convinced he'd only eaten that to be polite.

To her credit, Danielle had created a halfway decent salad using the bottled dressing. But then who could go wrong with store-bought dressing?

"What are Mom and Ted doing now?" Sophie asked.

Bailey peeked out the swinging door, stepping around her sister. She saw that her mother and Ted had returned to the dining room table and were finishing their coffee. The atmosphere was almost...intimate, vastly different from what it'd been earlier. His arm across the back of an empty chair, Ted was leaning back, speaking animatedly about one thing or another. Whatever he was saying obviously amused Beth, who laughed more than once. She looked relaxed and at ease.

This wasn't how it was supposed to be! It should be Dad in that chair. It should be Kent laughing with Mom. Not Ted Reynolds. Bailey didn't have anything against him; he was a decent guy. But he wasn't their father.

"Well?" Sophie said from behind her.

"They're getting along just fine," Bailey muttered.

"We should break it up," Sophie said, drying her hands on a kitchen towel. Everything was inside the refrigerator and the counters were wiped clean.

Bailey swung open the door. "Okay if we join you?" she asked, feigning cheerfulness.

"By all means." Ted removed his arm from the back of the chair, straightened and set his cup on the table.

"How long have you two known each other?" Sophie asked.

"A while." Beth was the one who answered. "I've brought more than one dog to Ted. He helps me with the rescues, too."

"You must like animals," Sophie went on.

Bailey thought that was a dumb remark. The guy was a vet; obviously he liked animals.

"I do." Ted hesitated. He must've thought it was a dumb remark, too. But then he added, "And I like your mother."

His announcement fell like bricks from the sky.

"What about my dad?" Bailey asked.

"Yeah, our dad," Sophie echoed plaintively.

"Oh, dear," Beth whispered. "If you two have any hopes that your father and I are getting back together, you need to forget them. It's much too late for that."

Fourteen

"Who'd be calling on Christmas Eve?" Bobby Polgar asked when Teri hung up the phone. It was after dinner, and the children were—finally—all snug in their beds.

"Beth Morehouse," Teri said. "She wants to know if it would be all right if she dropped the puppy off tonight instead of in the morning." Actually, it sounded as though Beth needed to get out of the house.

"What did you tell her?"

"I said come on over."

Bobby glanced into the family room, where he had three scooter-riders out of the boxes ready for assembling. The triplets were eight months old now and crawling. Robbie, the firstborn, was already standing on his own. Teri figured he'd be walking soon; the boy was fearless. Little Jimmy, the middle child and the smallest, was content to continue crawling, and Christopher, the youngest by a couple of minutes, loved sitting on the floor, banging pots and pans. Bobby felt sure their son was destined to be a drummer.

"I asked James to give me a hand assembling these," Bobby admitted a bit sheepishly.

"You'll do fine." Her husband might be a chess genius, but he didn't excel in certain other areas—like household repairs. Or "assembly required" toys.

"Are the boys down for the night?" Bobby asked.

Teri nodded, too exhausted for a detailed description of what it took to get all three to fall asleep at roughly the same time. Their nanny had the next two days off to spend the holidays with her family, and it felt like she'd been gone for a month. Teri's sister, Christie, had agreed to help make Christmas dinner and look after the triplets.

"Come and sit with me," Bobby said, holding his arm out to Teri.

She sat beside him on the sofa and laid her head on his shoulder. Bobby was semi-retired these days, following the birth of his sons, and Teri was grateful. Bobby and his best friend, James, had developed a chess-based computer game that consumed a great deal of their time, since they were now working on the second version. Still, Teri was glad to have her husband at home instead of on the road.

Closing her eyes, she remembered how she'd met Bobby Polgar. It had definitely been an unusual introduction.... He was in a championship chess match in Seattle and to everyone's shock he was losing. The chess world was aghast that the great Bobby Polgar could be toppled. One look at the chess player on the TV screen told Teri what his problem was. Bobby was distracted by his hair, which was too long and kept flopping in his eyes. He needed a cut.

In retrospect she was astonished that Security had let her through to see him. When she explained why she'd come, Bobby had stared at her as if she was some kind

OFFICIAL OPINION POLL

Dear Reader,

Since you are a book enthusiast, we would like to know what you think.

Inside you will find a short Opinion Poll. Please participate in our poll by sharing your opinion on 3 subjects that are very important to all of us.

To thank you for your participation, we would like to send you **2 FREE BOOKS** and **2 FREE GIFTS!**

Please enjoy them with our compliments.

Sincerely,

Pam Powers

For Your Reading Pleasure...

Get 2 FREE BOOKS that will fuel your imagination with intensely moving stories about life, love and relationships.

Free

Your **2 FREE BOOKS** have a combined cover price of $15.98 in the U.S. and $19.98 in Canada.

Peel off sticker and place by your completed poll on the right page and you'll automatically receive **2 FREE BOOKS** and **2 FREE GIFTS** with no obligation to purchase anything!

We'll send you two wonderful surprise gifts, (worth about $10), absolutely FREE, just for trying our Romance books! Don't miss out — MAIL THE REPLY CARD TODAY!

Visit us at:
www.ReaderService.com

YOUR OPINION POLL
THANK-YOU FREE GIFTS INCLUDE:

▶ **2 ROMANCE BOOKS**
▶ **2 LOVELY SURPRISE GIFTS**

OFFICIAL OPINION POLL

YOUR OPINION COUNTS!
Please check TRUE or FALSE below to express your opinion about the following statements:

Q1 Do you believe in "true love"?

"TRUE LOVE HAPPENS ONLY ONCE IN A LIFETIME."
○ TRUE
○ FALSE

Q2 Do you think marriage has any value in today's world?

"YOU CAN BE TOTALLY COMMITTED TO SOMEONE WITHOUT BEING MARRIED."
○ TRUE
○ FALSE

Q3 What kind of books do you enjoy?

"A GREAT NOVEL MUST HAVE A HAPPY ENDING."
○ TRUE
○ FALSE

YES! I have placed my sticker in the space provided below. Please send me the **2 FREE books** and **2 FREE gifts** for which I qualify. I understand that I am under no obligation to purchase anything further, as explained on the back of this card.

194/394 MDL FEPX

FIRST NAME | LAST NAME

ADDRESS

APT.# | CITY

STATE/PROV. | ZIP/POSTAL CODE

of lunatic, but he'd allowed her to trim his hair. Then she'd quietly left. Bobby had gone on to win the match and afterward he'd sought her out. Crazy as it sounded, that was how it all began.

She wasn't quite sure when she fell in love with him. In the beginning, she'd fought against having any feelings for this man. Really, what could come of it? She was a hairdresser from a little backwater town and Bobby Polgar was a champion chess player admired by the whole world. He might be infatuated with her for a while, but his affection would quickly wane. She'd bore him, and Bobby would soon grow tired of her.

Talk about an odd couple! But fall in love with him she did, despite her efforts not to. And when she fell, she fell hard.

She'd questioned why an intellectual like him—a celebrity to boot—would love someone like her. He'd said that she brought emotion into his life, that he liked her practical and intuitive approach, that she'd taught him how to *feel*.

Before that tournament in Seattle, every minute of Bobby's life had been involved with chess. He lived, breathed and slept chess. It was all he thought about, all he cared about…until he fell in love with her.

"You're smiling," Bobby said now, brushing the hair off her forehead almost as if she were a child.

"I was remembering our honeymoon." They got married in Las Vegas. Bobby had been in a chess competition there, and they were given the most luxurious penthouse suite in the hotel. The morning after their wedding night, Bobby had to leave for a chess match. Teri had stayed in bed and turned on the television to watch her husband play.

She knew from the first move he made that his mind wasn't on the game. He was thinking about *her,* thinking about coming back to the room and making love to her again. Then something happened; she could almost see the transformation taking place.... His expression changed. Even his posture changed. Bobby had realized that the sooner he won, the sooner he could return to their room. His focus, his attention, went straight into the game. His opponent didn't stand a chance. The poor man lost in record time. A second later, Bobby popped out of his seat and raced for the elevator, the camera crew on his heels.

Teri had been waiting for him....

The doorbell chimed and Teri sighed, not wanting to leave the comfort of her husband's arms and the warm memories that had wrapped themselves around her. She started to get up, but Bobby stopped her.

"I'll get it."

As Bobby was rising to his feet she slipped her hand around his neck and brought his mouth down to hers for a lengthy kiss. They broke it off when the doorbell chimed again.

Bobby's glasses were askew and his face flushed by the time he moved away from her. He cleared his throat. "You need to warn me before you do that," he muttered.

"Okay, I will," she said, smiling up at him. "That was just to say how much I love you."

Bobby cleared his throat again and gave her a small, crooked smile. He never quite knew how to respond when she mentioned love. "Thank you," he whispered, then hurried to the door.

In a minute he was back with Christie and James. They were another odd couple, Teri mused. When she'd first met James Wilbur, she hadn't known what to think of the tall, exceptionally thin man who served as Bobby's driver. It wasn't until much later that she discovered James was Bobby's dearest friend. He'd been a chess prodigy like Bobby, but James had suffered a breakdown caused by all the pressure. He'd disappeared from the public eye and been forgotten by everyone except Bobby. Her husband refused to abandon his friend, so he'd hired James as his driver. For years no one had recognized Bobby's chauffeur as the teenager who'd made chess history along with Bobby Polgar.

As soon as James met Christie, he fell for her. Teri hated to be the one to tell him, but her younger sister came with plenty of baggage, just like she had. To her complete surprise, Christie had fallen in love with James. Their relationship had been a series of stops and starts, had taken a number of unexpected turns. But in the end Christie had dumped the losers who'd taken advantage of her, gone back to school and straightened out her life.

A year ago, over Christmas, she'd split up with James. A story in the press had identified him as James Gardner, the prodigy who'd disappeared. It might not have been such a big news item if not for the fact that he'd still been part of the chess world all that time. He hadn't played in years, not since his collapse, but he enjoyed belonging to that world. Christie hadn't been able to tolerate his deception, his inability to trust her with his secret. Eventually, however, they'd reconciled and their estrangement had led them to a greater understanding of each other.

Teri realized James was like Bobby, in that chess was all he knew. He'd acknowledged he no longer wanted to play high-pressure big-money chess, but liked being close to the game—and close to the one friend he could count on, Bobby Polgar.

"We're here to help with the kids' Christmas gifts," Christie announced.

"Wonderful." Teri patted the empty space next to her on the sofa. "We'll let the men put together these toys while you and I visit."

"Sounds like a great idea to me," Christie said. "By the way, the house looks gorgeous." She gestured at the candles arranged on the fireplace mantel and at the Christmas tree, its lights reflected in the picture window overlooking Puget Sound.

Falling in love had changed Christie, just as it'd changed Teri. The hard edges of her personality had softened. She'd proven to herself she could get whatever she wanted as long as she worked hard and persevered. Christie had recently graduated from Olympic Community College, and she planned to start her own business, photographing the contents of houses for insurance purposes. Teri was proud of her little sister.

"I heard from Johnny this afternoon," she told Christie. Johnny was their younger brother. He was in school, attending the University of Washington. "He'll come over for dinner tomorrow. With his new girlfriend." Johnny never lacked for girlfriends, but he hadn't met anyone who was going to change *his* life. Not yet.

Teri had been more of a mother to him than their own. Another memory floated into Teri's mind. Soon after she'd married Bobby, Teri had made a huge dinner and invited her family to the house to meet her husband.

Sadly, her mother had arrived half-drunk, and from

the moment Ruth stepped through the door, she did nothing but find fault with Teri.

Bobby wasn't about to let his mother-in-law insult his wife and had handled the situation in a firm, yet subtle way. He'd wordlessly picked up Ruth's purse and set it by the front door, indicating it was time for her to leave. Ruth had immediately taken offense and, dragging her fourth—or was it fifth?—husband, she'd stomped out.

"James, what do they mean by a flat-head screwdriver?" Bobby and James sat on the family room floor with the pieces of one scooter scattered about the room. Bobby held out the instruction sheet, frowning at the diagrams. Then he turned it upside down before turning it right side up again.

"I didn't know there was more than one kind of screwdriver," James confessed.

"You learn something new every day, right?"

"Right," James agreed.

"I'll get a flat-head screwdriver for you," Teri said, sliding off the sofa.

Bobby gazed up at her as if she were the most brilliant woman who'd ever lived. "You have one?"

"That and a Phillips and a square tip…" She went to the kitchen drawer and returned with the required screwdriver.

"Do you need anything else?" she asked, handing it to him.

"Uh…" He showed her the instruction sheet. "Can you tell me what I'm supposed to do with that?" He pointed to the drawing of a part.

"Teri," Christie said, getting up from the sofa. "It looks like these two are going to need a bit of assistance."

"Looks that way," she concurred.

"We can do this," Bobby insisted.

"Yeah," James echoed, but without much conviction.

"Do you want them to help us?" Bobby asked his friend.

James regarded Christie, and then Teri. "I don't think it would hurt. What about you?"

"I don't need help," Bobby said, "but if Teri wants to volunteer I won't stop her."

Teri and Christie exchanged an eye-rolling glance.

All of them were on the floor when the doorbell chimed yet again.

"That'll be Beth Morehouse," Teri said.

"Oh, were you expecting her?" Christie asked. "Why's she here?"

"Delivering a puppy," she said on her way to the door.

"Teri, don't tell me you and Bobby are getting a puppy!" Christie called after her.

"No," James answered on her behalf. "We are."

"James!" Christie yelped. "Isn't this something you should've discussed with me first?"

"Well…"

Before he could respond, Teri walked into the living room, followed by her guest. Beth held a basket—with a small black puppy staring out. The little creature wore a pink bow that contrasted with its glossy fur.

"Oh, she's adorable."

"Yes, and she's all yours," James told her. "Merry Christmas, darling."

"Merry Christmas," Christie said, her voice choked.

"Why are you crying?" James asked, drawing his wife into his arms.

"I...I always wanted a...dog."

"I know."

Christie threw her arms around James's neck.

Teri took the basket out of Beth's arms. "Thank you so much for bringing over the puppy."

"I was happy to," Beth said. "I know this little girl will have a wonderful home, so thank *you*."

"Our pleasure," Christie murmured.

James kissed her forehead. "Merry Christmas, my love," he said again. "I thought we could name her Chessie."

"Chessie! Of course." Christie laughed.

"You'll get your gift later," she promised in a husky voice.

James turned three shades of red. "I'll hold you to that," he said. "Now come and meet your dog."

Fifteen

After dropping off the puppy at the Polgars', Beth headed back to her house on Christmas Tree Lane. She'd enjoyed her brief visit with Bobby and Teri and James and Christie. The two couples were obviously devoted to one another. Watching them all working together, assembling toys for the triplets, reminded Beth of those early years with Kent. Finances had been tight back then, but they'd managed; their happiness had more than compensated for the luxuries they'd done without. She missed those times, and yes, she missed Kent, too.

On the way home Beth felt empty inside. For three years she'd pretended she was happy. Pretended she'd rather live her life without Kent. It'd all been a lie.

And now it was too late.

The girls would be getting ready for evening services at the church and the three of them would arrive together. Kent had said he might attend, as well, but she knew he'd sit with Danielle, not with Beth and the girls. That made sense, but it was another blow she wasn't ready to deal with.

While waiting at a red light, she saw the open sign

at Mocha Mama's. Because she didn't want to return home until she'd regained control of her emotions, she decided to go in. Stopping for a quick cup of coffee would give her a chance to sort through her feelings, to better understand what was happening and accept the reality that she had lost Kent for good. The life they'd once had was truly over.

She pulled into a parking space and turned off the engine. Sitting in the car, she pressed her hand over her eyes as unfamiliar and unwelcome emotions swirled through her. This Christmas was nothing like she'd anticipated. For weeks she'd looked forward to her children's visit. She'd carefully planned events, shopped, wrapped gifts, cooked their favorite meals. What she realized now was that she'd done it for Kent, too. Since he was coming to Cedar Cove for the holiday, she'd wanted to remind him of what they'd had. Of everything that was gone now, but could…perhaps…be recovered. She hadn't even acknowledged this to herself. Not really.

What made it all so impossible was Danielle. Facing the ghosts of Christmas past, back when she and Kent were so much in love, only depressed her now.

When Beth entered the coffee shop, she saw that it was nearly deserted. A teenager stood behind the counter, playing a handheld game. He didn't seem to notice he had a customer.

"Hello! I'd like a decaf Americano," she said briskly.

Startled, the kid glanced up. He blinked and reluctantly set aside his game. "Anything else?"

"No, thanks." She paid, adding a nice Christmas tip, and waited for her coffee.

A couple of minutes later he delivered it in a to-go cup, which was fine, although she wasn't in any rush to leave. Carrying it with her, she chose a table by the window, one that overlooked Harbor Street.

She gazed out at the serene and yet festive view of the town's main street. Garlands were strung across it. Silver bells dangled from the lampposts, and the town had never seemed more inviting. A light dusting of snow glistened on the large Christmas tree, which blinked red and green lights, outside city hall, while Christmas carols were broadcast from the bell tower.

"I wondered if that was your car outside."

Stunned by the familiar voice, Beth turned. Kent stood next to her small table, although she hadn't seen him come in.

"What are you doing here?" she asked breathlessly.

"I decided to take a drive—"

"Where's your friend? Danielle?" she interrupted.

"At the Thyme and Tide. Resting. And, Beth, she really is a friend."

Sure she was. Ex-husbands usually traveled with *friends*. But apparently the headache was real.

"She took a couple of aspirin and is lying down."

Beth cupped her hands around the paper cup, the heat of the coffee stinging her palms. "I hope she feels better soon."

"She'll be fine." Without waiting for an invitation, Kent pulled out a chair and sat down across from her.

"You want a coffee, sir?" the kid behind the counter called out.

"Sure. I'll have whatever she's having," he said.

"You got it," Mr. Gameboy said with a promptness he hadn't demonstrated earlier. Maybe her generous tip had something to do with it.

"You looked deep in thought when I walked in," Kent

said, relaxing against the back of the chair. He extended his legs into the aisle, crossing them at the ankles. He seemed so comfortable, so calm, as if he hadn't a care in the world.

Beth stared at her ex-husband, unable to grasp how he could remain so unaffected by what had happened between them.

Perhaps Beth was the only one who had regrets, who wanted to examine the reasons their marriage had failed. What did it matter, anyway? she reflected darkly. Kent was with Danielle. He'd moved on, and she should, too.

"Beth?" he said, breaking into her thoughts.

She looked over at him, wondering what he'd just said.

"You worried about something?"

"Of course not," she said, forcing a brightness into her voice. "Why would you think that?"

"You never were much of a liar."

Beth shrugged, knowing it was true.

"Why are you out here, anyway?"

"I dropped off a puppy. A Christmas gift."

He seemed to be waiting for her to explain why she hadn't gone directly home. If she knew the answer to that question, she wouldn't be sipping blistering hot coffee and feeling as if the entire world was against her.

"So, how long have you and Ted been…friends?"

"Oh, for some time now."

"Is it serious?"

"No." She managed a nonchalant smile. "Perhaps I should've clarified that. I routinely see Ted on a professional basis—and yes, we've been out socially." She didn't mention the few kisses they'd shared because, frankly, it wasn't any of his business. When it came to *his* friend, she'd rather not know.

"But it could develop into something serious?" he asked.

This was even more difficult to answer. "I suppose. If we both wanted it to."

"And do you?"

She stared down into her coffee to avoid looking at him.

"No." Then she quickly shook her head. "Well, maybe."

"Maybe," he repeated slowly.

"It depends."

"On what?" he prodded.

Beth straightened. "I'd rather not talk about Ted and me. I didn't ask you about Danielle."

"True." He nodded. "All right, what *do* you want to talk about?"

"Do we need to talk about anything?"

He hesitated. "I guess not."

The kid brought over Kent's coffee and he paid for it. He was about to take his first sip when Beth warned him, "Careful, it's hot."

Kent sipped his coffee guardedly and grimaced. "You're right."

Beth took another sip of her own coffee, which had cooled slightly. "The puppy I delivered—it was to the Polgars."

"Polgar. That's an unusual name. As in Bobby Polgar, the chess champion?"

"Yes, he lives in Cedar Cove."

"Bobby Polgar lives here?" Kent arched his brows, clearly impressed.

"His wife is, or rather was, a local hairdresser. She's a wonderful, wonderful person."

"You mean to tell me Bobby Polgar married a beautician?" Kent grinned, as if the idea amused him.

"Don't say it like that. Teri's perfect for Bobby and now they have triplet sons...."

"And they took a puppy?"

"Actually, no. The puppy was for Teri's sister."

"What did you want to say about the Polgars?" Kent asked.

"I...I was remembering how it was with us when the girls were little."

"We talked about that earlier."

"We did," she agreed. "Those early Christmases, the basement apartment, those silly gingerbread decorations I sewed."

"What you're really saying is that you wonder what happened to us."

So Kent was the one brave enough to lay it on the table, the subject neither of them had been willing to broach until now.

Beth suppressed the urge to say it was too late. All of a sudden, she didn't want to dig up the past anymore, a past that was full of hurts and slights committed on both sides. If they dug too deep, she didn't know what they might uncover. Anyway, what was the point? They weren't together anymore. He had a new life and so did she.

Another part of her, the more rational part, recognized that unless she knew why her relationship with Kent had dissolved, history might repeat itself. If she did fall in love with Ted, she could revert to the same pattern that had destroyed her marriage to Kent.

"I don't think we can or should assign blame," Kent said, sitting up. He leaned forward and extended his arms, cupping his coffee between his hands. "So...I guess we should figure out what went wrong."

Beth swallowed hard, unsure where to start. She couldn't.

"Do you want to go first?" he asked. Kent, too, apparently found it difficult.

"No. You go."

"All right." He took a breath. "Once the girls got their driver's licenses, they didn't seem to need me anymore. They had their own lives. And that's the way it should be."

"A father's more than a chauffeur," she said with the glimmer of a smile. "But I know what you mean. They were becoming adults, so our role as parents changed."

He nodded. "And you had your career, while I had mine."

"At some point, without even being aware of it, we lost sight of what's important," Beth said. "And then it became a matter of pride, as if the most vital thing was proving how little we needed each other."

He nodded again.

"You stopped attending college social functions with me, and I retaliated by not attending your business dinners."

He lowered his gaze. "I'm sorry, but I found them boring."

"They were." She'd be the first to admit it.

"You always made them fun, though—in a slightly scandalous way," he said, grinning. "I got all the gossip. We'd stand in a corner and you'd tell me the most inappropriate stories."

"And you'd embarrass me by laughing at the most inappropriate times," she reminded him, and had trouble not breaking into giggles right then.

They looked at each other in silence.

"We both got absorbed in our lives, apart from each other," he finally said.

"We became strangers who happened to be married."

"I can't think of a single defining incident, an event that triggered the end of our marriage. Can you?"

"Not really." It was more an accumulation of grudges, of minor slights and careless acts. Oh, there were plenty of small decisions Beth had made through the years. Decisions that seemed inconsequential, insignificant. For some reason she thought of the morning Kent had asked her to drop off a letter at the post office. It was on her way to the college, while he was driving in the opposite direction. She told him she couldn't because she was running late. Really, how much time would it have taken? A minute? Two? Kent hadn't complained. He'd dropped off the letter himself.

Then there was the night she'd phoned and asked Kent to pick up bread and milk on his way home from work and he forgot. Such a little thing, but it had annoyed her no end.

At some stage she must have decided to ask nothing more of Kent. Was that when the pettiness began? When they turned to a silent battle of wills? How ridiculous they'd been. How silly and selfish and juvenile. No wonder their marriage had crumbled into pieces....

Beth visualized the slights, the put-downs, the irritations on both sides as pebbles, each a small stone in the growing pile that eventually crushed their marriage. Kent was right; it hadn't been any one thing.

Nothing big. No infidelity. No drugs or alcohol abuse. No money problems.

"Folks," the teenager said. He stood in front of their table with a tray and a white rag. "We're closing now."

"Oh." Feeling disjointed, Beth looked up.

"Normally I wouldn't mind staying while you finished your coffee, but it's Christmas Eve and my grandma's at the house."

"No problem," Kent said. He took one last drink of his coffee and left the cup on the table. "Thanks, and merry Christmas."

"Merry Christmas," Beth echoed. She left her cup behind, too.

Kent walked her to her car. He seemed to have more he wanted to say. Beth knew she did. Perhaps later…

"I'll see you at the church in twenty minutes," Kent said. He tucked his hands inside his pockets. "Bob at the B and B told me where it is."

"I'm going to pick up Bailey and Sophie. We'll see you there."

He started to turn away, but Beth stopped him.

"Kent…"

"Yes?"

"Would you mind sitting with the girls and me?"

He smiled. "I'd be happy to," he said.

Beth smiled back. Even if that meant Danielle joined them—well, she could tolerate that. It was the season of goodwill, after all. The important thing was for their family to be together.

Sixteen

Emily Flemming blew out the last candle after the seven o'clock Christmas Eve service at the Methodist church where her husband, Dave, was pastor. Every pew had been filled and the choir had sounded glorious. Both of their sons had gone back to the house with her parents. Emily appreciated the fact that the service was relatively early. Some churches waited until after nine, and the Catholic church always had a midnight mass.

Dave finished greeting the last of his parishioners, Bible in hand, as Emily joined him in the vestibule.

"That was lovely, sweetheart," she told her husband. Dave worked hard on his sermons, heading over to the church two hours before the first service in order to practice and pray. He took his responsibilities seriously and looked after his flock.

"Thank you." Dave slipped his arm around Emily's waist. "Did you see the man with Beth Morehouse?"

Emily had noticed him, and it wasn't the local veterinarian. Emily had suspected for some time that a romance between Beth and Ted Reynolds was in the offing. But when she'd seen Beth with this other man, she'd changed her mind. Judging by the electricity that sizzled between them, they were more than acquaintances or even friends. "I saw him."

"That's her ex-husband. His name is Kent."

"Her ex-husband?" They sure didn't act like exes, Emily thought. They'd exchanged frequent looks throughout the service and seemed keenly aware of each other. At first, Beth's glances had been shy, but as the service progressed, she'd grown bolder. Several times their eyes had met, and neither seemed inclined to look away.

The two girls had been sitting on one side of Beth, with Kent on the other, closest to the aisle. The girls hadn't exactly hidden their delight.

"On her way out of church, Beth mentioned a litter of part-Labrador puppies that were left on her doorstep. Ten in all."

"Ten? But I thought she was leaving for a short vacation with her daughters."

"She is, so she needs to find homes for these puppies quickly. She's only got two left and wanted to know if we're interested."

"Are we?" Emily asked, almost afraid of the answer.

"I was thinking a couple of puppies would help teach Mark and Matthew a sense of responsibility."

"Mark's been asking for a dog," Emily added with some reluctance. Her fear was that her son would lose interest and she'd be the one taking care of his dog. She had no concerns about Matthew; he was the dependable one.

"I was thinking—"

"Dave, before you say anything, we need to consider

this very carefully. A puppy, let alone two, is a lot of work and—"

"Mark's old enough to understand that. Besides, Beth sounded desperate to find a good home for these dogs. Especially at this late date."

Emily could feel herself weakening. Especially when her husband was regarding her with a puppy-dog look of his own....

"I had a Lab while I was growing up," Dave said.

Emily nodded, remembering his fond stories about the family pet.

"We named him Blackie," David went on. "Not very original, but, oh, how I loved that dog."

"In other words, you'd like our sons to have the same wonderful experience with a dog that you did?"

Dave smiled sheepishly. "But only if you agree."

While she wasn't one hundred percent sold, Emily was willing to take a chance.

"Can we at least look at them?" Dave asked, his eyes alight with excitement.

"Tonight?"

"Well, yes. It would be perfect. The boys are with your parents and we can drive out to Beth's place. By the time we get back, Matthew and Mark will be asleep. When they wake up in the morning, the puppies will be there—the best Christmas gift ever."

Clearly, her husband had worked this all out.

"All right," she said, holding back a smile. "We can go see the puppies, but there are no guarantees. Understand?"

"Definitely," he assured her. "We'll go to Beth's and look at them, and if you don't think it'll work, or you take an instant dislike to either dog or whatever, then we'll leave."

She raised her eyebrows. Dave knew her far too well. The minute she laid eyes on those puppies she'd be lost. She couldn't possibly say no. Especially since he wanted to provide his sons with the same childhood experience that he'd enjoyed.

During a quick phone call to the house, Emily told her mother that she and Dave had an errand to run. She explained what it was, and her mother promised that the boys would be in bed when Emily and Dave returned.

While Emily was talking to her mother, Dave contacted Beth, who said it would be fine to stop by the house that evening. In fact, she wished he would, because she planned to leave with the girls early on the morning of the twenty-sixth, so the sooner these last two puppies found homes, the better.

In the car on the way to Beth's house, Emily gazed out at the sky. The night was clear, with a million stars twinkling like jewels, but far more precious than any stone she'd ever seen. Her eyes fell to the wedding ring on her left hand. She'd almost removed it when she believed Dave was having an affair. Those had been dark days in their marriage and she'd been so sure, so completely convinced, that her husband was seeing another woman. It wasn't as if pastors were exempt from temptation.

In retrospect, she felt embarrassed that she'd suspected Dave of anything so underhanded. Yet what else was she to believe? He was gone almost every night and, well…thankfully those days were over. Probably every marriage went through at least one rocky period.

"Dave?"

"Yes, love?"

"I think Beth and her ex-husband still have feelings for each other."

Dave didn't speak for several minutes. "I had the same impression," he finally said.

"What do you suppose went wrong between them?" Emily asked.

"Probably the same thing that went wrong with us."

"Lack of communication," she murmured. "I guess it almost always comes down to that."

They pulled into Beth's yard and saw another vehicle parked next to hers.

"Maybe Kent's still with her," Dave commented.

Emily had heard Kent was staying at the Beldons' B and B. Rumor had it that he hadn't arrived alone, but if so, whoever he'd brought hadn't been at the church.

The front door opened and Beth stepped onto the porch to greet them. "Welcome, welcome! Please, come inside."

Dave held Emily's hand as they walked into the gaily decorated house.

"The girls have hot cocoa on the stove. I hope we'll be able to interest you in a mug."

"With whipped cream," Kent added, joining Beth.

He extended his hand to Dave. "We met in church earlier. Kent Morehouse."

"Dave Flemming, and my wife, Emily."

"Hi, Emily. Good to see you again, Dave."

Beth led the way into the kitchen. She opened the door leading to the laundry room and returned a moment later with two beautiful black puppies. They wore the saddest, most forlorn looks Emily could imagine.

"These two are the last of the litter, both males." Beth handed one to Emily.

"They're gorgeous," Emily said, falling hard and fast. All it had taken was one look, and she was convinced these puppies needed to be part of their family.

She sat on one of the kitchen chairs, holding the puppy on her lap. The little creature licked her hand, then immediately curled up and went to sleep. Yup, Emily was lost. Mark would love this dog and she felt confident he'd do a good job of feeding, training and caring for this puppy. Matthew, too, would love and train his dog.

When Emily glanced up she saw that Dave was holding the other puppy, all the while engaged in conversation with Kent Morehouse.

"The sermon tonight really touched me," Beth said. "I've heard the Christmas story all my life. But I'd never really considered the role Joseph played. How he must have loved Mary."

Emily agreed. "It's a beautiful love story and one that's often overlooked." This was Dave's gift. He looked at Biblical stories in ways that stirred people's hearts and brought them closer to God. He could take familiar passages and study them from a different point of view, bringing contemporary relevance and new insight.

Beth returned to the stove, and removed the pan from the burner. Bailey and Sophie, who'd poked their heads in to say hello, were playing a computer game in the family room.

"Girls! Cocoa," Beth called out.

Neither seemed to hear her, too engrossed in their game. Shaking her head, Beth finished filling the mugs and brought two of them to Emily and Dave, both sitting at the kitchen table.

Kent picked up the other two, then he and Beth sat down with her guests.

"I see they've taken a liking to us," Dave said, motioning to the puppy on his lap. The second one was asleep, too, chin now resting on Emily's arm.

"You know what a soft touch I am," she complained laughingly.

"Yeah, I guess we're a two-dog family now."

"Dave was telling me he likes to golf," Kent said to Beth a moment later.

"It's a prerequisite for pastors," Dave joked. "A lot of men bond over the sport."

"There was a time not so long ago when Dave gave it up, though," Emily said. "We were going through a difficult financial period and he didn't want me to know how bad things were. The idiot let me think he was out golfing when he was actually working at a second job." Emily wasn't sure about confiding anything so personal, but she felt this was something Beth and Kent might benefit from hearing.

"How did you find out?" Beth asked.

"Peggy Beldon casually mentioned that Bob missed seeing Dave on the golf course."

"Of course, Emily didn't say anything at the time. She just waited for me to come back to the house. She was cool as a cucumber—until I walked in the front door."

"Was that before or after I dyed my hair blond?"

Beth stared at her. "You went blond?"

"It was stupid, but we do stupid things when we're desperate."

"We do," Kent agreed far too quickly.

"In the end we worked everything out, thank God," Dave said. "I made such a mess of my marriage. I nearly destroyed my wife's faith in me."

"And then there were those missing jewels," Emily added. There was far more to the story.

"Oh, yes, the jewels." Dave sighed, lifting his mug of cocoa.

"Missing jewels?" Kent asked, looking from one to the other.

"It's a long story, so allow me to condense it. One of the older ladies in the church, Martha Evans, died and several pieces of her jewelry turned up missing."

"Dave was the last person to see her alive," Emily said. "Which immediately threw suspicion on him."

"So everyone assumed I was the one who took the jewelry—even my wife," Dave said, grinning at Emily.

She smiled back. "What else was I supposed to believe?" she murmured. "Besides, I found Martha's earring in his suit pocket. Only I didn't know it belonged to Martha or that someone had purposely placed it there. At the time, I imagined my husband was having an affair."

"My goodness, you two had quite a few troubles, didn't you?" Kent glanced at Beth.

"What saved your marriage?" she asked.

"Prayer," Emily said, "and the two of us talking honestly. Dave finally admitted we had more bills at the end of the month than money, and that he was doing two jobs."

"And Sheriff Davis was instrumental in capturing the man responsible for the theft of Martha's jewelry," Dave explained, "with Roy McAfee's help."

"What an incredible story!"

"It really is, and I'll fill in the missing pieces the next time we see you," Emily promised. She took a last swallow of her cocoa and stood, the puppy in her arms. "We need to head home. My parents are looking after the boys."

"Wait," Kent said. "I want to know who actually took the jewelry?"

"Someone who worked on Martha's will, a paralegal," Dave explained. "His name is Geoff Duncan. He's serving prison time now. He was trying to impress his fiancée's family, so he stole the jewelry, pawned it all and spent the money."

"Lori Bellamy, the fiancée, didn't have a clue what Geoff had done," Emily said. "She's Lori Wyse now. She got married not long ago to Lincoln Wyse, who opened a body shop in town earlier this year. They seem to be a good match, although they had a few problems with Lori's family. But apparently that's all settled now."

"This Geoff guy. Did he have a grudge against you?" Kent asked.

"Not that I know of. I was just the perfect candidate for him to frame because, as Martha's pastor, I spent a lot of time with her. Like I said, I seemed to be the last person to see her alive, and I was also the one who found the body. The obvious suspect." He shook his head. "Thank goodness Sheriff Davis and Roy McAfee looked beyond the obvious."

"It must've been a terrible time for you," Beth said sympathetically.

"The worst, but we made it through and I'm so grateful we did."

"I can imagine."

"Some people are far too willing to give up on..." She let the rest fade once she realized what she was about to say. Emily didn't want to embarrass the divorced couple.

Kent moved closer to Beth. "I agree."

"So do I," Beth said, almost before the words had left Kent's mouth.

They looked at each other, but the moment was broken by the sharp peal of Kent's cell phone.

He answered it on the second ring, and although Emily couldn't make out what was being said, the person calling him was clearly female—and clearly upset.

"Yes, of course," he said. "Yes, I know." He closed his cell with a snap. "I apologize, but I need to leave."

He reached for his coat and, after a few words of farewell, was out the door.

"I know it's none of my business, but who was that?" Dave asked Beth.

"His...friend," Beth said.

Emily looked at Dave just as he turned to look at her. So the rumors of a female companion had been correct, and for some reason this woman had stayed back at the B and B. There were more obstacles to a reconciliation between Beth and her ex-husband than either of them had guessed.

Seventeen

"**D**id you see the way Dad looked at Mom during the service?" Bailey whispered to her sister in the darkened bedroom. Sophie was in the twin bed next to hers. Although she'd turned out the lights several minutes ago, Bailey was too excited to sleep.

"Yes, I know but—"

"They're falling in love all over again," Bailey broke in. "I can *feel* it."

"Well, maybe, but…"

"But what?" Bailey muttered. Sometimes her sister could be so…negative. Well, she refused to allow Sophie's skeptical remarks to dampen her good feelings. For a time it seemed that everything they'd planned was about to fall apart. Then, at the very last minute, their father had shown up at the church…alone. It'd been perfect. Just perfect.

Bailey hadn't asked about Danielle and neither had Sophie. Their dad had slipped into the pew next to Beth, and their mother had smiled over at him and…

Oh, it'd been sheer bliss. Love radiated between them. If this were a movie, a crescendo of music would have burst forth, and there would've been joyful singing in the background. Actually, there *was* music, but it had come from the church choir. Still, the effect was pretty satisfying.

"Can I talk now?" Sophie asked impatiently.

"Oh, all right."

"I have a question."

"Ask away." Bailey sighed, suspecting that Sophie was going to ruin Bailey's Christmas Eve by casting doubt on the likelihood of their parents reuniting. Her father had introduced Danielle as a "friend." *They* were the ones who'd made the assumption that she was more than that.

"What about when Danielle phoned? Dad left in a mighty big hurry after that."

"Yeah, I know," Bailey admitted with more than a little reluctance.

"He's still at Danielle's beck and call."

"But we can't be sure of all the circumstances and—"

"There are no *buts* here," Sophie fumed. "I don't know what Dad sees in Danielle, but there's obviously something."

"Whatever it is, I trust Dad to do the right thing." Bailey rolled onto her back and stared up at the ceiling. Leave it to Sophie.... Now she was worried again. Their father was smart—she hoped. Deep down, she couldn't believe he was involved with Danielle. In fact, the more she thought about it, the more certain she was. He might have brought Danielle with him, but from the moment he arrived Kent only seemed interested in Beth. Danielle was far more attached to her cell phone than she was to their father.

"Mark my words, Dad doesn't care about Danielle," Bailey insisted in a confident voice.

Sophie sighed loudly. "I wish I could believe that."

"Maybe we should help him along."

"Bailey, no!"

"No?"

"No," she repeated. "If we step in now, it'll just complicate everything. Dad has to do this on his own. Otherwise, we'll sabotage the whole reconciliation."

Bailey slowly absorbed her sister's words. Although Sophie was younger—and not studying psychology—she could occasionally be really smart. "Have you ever thought of going into diplomacy? You'd be great."

"You think so?" Sophie loved getting compliments.

Well, everyone did, but her sister was so transparent. She made no effort to hide how much she enjoyed hearing nice things about herself. Bailey could almost see Sophie's self-congratulatory little smile.

"Trust me," Bailey said, returning to the subject at hand. "Mom and Dad are going to remarry. I can feel it."

"Well…we can wish."

"Oh, come on," Bailey urged. "*Believe* it."

"You really buy into that positive thinking idea, don't you?"

"Yes," Bailey concurred. "And you should, too." In her opinion, it would go a long way toward raising Sophie's spirits.

"I'll consider it," Sophie said.

Pulling the sheet and blanket up over her shoulder, Bailey shifted onto her right side, her back to her sister. Despite Sophie's pessimism, Bailey believed with all her heart. She remembered the look her parents had exchanged in church that night. The look of love, of re-gret and the promise of reconciliation.

Tomorrow morning, when it was Christmas, the biggest and best present wouldn't be under the tree. It would be the fact that her parents still loved each other and wanted to remarry.

On Christmas Day, they'd finally acknowledge their feelings, and the rest of their lives would begin.

Bailey was sure of it.

Eighteen

"Merry Christmas," Bruce Peyton whispered as he drew Rachel into his arms.

Smiling, Rachel arched her back and yawned. "Is it morning already?"

"It sure is. I've got coffee brewing and Jolene's up."

Rachel turned her head to look at the clock. "Bruce, it isn't even eight." She could easily have slept another hour. Or two.

"I know, but Jolene's anxious to get to the presents."

With some effort, Rachel sat up. She was noticeably pregnant now and the baby was more active every day. Thankfully the worst of the morning sickness had passed.

The pregnancy had been unplanned and Jolene, her thirteen-year-old stepdaughter, hadn't yet adjusted to her father's remarriage when she was forced to deal with the news about the baby. The marriage itself had resulted in a difficult transition for the girl, but the pregnancy complicated everything that much more.

Her relationship with Jolene had grown tense. The stress became too much for Rachel and eventually she felt she had no choice but to move out of the family home. Only recently—just weeks ago—had she returned.

The counseling sessions had helped a great deal and they were learning to coexist and work together as a family. Rachel was excited about spending Christmas with her husband and stepdaughter. She and Jolene had planned the dinner menu together and they'd spent most of yesterday in the kitchen, preparing vegetables and side dishes and dessert.

During the afternoon they'd also made a breakfast casserole to put in the oven Christmas morning while they opened gifts. And Jolene had baked her first cinnamon rolls from scratch. Rachel hadn't told her, but this was her first experience, too. The rolls had turned out well, if Bruce's lavish praise was anything to go by.

All the while, Poppy, their new dog, had lounged in the warm kitchen, with occasional bursts of activity and escorted trips to the backyard.

"Would you like tea in bed?" her husband asked her.

"I'd love some."

"And I'd love to bring you some," he said, grinning. "In fact, I'll do anything. I'd stand on my head in the middle of the street in a snowstorm if it meant you'd be with me every Christmas morning for the rest of my life." Leaning forward, he pressed his lips to hers. "Merry Christmas, my beautiful wife."

"Merry Christmas, my silly husband."

"I'll be back in a minute with your tea." Bruce kissed her again, and then he was gone.

Rachel sat up in bed and rearranged her pillows. She held one hand over her stomach, letting her unborn daughter know how much she was loved. Next

Christmas, this little one would be crawling around, eager to tear open packages. Rachel closed her eyes, savoring the vision of all the wonderful things the next year would hold.

Bruce returned with a steaming cup of tea, which he handed her just as Jolene burst into the master bedroom, carrying Poppy.

"Rachel, you're awake, aren't you?"

"I'm getting there."

"Hurry up," the girl said, holding the puppy close to Rachel. "There are gifts out there just waiting to be opened."

"Okay, okay," Rachel said, squinting as Poppy licked her face. "Give me five minutes."

"That long?" Jolene whined, and then laughed out loud, sounding young and carefree.

"You're certainly in a good mood," Bruce teased, hugging his daughter.

"Daddy, it's Christmas. Everyone's in a good mood on Christmas Day."

If only that was true. Memories of her childhood drifted into Rachel's mind. After her mother's death, she'd gone to live with an unmarried aunt who'd seen Christmas as a commercial wasteland and refused to partake in anything so frivolous. There'd been no tree, no presents. It was just like every other day, except that Rachel didn't have to go to school.

She'd listened attentively as her friends told of their wonderful holidays and longed for the time when she'd celebrate Christmas with a family of her own. And here it was, unfolding right before her eyes.

Setting her mug aside, she tossed back the covers

and slid out of bed. "Did someone say something about presents?" she asked.

Jolene placed Poppy on the floor, grabbed Rachel's hand and led her into the living room. "I put the casserole in the oven."

"Great. Did you preheat it to three hundred and fifty degrees first?"

"Yes, I did."

"You're going to be a terrific cook."

"I already am," Jolene said. "I made dinner the whole time you were gone and I did a good job, didn't I, Dad?"

"Yup." Bruce joined Rachel on the sofa. "Unfortunately, I didn't have much of an appetite."

Jolene sighed. "All he could think about was you and the baby."

"But Rachel's with us now, and that's what matters."

"Hey," Rachel said, "are we going to sit around all morning discussing the past or are we going to open gifts?"

Her question got the desired results. "Open gifts!" Jolene said with renewed energy.

Rachel went back to the bedroom for her robe and tied it loosely about her waist as she slipped her feet into fuzzy slippers.

Bruce had a nice fire going in the fireplace, and Poppy lay stretched out in front of it, snuffling in her sleep. The radio was tuned to a station that played Christmas music without any commercial interruptions. The casserole was baking in the oven, and the scent of bacon and cheese wafted into the room. This was as idyllic a picture as Rachel could ever have conjured up in some blissful fantasy.

"Who gets to open a gift first?" she asked, settling onto the sofa with her husband.

"I have to sort through them all before we open any," Jolene said. "I'll hand everything out and *then* we open them. One at a time," she ordered.

"Then get to it, girl," Bruce said with a laugh, reaching for Rachel's hand.

Jolene walked over to the lighted tree, which they'd just finished decorating yesterday, and got down on all fours, rooting through the gifts. She pulled one out and sat back, checking the name tag.

"This one's for Dad," she said and, stretching forward, passed it to Bruce.

He held the rectangular package close to his ear and shook it. "Who's it from?"

"Rachel," Jolene said. "Looks like a shirt to me."

"Don't spoil the surprise."

"Dad, it's obvious." Jolene grinned from ear to ear. She disappeared again, foraging under the tree.

"What are you looking for now?" Bruce asked, setting the box at his feet.

"A special gift," Jolene said, her voice muffled.

"Who's it for?"

"Rachel, from me."

"Oh, I love getting gifts." Rachel smiled at Bruce. Considering the months of tension between her and Jolene, she was pleased that her stepdaughter was so eager to give her presents. She leaned her head against her husband's shoulder. This was what she'd always hoped Christmas would be like, surrounded by people she loved and who loved her.

"Here it is," Jolene announced, scooting out backward from beneath the huge tree.

Rachel took the package from her. It was the size and shape of a shoe box.

"Can Rachel open it now?" Jolene asked her father. "Even though that's not the rules."

"That's up to Rachel."

Jolene looked at her, eyes dark and serious. "Will you, Rach?"

"If you want me to."

"I do." She sat on the floor as she waited for Rachel to unwrap her gift.

"I made it myself," Jolene said, her eyes bright as she bit her lower lip. "I hope you like it."

"I'm sure I will." Rachel carefully slid the ribbon off and peeled back the decorative paper. The box had, indeed, held Jolene's new gym shoes. Rachel lifted the lid and stared down at a white hand-knit baby blanket, enfolded in pink tissue. Rachel hardly knew what to say. "You...you knit this yourself?" She drew it out, marveling at the complexity of the design.

Jolene nodded. "We learned how to knit in an after-school class. I bought the pattern and the yarn at that craft shop downtown, the one where Mrs. Flemming works. I worked on it every day. I made a lot of mistakes," she admitted. She hurried to Rachel's side, kneeling in front of her. "See? Here's one."

It was so small Rachel had to squint to see it.

"There are other mistakes, too."

"Oh, Jolene, it's *perfect*." Rachel struggled to hold back tears. "I'll bring your sister home from the hospital in it."

"You will?"

Rachel leaned forward and brought Jolene toward

her, kissing her hair. "I'll always treasure it, because you made it for me and the baby."

"Don't tell me you're both going to get all weepy on me," Bruce groaned.

"I might," she said, struggling to hold back the tears.

Jolene raised her arms and wrapped Rachel in a big hug.

"I love you, Jolene," Rachel whispered.

"I love you, too… You're going to be a great mother."

Bruce put his arms around them both. "She already *is* a great mom," he said.

Jolene nodded and met Rachel's eyes. "Yes, she is."

Nineteen

This was Sheriff Troy Davis's first Christmas with his wife, Faith. It was a second marriage for both. Each of them had been blessed with a long and happy first marriage and each had suffered the loss of their beloved partner. Recently, they'd found a renewed sense of purpose and love with each other.

As it was their first major holiday together, they'd divided the time between his daughter, Megan, and her family and Faith's son, Scott. Christmas Eve had been spent with Megan, her husband, Craig, and their infant daughter, Cassandra.

Today, Troy and Faith were headed for Scott's home. Late Christmas morning, Troy loaded up the car with the Christmas gifts and treats Faith had prepared for her son's family. They'd delivered a carload of presents and homemade sweets to Megan the night before, as well. Faith had been baking for weeks, not that Troy was complaining. He hadn't enjoyed the holidays this much in a very long while. During the last years of her life, Sandy had been in a nursing home, and Troy hadn't bothered with decorating their house or putting up a tree. For the first time since Sandy went into the care facility, it actually felt like Christmas to him. He hadn't realized how much he'd missed all the fuss and bother.

"Can we make one stop?" Faith asked as she climbed into the front seat beside him.

"Sure," he said. "Where?"

"The Beldons'. Peggy and Bob were so kind to bring us that plate of goodies. I'd like to reciprocate."

"The Beldons probably have more than their fair share of candy and cookies."

"This is a peach-and-raspberry cobbler. They can eat it now or put it in the freezer. Peggy's always thinking of others, and I wanted to do something nice for her."

"Then of course we'll drop by."

"It'll just take a moment," Faith promised. "In fact, you don't even need to get out of the car."

Troy reached for his wife's hand and gave it a gentle squeeze. He loved Faith. He'd loved her when they were in high school, and he loved her now. After Sandy died, Troy had never expected to marry again. And then... Faith came back into his life. Their courtship had had its ups and downs, but despite some confused and difficult times, Troy wouldn't change a thing. Faith was with him now. Nothing else mattered.

The Beldons' Thyme and Tide Bed-and-Breakfast on Cranberry Point was en route to Scott's house, so it really wasn't out of their way. Troy entered the long driveway and noticed three vehicles parked in the area reserved for guests. He remembered that Bob had mentioned that their children would be visiting from Spokane, which accounted for two cars. The other must be a guest.

"I'll be right back," Faith assured him as he eased to a stop.

She got out of the car, opened the rear passenger door and took out the cobbler in its lidded plastic container. She'd put a bow on top, giving it a festive look. He hoped she'd tucked one in their freezer for him—and he didn't need the bow!

Bob Beldon answered the door and Faith went inside. Troy listened to Christmas music and sang along with Burl Ives on the car radio. Two or three minutes later, Faith reappeared and motioned for him.

Troy turned off the engine and started toward the house. Something was definitely wrong. He could see it in Faith's stance as she stood in the doorway, waiting for him.

When he approached, Faith said, "Oh, Troy, I'm afraid there's a bit of a…situation here. I think you might be able to help."

"What kind of situation?"

She moved aside and he walked into the house. The instant he did, he heard a woman shrieking and crying uncontrollably in the background. She seemed to be having some sort of temper tantrum. Troy heard things being thrown against the walls.

"It's one of our guests," Bob said, coming toward him. "She arrived with Kent Morehouse, Beth's ex-husband. We thought they were a couple—but apparently not. Seems she was supposed to meet up with a sailor from the navy base, but something happened. She hasn't been able to tell us what."

"So what's her relationship with Kent?"

"Friends, I guess. She works for him."

Kent wandered into the foyer with his hands in his

pockets. He looked completely baffled. "I'm sorry," he said. "I tried talking to Danielle, but she's too upset to make much sense. As far as I can tell, the young man she came to see has decided to dump her."

"On Christmas Day?" Troy wasn't impressed with the sailor's timing.

"She hasn't stopped crying...."

"For hours," Peggy inserted. "And throwing stuff. I don't know if she's broken anything but..."

"She refuses to answer the door," Bob added. "She must have blocked it with a chair or something, because we can't get in."

Troy could well imagine what this was doing to the family's celebration.

"I think all Danielle wants to do now is get back to California. I went on the internet to find a flight, but talking to her is impossible." Kent shook his head.

Troy moved down the hallway to the guest bedrooms and knocked on the door. It wasn't hard to tell which room was Danielle's.

"Sheriff Troy Davis," he announced authoritatively.

Silence followed, which was a blessing after the racket of the past several minutes. Then they heard the unmistakable sound of furniture being moved.

"What seems to be the problem here?" he asked when Danielle slowly opened the bedroom door.

"I have to get out of here," Danielle said, dabbing her eyes with a wadded tissue. "I *hate* this place."

"I found a flight that can get you to LAX, leaving Sea-Tac in a few hours," Kent rushed to say. This was obviously the information he'd been wanting to tell her for some time.

"Fine," she said, slamming her suitcase shut. It was

on her bed, although little else was. In fact, the room looked as if it'd been hit by a hurricane. Bedding lay on the floor. So did a potted poinsettia, with dirt scattered everywhere, and a framed picture, its glass now broken. And that wasn't all....

"I'm really sorry about this," Kent said, apologizing to the Beldons.

Danielle seemed to think he was talking to her. "Why didn't Hunter tell me sooner?" she wailed. "It worked out so well that I could come here for Christmas.... He said he'd be tied up, but I said that was fine because my boss invited me to visit his family until Christmas Day and then...then..." She broke into a fresh bout of tears. Angrily, she grabbed the tissue box from the floor and jerked out three. "Then Hunter waited until this morning to tell me.... He didn't even do it to my face. Instead, he sent me a text message and said he was seeing someone else. He let me come all this way and make a fool of myself." She dabbed at her eyes again. "Now all I want is to get away from this horrible town...."

"We'll need to get her to the airport."

Kent shifted uncomfortably. "I had plans with my family but I feel responsible for her. I'll drive her to the airport."

"I want to go home!" Danielle screamed. "I don't care who takes me to the airport. Isn't there a taxi or something?"

"I have a friend who owns a car service," Troy offered. "He can drive you to the airport."

"Fine!" Danielle shouted. "I want to leave *now*."

"Please call your friend," Kent said. "And I'll pay whatever it costs."

The small group watched as Danielle finished gathering up the last of her things, stuffing them in her carry-on. Kent seemed relieved not to be taking her to the airport. She swung the suitcase off the bed, and it landed on the floor with a loud thump. Straightening her shoulders, she wheeled her bag out of the room, ignoring everyone.

As soon as she'd left, Kent slumped on the edge of the bed and heaved a sigh. He lowered his head and plowed his fingers through his hair.

"You all right?" Troy asked.

Kent nodded. "I've made a big mess of things."

"It's not your fault the sailor broke it off."

"No," Kent said. "My mistake was taking her out to meet Beth and the girls. I let them assume Danielle and I were romantically involved. It was a stupid thing to do and I regretted it almost immediately." He looked disgusted with himself. "Danielle went along with it, since she knows I still love my ex-wife and she wanted to do me a favor. But she totally overplayed her role." He sighed again. "I wanted to tell Beth last night, but before I had a chance Danielle phoned in hysterics because she couldn't get hold of her boyfriend. After that, the situation went from bad to worse." He gestured around him. "I've botched everything."

"Don't be so sure," Faith said, coming to stand next to Troy.

"Do you think there's a way to salvage this?" Kent asked hopefully.

"Troy and I were in the pew behind you and Beth at the service last night. I believe if you speak to Beth honestly, you'll discover she feels the same way."

Kent's eyes brightened. "Really?"

Faith nodded.

"First let me see if I can arrange this airport ride," Troy said, reaching for his cell. He punched in the appropriate number and waited. Logan, the son of a friend, had recently started a car service, focusing on airport transportation. He was hungry enough to take the fare, even if it was Christmas Day.

After a short conversation, Troy closed his cell. "He'll be here within thirty minutes."

"Have you ever done anything so stupid you wonder what you could possibly have been thinking?" Kent asked Troy.

The sheriff wasn't sure whether this was a real question or a rhetorical one. He decided to answer it anyway. "We all have, at one time or other. All you can do is learn from it—and you've certainly done that. And like Faith says, things will probably turn out okay."

Kent looked up and gave a slight nod. "I appreciate the encouraging words."

After a few minutes, Troy returned to the kitchen. The Beldons had gathered there. Danielle sat in the living room next to her suitcase, crying quietly. He did feel sorry for her. This couldn't be easy; no broken relationship was.

Kent wanted to pay for the damages, but the Beldons refused. And at their insistence, no charges would be laid. They, too, sympathized with Danielle, despite their exasperation with her out-of-control behavior.

To be on the safe side Troy and Faith remained at the B and B until Logan arrived and Danielle departed.

They left a few minutes later. Faith sighed as Troy turned out of the driveway.

"Well, that was an unexpected interlude," she said in a good-humored voice. "I don't know what would've happened to that poor girl—and Kent—if we hadn't got there when we did. You're my hero, Troy Davis."

"And you're my sweetheart," he returned, smiling in her direction.

Twenty

"Now what?" Will Jefferson asked. He held his gloved hands upright like a surgeon about to enter the operating theater.

"It's a turkey," Miranda Sullivan teased, "not an appendectomy."

Will lowered his arms.

"We're going to stuff it," Miranda said.

"You mean I'm actually going to put my hands *inside* that bird?" His look was incredulous.

"Yes." It was difficult to keep a straight face when Will took everything so seriously.

"I've never done this before."

Miranda rolled her eyes. "Really? You could've fooled me."

"Are you making fun of me?" he asked, eyebrows raised.

"I'm doing my best not to."

Will grinned. "Well, this is hard work. First time in my life that I've cooked a turkey."

"We'll do fine."

"I'm glad you're with me," he said, "and not just because of the turkey."

"I'm happy to be here."

Quite unexpectedly, Will had invited Miranda to spend Christmas Day with him. They'd worked together at the Harbor Street Art Gallery for the past several months. She'd started as part-time help, working a couple of days a week. Gradually, Will had increased her hours.

In the beginning they hadn't gotten along. He thought she was too opinionated; she thought he was stubborn and dictatorial. But as the weeks progressed they'd formed a strong friendship. She'd taken a step toward compromise and he'd taken one, too, and they'd met in the middle.

Recently…well, *very* recently, that friendship took another turn. Miranda wasn't ready to put a name to it; she wasn't sure it was safe for her heart to define it. Not yet. But…there was definitely a sense of excitement that sizzled between them.

They'd kissed. She'd kissed him once, shocking herself far more than she'd shocked Will. And he'd kissed her. More than once.

Will had moved into his childhood home a few weeks earlier, purchasing the residence on Eagle Crest Avenue from his mother. This made it possible for Charlotte and Ben to move into the Sanford assisted-living complex without the additional worry of what would happen to their home.

Will and his sister, Olivia, had come up with the idea and coincidentally the move had benefited Miranda, too. She lived near Gig Harbor, a twenty-minute drive from Cedar Cove. The lease on her apartment was up, and she'd been hoping to move closer to the art gallery when Will approached her about living in his apartment on the premises. He'd had it remodeled and she could move in whenever she wished.

It was an offer too good to refuse. Her best friend, Shirley Bliss, had urged her to accept. Miranda grew a bit sad as she thought about Shirley. They'd become close after they'd both lost their husbands. Miranda had been married to an artist and Shirley was one herself. They'd helped each other adjust to widowhood.

Shirley had remarried a couple of months ago, and as soon as Tanni, her daughter, graduated from high school, Shirley planned to move to California with her new husband, Larry Knight, who was a nationally known and highly respected artist.

It would be hard to see Shirley leave the area and yet Miranda couldn't begrudge her friend this happiness. They'd stay in touch, of course, but…it wasn't the same.

Will had been attracted to Shirley. His ego had taken a beating when she chose Larry Knight over him. The fact that he'd introduced Shirley to Larry had made the whole situation especially galling for Will; Miranda understood that. When he'd first started paying attention to *her,* Miranda had reason to think he was trying to make Shirley jealous. She wouldn't stand for that and made sure Will knew it.

Lately, however, there'd been a shift in the way he treated her. But his first tentative attempts to deepen their relationship didn't work, mainly because Miranda didn't trust him. He'd invited her to dinner and she'd refused. Later, she felt bad about that and she'd taken him a store-bought chicken. So they'd ended up having dinner together, after all. That was the night he'd invited her to spend Christmas Day with him.

"Now what?" Will asked. He was pushing the home-made stuffing into the cavity.

"Keep going until you can't get any more inside."

"Okay. Although this is kind of a revolting activity."

She laughed. "Will, why did you buy a twenty-three-pound bird for just the two of us?" she asked.

"I don't know… At least there'll be plenty of left-overs."

"Enough to feed an army," she muttered.

"And a navy," he added.

He finished with the stuffing, and washed his hands while Miranda basted the turkey and placed an aluminum-foil tent over the top. "Okay, it's ready for the oven," she said.

She held open the oven door and Will slid the turkey inside. "How long will it take?" he asked.

"Twenty minutes a pound, so do the math."

"Seven and a half *hours?*"

"You'll build up an appetite," she said. "And we can have some crackers and cheese while we wait."

"And a nice glass of wine…" Will pulled off his oven mitts. "Any other suggestions?"

"As a matter of fact, yes." She left the kitchen and went into the living room to collect her bag. Reaching inside, she took out a wrapped gift. "For you," she said playfully, handing him the large square box.

Will looked a bit uneasy, which told her what she already suspected. He hadn't purchased her a gift. She hadn't really expected him to. Besides, this was more of a thank-you for having her over.

"It's small, just a token," she said. She didn't want

to embarrass him or make him feel guilty for not re-
ciprocating.

"Go ahead and open it," she urged.

"You shouldn't have," he said theatrically. He sat
down on the sofa and tore away the paper. When he
saw the jigsaw puzzle, he grinned. The picture was a
seascape, with dolphins and tropical fish swimming in
a blue, blue ocean. "Hey, good idea! We can put it together this afternoon."

Miranda stood and started to clear off the table. "I
used to enjoy doing puzzles," she told him. "This table's
big enough to lay out all the pieces."

"Here. Now you open my gift," Will said.

Miranda turned around, leaning against the table's
edge. She frowned as Will gave her the small, beautifully wrapped gift. The shape and size hinted that it'd
come from a jewelry store.

"Is this a marriage proposal?" she joked, and then
laughed nervously, wondering how she could have asked
something so idiotic.

"Not yet," he returned quite seriously.

Miranda stared at the package, almost afraid to re-
move the wrapping.

"Open it," he said.

Reluctantly, she untied the ribbon. "You didn't wrap
this yourself."

"You're right, the store did." He stood next to her
and nudged her to continue unwrapping.

"I…wasn't expecting anything like this," she said.
"All I got you is a puzzle."

"I know you'll be surprised, which makes it all the
more special."

Her hand trembled as she carefully slipped off the

paper. Holding her breath, Miranda lifted the lid of the small blue box. Inside was a gold coin, a very old one, she guessed, framed by a gold bezel.

"It's from a sunken treasure ship found off the Florida coast," Will explained.

Taking it from the box, she saw that the coin was attached to a fine gold chain. Will took it out of her fingers, placed it around her neck and secured the clasp. She could feel the coin resting at the base of her throat, the metal smooth and cool. Automatically, she pressed her hand over it.

"It's treasure, Miranda," Will whispered. "Just like you are to me."

She blinked a couple of times, hardly able to fathom that Will Jefferson would do this for her. Or that he'd say such a thing.

"I..." Speaking seemed impossible, and whatever she said, whatever words of appreciation she managed to form, would never be enough. "I don't know how to...thank you."

"You're kidding. You, speechless? I don't believe it."

"Don't joke, Will. I mean it. I don't think anyone's ever done anything like this for me."

Will kissed her then. Really kissed her. He was gentle and loving, and when he raised his head, his eyes were filled with promise.

Twenty-One

"Mom, what time will Dad get here?" Sophie asked, as she and Bailey hurried into the kitchen. "Is Danielle coming, too?"

Beth had expected them long before now. She was clearing away the last of their brunch dishes, irritated that she hadn't heard from Kent. She was determined not to contact him, although she considered it bad manners to keep his family waiting on Christmas Day. "I don't think your father actually gave us a time," she said with more generosity than she felt. He'd certainly implied it would be that morning.

"Oh," Sophie murmured.

"It's already afternoon," Bailey said. "We've never opened our gifts this late."

That seemed like a minor complaint to Beth. The thought of spending Christmas Day with Kent's…friend was enough to make her feel like going back to bed. Playing hostess to Danielle was above and beyond the call of duty.

It hadn't bothered her nearly as much until she'd realized how deeply she still loved Kent. For the past three years, she'd been able to live with a degree of content-ment, refusing to acknowledge how lonely she was.

"Mom, call Dad and ask when he's going to be here," Bailey said.

"Why don't *you* phone him?" Beth suggested. She purposely banished the picture of Kent and Danielle cuddled together while their daughters impatiently awaited his arrival.

"Okay."

Cell phone in hand, Bailey sat down, propping her elbows on the kitchen table.

Beth tuned out her daughter's conversation as she silently prayed for the strength to get through the day. Depression weighed heavily on her. If she managed to survive this Christmas, she'd tell Kent she'd made a mistake. She loved him and wanted him back in her life. Only she couldn't tell him that in Danielle's presence.

No, she might as well forget any hope of a reconcili-ation, she told herself. Danielle was young and beauti-ful and competitive. She wouldn't give Kent up easily. Beth had made the mistake, and now she had to live with the consequences.

"Mom? Mom?"

"Yes," Beth said, turning her thoughts away from her ex-husband.

"Did you hear what I said?"

"Sorry, no."

"Are you feeling all right?" Sophie asked, joining her sister at the table.

"I...don't know." What Beth really wanted was to es-cape to her room with a fake flu bug and leave the girls to celebrate Christmas with Kent and Danielle. But she couldn't do that to her daughters. She'd muddle through and somehow find the strength to pretend all was well.

"Dad's on his way," Bailey told her.

"Good." She forced a smile. Turning from the sink, she grabbed a dish towel and wiped her hands dry. Needing fortification, she went to freshen her makeup.

Upstairs in her bathroom, she stared at her reflection in the mirror. Sad. Sad. Sad. She straightened her shoulders, saying, "You can do this. You can do this."

When she walked down the stairs she found Kent standing by the front door. She stopped abruptly before she reached the bottom. He looked up at her; their eyes met, and her heart immediately reacted. She gave him a tentative smile.

Kent smiled back.

He spoke first. "Merry Christmas," he said.

"Thank you." Her voice sounded wispy. "Merry Christmas."

"Dad," Bailey said excitedly, rushing over to him. She paused and looked around. "Where's Danielle?"

Kent broke eye contact with her. "She isn't here."

"Isn't here? Did she stay at the B and B?"

"Not…exactly." He bent down to take off his boots.

"Then where is she?"

Kent glanced at his watch. "I imagine she's at the airport about now."

"The airport?" Sophie repeated. "I thought she was spending Christmas in Cedar Cove."

"That was her original plan. She came with me, hoping to meet up with a sailor she'd met when he was on leave in California. Apparently, she read more into the relationship than she should have."

"What?" Beth asked in shock. "She came to meet up with a sailor? But…"

"Danielle was hoping to see this guy, Hunter. She and I were talking about that, and I told her I still had feelings for you, but wasn't sure what to do when you asked me to come here for Christmas. She offered to come with me and—"

"Wait." Beth's hand flew to her chest. "I asked *you?* I think there's been some misunderstanding." Beth noticed that the girls had skittered off as she spoke.

Kent frowned. "You mean you didn't?"

Beth frowned, too. "Are you saying you *weren't* the one who wanted to spend Christmas as a family?"

"Bailey! Sophie!" Beth and Kent shouted at the same time.

"Bailey Madison. Sophie Lynn," Beth threw in for good measure.

Their two daughters reappeared, looking sheepish.

"Okay, we admit it," Bailey said, hands in her back hip pockets. "The thing is, Sophie and I think this whole divorce is wrong. We thought if the two of you were together at Christmas, you'd realize what a terrible mistake you made. Then Dad had to go and ruin everything by bringing Danielle."

"I didn't exactly bring her," he clarified. "Danielle told me she intended to visit the area at the same time, and we discovered we'd be on the same flight and had booked rooms at the same bed-and-breakfast."

"Just a minute," Beth said in confusion. "But she works with you, right? That's all true?"

"Yes. She works in the accounting department."

"Are…are you… Have you ever been involved?"

"Good heavens, no."

"But…"

Kent broke eye contact. "While we were at the airport waiting for the plane, we started talking. Just like I already told you, I explained that I wasn't sure how I felt about being here this Christmas. I missed my wife, but the girls had hinted that you were seeing the local vet and I didn't want to be a fifth wheel. So Danielle said what you needed was some competition and I… agreed. I felt it was worth a shot, anyway. So she put on this ridiculous act and—" He shrugged, glancing up the staircase at Beth. "I regretted the entire charade immediately, but by then it seemed too late. The whole thing had taken on a momentum of its own.…" He shrugged. "I just hope you can forgive me."

The girls sent each other a triumphant smile, as if they were personally responsible for this turn of events.

Kent continued to hold Beth's look.

She bit her lip and started down the remaining steps.

"Problem is," he told his daughters, "I don't know how your mother feels about me. It's been three years."

"Mom's crazy about you," Bailey said.

"Of *course* Mom loves you," Sophie added her voice to her sister's. "She'd be a fool not to."

"What about Ted Reynolds?" Kent asked.

"What about him?" Bailey returned. "Mom loves you, not Ted."

"I'd rather have your mother tell me so herself." Kent stood with one foot braced against the bottom step. He stretched out his arm to Beth.

She placed her hand in his. "Oh, Kent, I've never stopped loving you. I never will."

He grabbed her by the waist and lifted her down the last two stairs, setting her feet on the ground.

As Beth slipped her arms around his neck, she buried her face in his shoulder. "We've both been so foolish."

He kissed her again and then again, as if he couldn't get enough of her.

Cradling his face with her hands, Beth gazed into his eyes, aware of their daughters grinning from the sidelines.

"These girls have a lot of 'splainin' to do," Kent said in a stage whisper.

"It was Bailey's idea," Sophie maintained.

"Both of you were being ridiculous about this stupid divorce," Bailey said quickly. "We felt we had to do something." She obviously intended to share the blame—or the praise.

"So you conspired to bring us together," Kent muttered.

"You aren't mad, are you?" Bailey asked, moving closer to her sister.

Kent brought his attention back to Beth and kissed the tip of her nose. "Are *you* upset?" he asked.

With her husband's arms around her and the Christmas tree lights shining in the background, Beth had to admit she wasn't. "Not in the least. Actually, I think it was a brilliant idea."

"Okay, if you must know," Sophie said, "I did help Bailey a little."

"Isn't this the best Christmas ever?" Bailey exclaimed, hugging her sister. "And we haven't even opened our gifts yet."

Beth had to agree. This was the best Christmas of her life.

Epilogue

Valentine's Day

"This is so romantic," Bailey said to her sister. "I'm so happy, I want to cry." They left the kitchen, ready to set out the plates and forks to serve cake to their parents' guests.

"We did it," Sophie said, almost giddy with happiness. "I don't know *how,* but it worked. Mom and Dad are back together."

"Just like they were meant to be."

Their parents were remarried and their dad was now living at 1225 Christmas Tree Lane, where he planned to take on the business aspects of the farm.

Beth came down the stairs and into the living room, with Kent directly behind her. "Oh, girls, the table looks lovely."

"Thanks, Mom."

The coffee- and teapots were filled and the cake sliced. This wasn't a wedding reception, Beth had explained to her daughters. It was an opportunity to introduce Kent to her friends and neighbors in Cedar Cove.

Bailey thought her father had never looked handsomer or her mother more beautiful. They were constantly together now. It had started while they were all in Whistler during Christmas break. Bailey couldn't remember a time they'd had more fun as a family. After their short vacation, Kent had returned to California. Before he could move north to Washington State, he needed to make some decisions and changes.

Within six weeks he'd sold his engineering company to his partner, packed up his house and found responsible tenants. In between all those negotiations and all that packing, Kent flew up to Cedar Cove practically every weekend to be with their mother. It was the most romantic thing.

They'd remarried in a private ceremony on January twenty-eighth. Only the girls and Kent's brother Michael, who'd come in from California to act as best man, had been in attendance. Afterward, their parents had sent out announcements to family and friends. From the comments Bailey heard, everyone seemed to think this remarriage was wonderful. To Bailey and Sophie it was just plain…right.

"We have our first guests," Sophie called out, standing by the living room window. "It's Grace, the lady who has Beau."

"Grace Harding," Beth said. "And her husband, Cliff." She headed for the door.

"There are four of them," Sophie added.

"The other two are Olivia and Jack Griffin."

Their mother ushered their guests in out of the rain.

Grace and Olivia stepped inside the house and were warmly greeted by Beth and Kent.

"I think we might have met earlier," Kent said, shaking hands with the two men. "Didn't I see you at the Christmas Eve service?"

Both men nodded.

"Would you like some coffee and cake?" Bailey asked politely.

"Sure! Thanks." The two men eagerly accepted her offer while the women raised their hands to decline. "We're driving to Seattle for a Valentine's treat," Grace said. "I'm saving my calories for that."

"Me, too," Olivia chimed in. "By the way," she told Beth, "my mother sent you a small gift. The ladies in her knitting group made you several cotton dishrags. Not very romantic, perhaps, but Mom says everyone can use extras."

Beth took the package gratefully. "Charlotte is always so thoughtful."

"Oh, Ben and Mom both send their very best wishes. She wanted me to tell you that bringing the dogs to Sanford Suites has been a real blessing to everyone. They all just love working with those dogs."

"It's a help to me, too."

Bailey smiled. Apparently, her mother was using the senior citizens to help her with dog training. Beth claimed this provided two benefits in one: not only did the older people get a form of therapy spending time with the dogs, they also got a sense of purpose from it. The Reading with Rover program at the library was another of her successes.

Beth slipped an arm around Kent's waist. "I have to

admit that getting those dogs to Sanford Suites can be a bit of an ordeal."

"You won't need to do it alone anymore," Kent told her and, leaning over, gave her a quick kiss.

Seeing her parents like this, so openly in love, Bailey almost forgot her job.

"Since Olivia isn't having cake, you can give me a bigger slice," Jack whispered. Bailey threw him a conspirator's smile and willingly complied.

"I heard that, Jack Griffin," the judge said from the other side of the room.

"How's Beau?" Sophie asked.

"I believe he's the smartest dog I've ever owned," Grace said, beaming with pride. She entertained them all for several minutes with stories of the puppy's antics.

The sound of another car pulling into the driveway attracted everyone's attention. "Oh, good," Sophie said, peering out the window. "It's the couple who owns the bed-and-breakfast where Dad stayed during Christmas," she announced. "Oh, and look! They brought their dog."

"They named her Millie," Beth said. "I've been doing dog obedience classes with her and four of her siblings over the past two months."

Bob and Peggy Beldon sat down for cake and coffee just as the Griffins and Hardings left. Millie lay contentedly at Peggy's feet.

Bailey hurried into the kitchen for a doggie treat, returning just in time to hear Bob Beldon say to her father, "Welcome back to Cedar Cove." Bob dug into the white cake with raspberry filling.

"You'll never guess who we heard from," Peggy said

conversationally and then, before anyone could guess, she answered her own question. "Danielle!"

Bailey was all ears. Sophie, too. Her sister set down the coffeepot and waited for the punch line.

"And?" Their dad frowned; clearly, Danielle wasn't a good memory.

"She sent a check to pay for the damage she did and wrote a letter of apology."

"I'm glad she apologized," Kent said. "She caused quite a scene."

"I'll say," Bob muttered between bites of cake. "I've been in theater for twenty years, and I've never seen more of a drama queen than that woman."

"But she had a broken heart," Sophie said, looking at Bailey. "Right?"

Her younger sister was far more charitable than Bailey was inclined to be. She had a point, though. They could afford to be generous. Their parents were together again, and, after all, Danielle's plan to make their mother jealous had started out as a misguided favor to their dad.

"In my opinion, the sailor who dumped her made a lucky escape."

"Bob," Peggy said pointedly. "Be kind."

"Okay, okay. At least she was responsible enough to pay for the damages and send us a note of apology."

"I still feel bad about all of that," Kent said. "I had no idea she'd react the way she did."

"It wasn't your fault," Bob told him. "We appreciated your offer to pay for the damages, but you weren't the one who created the mess. We mailed Danielle a letter after the first of the year, and three weeks later the check arrived." They chatted for another twenty minutes, and then the Beldons went home, with Millie heeling very nicely.

The Flemmings and their two sons stopped by next, passing the Beldons in the driveway. The dogs were at home, but Matthew and Mark spoke animatedly about their puppies whom they'd named Charlie and Sam. It was obvious that the boys had taken very successfully to dog ownership. Bailey remembered when she and Sophie had become dog owners for the first time. Watching the two brothers reminded her of the summer their parents had allowed them each to choose a puppy at the local animal shelter. Bailey got a beagle and Sophie had an Australian shepherd. They'd named them Barney and Fi Fi, and those dogs had been their companions for more than ten years.

Over the course of the next two hours, more people than Bailey could keep track of came and went. Bruce and Rachel Peyton arrived with their newborn daughter, Corinna. Jolene had gotten one of the puppies for Christmas, too, and bragged equally about Corinna and Poppy, her dog.

Troy and Faith Davis came by for cake and to chat with their parents. So did the McAfees, who were full of compliments about *their* puppy, Asta—as smart and charming as the dog in those movies, Roy bragged. Everyone was so friendly. Bailey was in charge of serving cake and Sophie busied herself with coffee and tea.

Soon after, Teri and Bobby Polgar, plus Christie and James Wilbur—proud owners of Chessie—dropped over with a bottle of champagne. Then Will Jefferson and Miranda Sullivan, sporting an engagement ring, brought *another* bottle.

By the end of the afternoon it seemed as if everyone

their mother knew in town had made the effort to welcome Kent to Cedar Cove.

Everyone, that is, except Ted Reynolds, the veterinarian.

Briefly, Bailey had wondered if her mother's friend would stop by. No one said anything, but Sophie noticed and so did Bailey. That saddened her a little because she knew that Ted and her mother were fond of each other.

"Well, that looks like everyone," Beth said, carrying the leftover cake into the kitchen.

"You girls did a great job."

"Wait!" Sophie cried out. "I see a car coming down the driveway."

"It's Ted," Bailey said excitedly.

"Ted?" Beth pushed open the kitchen door and stuck her head out. "Oh, I was hoping he'd have a chance to come." She brought out a piece of cake and set it on the table, as if it'd been there all along just waiting for Ted's arrival.

Kent opened the front door and extended his hand. "Good to see you, Ted."

"You, too. I'd like you to meet my friend Lana."

Ted had a female friend? Bailey met her sister's eyes.

"Ted," Beth said, holding out her hand to him. "I'm so glad you brought Lana. I've been wanting to meet her."

Mom knew about this? Bailey thought that was a good sign. Lana was a petite attractive blonde who seemed as effervescent as Ted was low-key.

Ted stood with his hand protectively around Lana's waist. "Everyone, this is Lana Carr."

Bailey and Sophie introduced themselves after their parents did.

"Sit down, please," Beth said and gestured Ted and Lana toward the chairs. While they took their seats, Bailey and Sophie handed them plates with cake and took drink orders.

"You know, your mother and I haven't had any cake yet," their father said. "I don't suppose we could get a slice, too?"

"Sure thing, Dad."

Bailey cut two additional slices and brought them in while Sophie prepared coffee for their guests.

Bailey went back to the kitchen to start cleaning up, and Sophie joined her there a couple of minutes later. When she opened the kitchen door, the sound of their parents' laughter drifted toward her.

"Everyone seems to be getting along," Bailey commented.

"They are. I think Mom and Dad and Ted and Lana are going to be good friends. Did you hear how they met?"

"Mom and Dad?"

"No, Ted and Lana, silly."

"Tell me."

"She brought in a dog who'd been hit by a car. She used to work for a vet in Tacoma, a friend of Ted's, until she moved to Cedar Cove. His friend had mentioned Lana was single and wanted to introduce them, but Ted said the timing was bad."

"Yeah, he had his eye on our mother," Bailey murmured.

"Lana saw his picture and thought he looked like a nice guy, but let it go. She figured he'd contact her if he was interested."

"But he didn't."

"No. And then Lana found the injured dog and brought him to the nearest vet, not even knowing it was Ted until she got there. She helped him operate on the dog and did such a good job that he offered her a job at the animal hospital."

"And she accepted."

"That's such a romantic story," Sophie said.

Bailey nodded. "This is a romantic town."

Her sister gave a contented sigh.

"You know, I like Cedar Cove," Bailey said. "I like it a lot."

"I do, too."

It was the kind of town anyone would love to call home.

★ ★ ★ ★ ★

LET IT SNOW

For Virelle Kidder and Suzanne Carter
My Florida soul sisters

One

"Ladies and gentlemen, this is your captain speaking."

Shelly Griffin's fingers compressed around the armrest until her neatly manicured nails threatened to cut into the fabric. Flying had never thrilled her, and she avoided it whenever possible. It had taken her the better part of a month to convince herself that this trip would be perfectly safe. She told herself that of course the Boeing 727 that had taken off without incident from San Francisco almost ninety minutes ago would land unscathed just a little while from now in Seattle. Still, if it wasn't Christmas, if she wasn't so homesick, and if she'd had more than four days off, she would have done anything except fly to get home for the holidays.

"Seattle is reporting heavy snow and limited visibility," the captain continued. "We've been rerouted to Portland International until the Seattle runways can be cleared."

A low groan filled the plane.

She forced herself to relax. Snow. She could handle snow, right? She wasn't overjoyed at the prospect of having to land twice, but she was so close to home now that she would willingly suffer anything to see a welcoming smile light up her father's eyes.

In an effort to divert her thoughts from impending tragedy, she studied the passengers around her. A grandmotherly type slept sedately in the seat beside her. The man sitting across the aisle was such a classic businessman that he was intriguing. Almost from the moment they'd left San Francisco, he'd been working out of his briefcase. He hadn't so much as cracked a smile during the entire flight. The captain's announcement had produced little more than a disgruntled flicker in his staid expression.

She had seen enough men like him in her job as a reporter in the federal court to catalog him quickly. Polished. Professional. Impeccable. Handsome, too, she supposed, if she was interested—which she wasn't. She preferred her men a little less intense. She managed to suppress a tight laugh. Men? What men? In the ten months she'd been living in the City by the Bay, she hadn't exactly developed a following. A few interesting prospects now and again, but nothing serious.

As the plane made its descent, Shelly gripped the armrest with renewed tension. Her gaze skimmed the emergency exits as she repeated affirmations on the safety of flying. She mumbled them under her breath as the plane angled sharply to the right, aligning its giant bulk with the narrow runway ahead.

Keeping her eyes centered on the seat in front of her, she held her breath until she felt the wheels gently bounce against the runway in a flawless landing. She braced herself as the brakes quickly slowed the aircraft to a crawl.

The oxygen rushed from her lungs in a heartfelt sigh

of relief. Somehow the landings were so much worse than the takeoffs. As the tension eased from her rigid body, she looked around to discover the businessman slanting his idle gaze over her. His dark eyes contained a look of surprise. He seemed amazed that anyone could be afraid of flying. The blood mounted briefly in her pale features, and she decided she definitely didn't like his cold attitude, no matter how handsome he was.

The elderly woman sitting next to her placed a hand on Shelly's forearm. "Are you all right, dear?"

"Of course." Relief throbbed in her voice. Now that they were on the ground, she could feign the composure that seemed to come so easily to the other passengers.

"I hope we aren't delayed long. My daughter's taking off work to meet me."

"My dad's forty minutes from the airport," Shelly offered, hoping that he'd called the airline to check if her flight was on time. She hated the thought of him anxiously waiting for her.

The other woman craned her neck to peek out the small side window. "It doesn't seem to be snowing much here. Just a few flakes. They look a bit like floating goose feathers, don't you think?"

Shelly grinned at the image. "Let's hope it stays that way."

She remained seated while several of the other passengers got up and took advantage of the captain's offer to leave the plane during the delay. The businessman was among those who quickly vacated their seats. But since the captain had said he didn't expect them to be in Portland long, Shelly didn't want to take a chance of missing the flight when it was ready to take off again.

After checking her watch every ten minutes for forty

minutes, she was starting to think that they would never leave Oregon. The blizzard had hit the area, and whirling snow buffeted the quiet plane with growing intensity. Her anxieties mounted with equal force. Suddenly her dire musings were interrupted.

"This is the captain speaking." His faint Southern drawl filled the plane. "Unfortunately, Seattle reports that visibility hasn't improved. They're asking that we remain here in Portland for another half hour, possibly longer."

Frustration and disappointment erupted from the remaining passengers, and they all began speaking at once.

"This is the captain again," the pilot added, his tone one of wry humor. "I'd like to remind those of you who are upset by our situation that it's far better to be on the ground wishing you were in the sky than to be in the sky *praying* you were on the ground."

Shelly added a silent amen to that. As it was, she was beginning to feel claustrophobic, trapped inside the plane. She grabbed her purse and reached for her cell, then discovered when she tried to turn it on that she must have forgotten to charge it, because the battery was dead. Unsnapping her seat belt, she stood and headed down the narrow aisle toward the front of the plane.

"Do I have time to make a phone call? My cell is dead," she explained.

"Sure," the flight attendant answered with a cordial smile. "Don't be long, though. The conditions in Seattle could change quickly."

"I won't," Shelly promised, and made her way into the terminal. Thank heavens airports still had payphones, she thought as she found two lonely phones sandwiched between a newsstand and a bagel shop.

She claimed the only unoccupied one, then frowned when she saw the "Out of Order" sign taped over the credit card slot. It wasn't until she was sorting through her purse for change that she noted that the unsympathetic businessman from her flight was sitting at the other phone. Apparently even someone as focused as he seemed to be could forget to charge his phone, too.

"This is Slade Garner again," he announced with the faintest trace of impatience creeping into his voice. "My plane's still in Portland."

Shelly scowled at her wallet. She didn't have change for the phone.

"Yes, yes, I understand the snow's a problem on your end as well," he continued smoothly. "I doubt that I'll make it in this afternoon. Perhaps we should arrange the meeting for first thing tomorrow morning. Nine o'clock?" Another pause. "Of course I realize it's the day before Christmas."

Rummaging in her purse, Shelly managed to dredge up a token for the cable car, a breath mint and a lost button.

Pressing her lips tightly together, she mused about how coldhearted Slade Garner was to insist on a meeting so close to Christmas. Instantly she felt guilty because her thoughts were so judgmental. Of course he would want to keep his appointment. He obviously hadn't taken this flight for fun. Her second regret was that she realized she had intentionally eavesdropped on his conversation, looking for excuses to justify her dislike of him. Such behavior was hardly in keeping with the Christmas spirit.

Pasting on a pleasant smile, she stepped forward when he replaced the receiver, thinking to claim the working phone, but someone practically knocked her over and got there first.

"Excuse me," she said politely as Slade turned in her direction. He refused to meet her gaze, and for a second she didn't think he'd heard her.

"Yes?" He finally looked her way, his expression bored, frustrated.

"Have you got change, by any chance?"

He uninterestedly checked the contents of his pocket, then looked down at the few coins in his palm. "Sorry." Dispassionately he tucked them back in his pocket and turned away.

She was ready to approach someone else when he turned back to her. His dark brows drew together in a frown, something about her apparently registering in his mind despite his preoccupied thoughts. "You were on the Seattle flight, weren't you?"

"Yes."

"Here." He handed her what change he had.

The corners of her mouth curved up in surprise. "Thanks." He was already walking briskly away, and she was convinced he hadn't even heard her. She didn't know what difference it made that they'd shared the same plane, but without analyzing his generosity any further, she dropped the first coin in the slot, then shifted her weight from one foot to the other while the phone rang, hoping her father—one of the last holdouts against owning a cell—wasn't already at the airport waiting for her. She was pleased when he answered.

"Dad, I'm so glad I caught you."

"Merry Christmas, Shortcake."

Her father had bestowed this affectionate title on her when she was thirteen and her friends had sprouted up around her. To her dismay she had remained at a deplorable five feet until she was seventeen. Then, within six months, she had grown five inches. Her height and other attributes of puberty had been hormonal afterthoughts.

"I'm in Portland."

"I know. When I phoned the airline they told me you'd been forced to land there. How are you doing?"

"Fine." She wasn't about to reveal her fear of flying or how much she was dreading getting back on that plane. "I'm sorry about the delay."

"It's not your fault."

"But I hate wasting precious time sitting here when I could be with you."

"Don't worry about it. We'll have plenty of time together."

"Have you decorated the tree yet?" Since her mother's death three years before, she and her father had made a ritual of placing the homemade ornaments on the tree together.

"I haven't even bought one. I thought we'd do that first thing in the morning."

She closed her eyes, savoring the warm feeling of love and security that the sound of her father's voice always gave her. "I've got a fantastic surprise for you."

"What's that?" he prompted.

"It wouldn't be a surprise if I told you, would it?"

Her father chuckled, and she could visualize him rubbing his finger over his upper lip the way he did when something amused him. They chatted for another minute, and then she realized she should check on the status of her flight.

"I've missed you, Dad."

"I've missed you, too."

"Take care."

"I will." She was about to hang up, but then… "Dad," she added hastily, her thoughts churning as she focused on a huge advertisement for a rental car agency. "Listen, don't go to the airport until I phone."

"But—"

"I'll be hungry by then, so I'll grab some lunch and be waiting outside for you. That way you won't have to park."

"I don't mind parking, Shortcake."

"I know, but I'd rather do it my way."

"If you insist."

"I do." Her brothers claimed that their father was partial to his only daughter. It was a long-standing family joke that she was the only one capable of swaying him once he'd made a decision. "I insist."

They said their goodbyes, and she disconnected, feeling light-hearted and relieved. Instead of heading back down the concourse toward the plane, she ventured in the opposite direction, taking the escalators to the lower level, where the rental car agencies were located.

To her surprise, she saw Slade Garner talking with a young man at the first agency. Shelly walked past him to the second counter.

"How much would it cost to rent a car here and drop it off in Seattle?" she asked brightly.

The woman on duty hardly looked up from her computer screen. "Sorry, we don't have any cars available."

"None?" Shelly found that hard to believe.

"Lots of people had the same idea you did," the agent explained. "A plane hasn't landed in Seattle in hours.

No one wants to sit around the airport waiting. Especially at Christmas."

"Thanks anyway." Shelly hurried down to the third agency and repeated her question.

"Yes, we do," the agent said with a wide grin. "We have exactly one car available." She named a sum that caused Shelly to swallow heavily. But already the idea had gained traction in her mind. Every minute the plane remained on the ground robbed her of precious time with her father. And from what he'd told her, the snow was coming down fast and furiously. It could be hours before the plane was able to take off, if it took off today at all. She freely admitted that another landing at another airport in the middle of the worst snowstorm of the year wasn't her idea of a good time. As it was, her Christmas bonus was burning a hole in her purse. And this was a good cause. Surely there was some unwritten rule that stated every favorite daughter should spend Christmas with her father.

"I'll take the car."

She looked up and saw Slade Garner standing a mere six inches away. A wide, confident smile spread across his handsome features, and his aura of self-assurance bordered on arrogance.

"I'm already taking it," she said firmly.

"I have to get to Seattle."

"So do I," she informed him primly. And then, in case he decided to remind her that she was indebted to him, she added, "But give me an address and I'll make sure to reimburse you while I'm there."

"I've got an important meeting."

"As a matter of fact, so do I." Turning back to the

counter, she picked up a pen and prepared to fill in the rental form.

"How much?" he asked.

"I beg your pardon?"

"How much do you want for the car?" He slipped his hand into the pocket of his coat, apparently prepared to pay her price.

Squaring her shoulders, she exchanged looks with the rental agent, then turned back to Slade and said, "Get your own car."

"There's only one car available. This one."

"And I've got it," she told him with a deceptively calm smile. The more she saw of this man, the more aggravating he became.

His jaw tightened. "I don't think you understand," he said, and breathed out with sharp impatience. "My meeting's extremely important."

"So is mine. I'm—"

"You could share the car," the agent suggested, causing both Shelly and Slade to turn their eyes his way, shocked by his impromptu peacemaking.

Shelly hesitated.

Slade's brows arched and he met her eyes. "I'll pay the full fee for the car," he offered.

"You mention money one more time and the deal's off," she shot back hotly.

"Don't be unreasonable."

"I'm not being unreasonable. You are."

He rubbed a hand along the back of his neck and forcefully expelled his breath. "Do we or do we not have a deal?"

"I'm not going to Seattle."

He gave her a sharp look of reproach. "I just heard you say Seattle."

"I'm headed for Maple Valley. That's in south King County."

"Fine. I'll drop you off and return the car to the rental office myself."

That would save her one hassle. Still, she hesitated. Two minutes together and they were already arguing. How would they possibly manage three hours cooped up in the close confines of a car?

"Listen," he argued, his voice tinged with exasperation. "If I make it to Seattle this afternoon, I might be able to get this meeting over with early. That way I can be back home in San Francisco for Christmas."

Without knowing it, he'd found the weakest links in her chain of defense. Christmas and home were important to her.

"All right," she mumbled. "But I'll pay my share of the cost."

"Whatever you want."

For the first time since she'd seen him, Slade Garner smiled.

Two

"What about your luggage?" Slade asked as they strolled down the concourse toward the plane.

"I only have one bag. It's above my seat." Her honey-brown hair curled around her neck, and she absently lifted a strand and looped it over her ear. A farm girl's wardrobe didn't fit in with the formal business attire she needed in San Francisco so she had left most of her clothes with her father. And it hadn't been hard to fit four days' worth of clothes into her carry-on. The brevity of her vacation was turning out to be a blessing in disguise.

Her spirits rose as they neared the plane. She was heading home for Christmas, and she wasn't flying!

"Good. I only have a garment bag with me."

She hesitated. "I do have a tote bag filled with presents."

His gaze collided briefly with hers. "That shouldn't be any problem."

When he saw the monstrosity, he might change his mind, she mused with an inner smile. In addition to a variety of odd-sized gifts, she was bringing her father several long loaves of sourdough bread. The huge package was awkward, and she had required a flight attendant's assistance to fit it in the compartment above her seat. Normally she would have put everything in a second suitcase and checked it, but loaves of bread were so long—sticking out of her bag like doughy antennas—that none of her suitcases had been big enough.

The plane was nearly empty when they boarded, confirming her suspicion that the delay was going to be far longer than originally anticipated. Checking her watch, she discovered that it was nearly noon. The other passengers had probably gone to get something to eat.

Standing on tiptoes, she opened the luggage compartment.

"Do you need help?" Slade asked. A dark gray garment bag was folded neatly over his forearm.

"Here." She handed him her one small bag. She heard him mumble something about appreciating a woman who packed light and smiled to herself.

Straining to stretch as far as she could to get a good grip on her bag of gifts, she heard Slade grumble.

"Look at what some idiot put up there."

"Pardon?"

"That bag. Good grief, people should know better than to try to force a tuba case up there."

"That's mine, and it isn't a tuba case." Extracting the bag containing the bread, so the bigger bag would be easier to extricate, she handed it down to him.

Slade looked at it as if something were about to leap out and bite him. "Good heavens, what is this?"

What was it? What was wrong with his eyes? Bread had to be the most recognizable item in the world.

"A suitcase for a snake," she replied sarcastically.

The beginnings of a grin touched his usually impassive features as he gently moved in front of her. "Let me get that thing down before you drop it on your head."

She stepped aside so he could put the bread and their carry-ons on her empty seat.

"Suitcase for a snake, huh?" Unexpectedly he smiled again.

The effect on her was dazzling. She had the feeling that this man didn't often take the time to enjoy life. Only minutes before she'd classified him as cheerless and intense. But when he smiled, the carefully guarded facade cracked and she felt she was being given a rare glimpse of the intriguing man inside. And he fascinated her.

By the time they'd arranged things with the airline, the courtesy van from the rental agency had arrived to deliver them to their vehicle.

"I put everything in my name," Slade said on a serious note as he unlocked their car.

The snow continued to fall, creating a picturesque view and making her happier than ever that she wasn't getting back on that plane. "That's fine." He'd taken the small carry-on from her, leaving her to cope with the huge bag filled with Christmas goodies.

"It means I'll be doing all the driving."

After another glance at the snowstorm, she was grateful.

"Well?" He looked as though he expected an argument.

"Do you have a driver's license?"

Again a grin cracked the tight line of his mouth, touching his eyes. "Yes."

"Then there shouldn't be any problem."

He paused, looking down at her, and smiled again. "Are you always so witty?"

Shelly chuckled, experiencing a rush of pleasure at her ability to make him smile. "Only when I try to be. Come on, loosen up. It's Christmas."

"I've got a meeting to attend. Just because it happens to fall close to a holiday doesn't make a bit of difference."

"Yeah, but just think, once you're through, you can hurry home and spend the holidays with your family."

"Right."

The jagged edge of his clipped reply was revealing. She wondered if he had a family.

As they deposited their luggage in the trunk of the rented Taurus, she had the opportunity to study him. The proud, withdrawn look revealed little of his thoughts; there was an air of independence about him. Even after their minimal conversation, she realized that he possessed a keen and agile mind. He was a man of contrasts—pensive yet decisive, his highly organized façade covering his sense of humor.

The young man at the rental desk had given Slade a map of the city and highlighted the route to the nearest freeway entrance ramp, apologizing for the fact that the car's built-in GPS was broken. Since that explained why the car was available at all, neither she nor Slade had objected.

Now Slade pulled the map from his pocket and handed it to her. "Are you ready?"

"Forward, James," she teased, climbing into the passenger seat and rubbing her bare hands together to generate some warmth. When she'd left San Francisco that morning, she hadn't dressed for snow.

With a turn of the key, Slade started the engine and adjusted the heater. "You'll be warm in a minute."

Shelly nodded, burying her hands in her jacket pockets. "You know, if it gets much colder, we might get snow before we reach Seattle."

"Very funny," he muttered dryly, snapping his seat belt into place. Hands gripping the wheel, he hesitated. "Do you want to call your husband before we hit the road and I need you to navigate?"

"I'm visiting my dad," she corrected him. "I'm not married. And no. If I told him what we're doing, he'd only worry."

Slade shifted gears, and they pulled onto the road.

"Do you want to contact...your wife?"

"I'm not married, either."

"Oh." She prayed that her tone wouldn't reveal her satisfaction at the information. It wasn't often that she found herself so fascinated by a man. The crazy part was that she wasn't entirely sure she liked him, but he certainly attracted her.

"I'm engaged," he added.

"Oh." She swallowed convulsively. So much for that. "When's the wedding?"

The windshield wipers hummed ominously. "In approximately two years."

Shelly nearly choked in an effort to hide her shock.

"Margaret and I have professional and financial goals we hope to accomplish before we marry." He drove with his back suddenly stiff, his expression turning chilly. "Margaret feels we should save fifty thousand dollars before we think about marriage, and I agree. We both feel that having a firm financial foundation is the basis for a lasting marriage."

"I can't imagine waiting two years to marry the man I loved."

"But then you're entirely different from Margaret."

As far as Shelly was concerned, that was the nicest thing anyone had said to her all day. "We do agree on one thing, though. I feel a marriage should last forever." But for her, love had to be more spontaneous and far less calculated. "My parents had a marvelous marriage," she said, filling the silence. "I only hope that when I marry, my own will be as happy." She went on to explain that her parents had met one Christmas and been married less than two months later on Valentine's Day. Their marriage, she told him with a sad smile, had been blessed with love and happiness for nearly twenty-seven years before her mother's unexpected death. It took great restraint for her not to mention that her parents had barely had twenty dollars between them when they'd taken their vows. At the time her father had been studying veterinary medicine, with only two years of vet school behind him. They'd managed without a huge bank balance.

From the tight lines around his mouth, she could tell that Slade found the whole story trite.

"Is your sweet tale of romance supposed to touch my heart?"

Stung, she straightened and looked out the side window at the snow-covered trees that lined the side of Interstate 5. "No. I was just trying to find out if you had one."

"Karate mouth strikes again," he mumbled.

"Karate mouth?" She was too stunned by his unexpected display of wit to do anything more than repeat his statement.

"You have the quickest comeback of anyone I know." But he said it with a small smile, and admiration flashed unchecked in his gaze before he turned his attention back to the freeway.

Shelly was interested in learning more about Margaret, so she steered the conversation away from herself. "I imagine you're anxious to get back to spend Christmas with Margaret." She regretted her earlier judgmental attitude toward Slade. He had good reason for wanting his meeting over with.

"Margaret's visiting an aunt in Arizona over the holidays. She left a couple of days ago."

"So you won't be together." The more she heard about his fiancée, the more curious she was about a woman who actively wanted to wait two years for marriage. "Did she give you your Christmas gift before she left?" The type of gift one gave was always telling, she felt.

He hesitated. "Margaret and I agreed to forgo giving gifts this year."

"No presents? That's terrible."

"I told you. We have financial goals," he growled irritably. "Wasting money on trivialities simply deters us from our two-year plan. Christmas gifts aren't going to advance our desires."

At the moment Shelly sincerely doubted that good ol' Margaret and Slade *had* "desires."

"I bet she's just saying she doesn't want a gift," Shelly said. "She's probably secretly hoping you'll break down and buy her something. It doesn't have to be something big. Any woman appreciates roses."

Slade gave an expressive shrug. "I thought flowers would be a nice touch myself, but she claims they make her sneeze. Besides, roses at Christmas are ridiculously expensive. A total waste of money, when you think about it."

"Total," Shelly echoed under her breath. She was beginning to get a clearer and far less flattering picture of Slade Garner and his insanely-practical fiancée.

"Did you say something?" A hint of challenge echoed in his cool tone.

"Not really." Leaning forward, she fiddled with the radio, trying to find some decent music. "What's Margaret do, by the way?"

"She's a systems analyst."

Shelly arched both eyebrows in mute comment. That was exactly the type of occupation she would have expected from a nuts-and-bolts person like Margaret. "What about children?"

"What about them?"

She realized that she was prying, but she couldn't help herself. "Are you planning a family?"

"Of course. We're hoping that Margaret can schedule a leave of absence in eight years."

"Eight years?" She looked at him assessingly. "You'll be nearly thirty!" The exclamation burst from her lips before she could hold it back.

"Thirty-one, actually. Do you disapprove of that, too?"

She swallowed uncomfortably and paid an inordinate amount of attention to the radio, frustrated because she couldn't find a single radio station. "I apologize. I didn't mean to sound so judgmental. It's just that—"

"It's just that you've never been goal oriented."

"But I have," she argued. "I've always wanted to be a court reporter. It's a fascinating job."

"I imagine that you're good at anything you put your mind to."

The unexpected compliment caught her completely off guard. "What a nice thing to say."

"If you put your mind to it, you might figure out why you can't get the radio working."

Her gaze flickered automatically from Slade to the dial. Before she could comment, he reached over and pushed a button. "It's a bit difficult to hear anything when the radio isn't turned on."

"Right." She'd been too preoccupied with asking about Margaret to notice. Color flooded into her cheeks at her own stupidity. Slade flustered her as no man had in a long time. She had the feeling that, in a battle of words, he would parry her barbs as expertly as a professional swordsman.

She found a station playing Christmas carols, and music filled the car. Warm and snug, she leaned back against the headrest and hummed along, gazing at the falling flakes.

"With the snow and all, it really feels like Christmas," she murmured, fearing more questions would destroy the tranquil mood.

"It's caused nothing but problems."

"I suppose, but it's so lovely."

"Of course *you* think it's lovely. You're sitting in a warm chauffeur-driven car, listening to 'Silent Night.'"

"Grumble, grumble, grumble," she tossed back lightly. "Bah, humbug!"

"Bah, humbug," he echoed, and then, to her astonishment, he laughed.

The sound of it was rich and full, and she couldn't stop herself from laughing with him. When the next song was a Bing Crosby Christmas favorite, she sang along. Soon Slade's deep baritone joined her clear soprano in sweet harmony. The lyrics spoke of dreaming, and her mind conjured up her own longings. Despite his rough edges, she found herself comfortable with this man, when she'd expected to find a dozen reasons to dislike him. Instead, she'd discovered that she was attracted to someone who was engaged to another woman. A man whose responses showed he was intensely loyal. That was the usual way her life ran. She was attracted to a man she couldn't have, experiencing feelings that would lead nowhere. She wasn't even entirely sure that her insights about him were on base. As uncharitable as it sounded, she might be overestimating his appeal simply because she considered him too good for someone like Margaret.

Disgusted with herself, she closed her eyes and rested her head against the window. The only sounds were the soft melodies playing on the radio and the discordant swish of the windshield wipers. Occasionally a gust of wind would cause the car to veer slightly. She decided to ignore her troublesome feelings and lost herself in thoughts of Christmas.

The next thing she knew, she was being shaken by a gentle hand on her shoulder. "Shelly."

With a start she bolted upright. "What's wrong?"

Slade had pulled over to the shoulder of the freeway. The snow was so thick that she couldn't see two feet in front of her.

"I don't think we can go any further," he announced.

Three

"We can't stay *here*," Shelly insisted, looking at their precarious position beside the road. Snow was whirling in every direction. The ferocity of the storm shocked her as it whipped and howled around them. While she'd slept, the storm had worsened drastically. She found it little short of amazing that Slade had been able to steer the car at all.

"Do you have any other suggestions?" he asked, and breathed out sharply.

He was angry, but his irritation wasn't directed at her. Wearily she lifted the hair from her neck. "No, I guess I don't."

Silence seeped around them as Slade turned off the engine. Gone was the soothing sound of Christmas music, the hum of the engine and the rhythmic swish of the wipers. Together they sat waiting for nature's fury to lessen so they could get going again. Staring out at the surrounding area between bursts of wind and snow, she guessed that they weren't far from Castle Rock and Mount St. Helens.

After ten minutes of uneasiness, she decided to be

the first to break the gloom. "Are you hungry?" She stared at the passive, unyielding face beside her as she spoke.

"No."

"I am."

"Have some of that bread." He cocked his head toward the back seat, where she'd stuck the huge loaves of sourdough.

"I couldn't eat Dad's bread. He'd never forgive me."

"He'd never forgive you if you starved to death, either."

Glancing down at her pudgy thighs, Shelly sadly shook her head. "There's no chance of that."

"What makes you say that? You're not fat. In fact, I'd say you were just about perfect."

"Me? Perfect?" A burst of embarrassed laughter slid from her throat. Reaching for her purse, she removed her wallet.

"What are you doing?"

"I'm going to pay you for saying that."

Slade chuckled. "What makes you think you're overweight?"

"You mean aside from the fat all over my body?"

"I'm serious."

She shrugged. "I don't know. I just feel chubby. Since leaving home, I don't get enough exercise. I couldn't very well bring Sampson with me when I moved to San Francisco."

"Sampson?"

"My horse. I used to ride him every day."

"If you've gained any weight, it's in all the right places."

His gaze fell to her lips, and her senses churned in

quivering awareness. He stared into her dark eyes and blinked, as if not believing what he saw. For her part, she studied him with open curiosity. His eyes were smoky dark, his face blunt and sensual. His brow was creased, as though he was giving the moment grave consideration. Thick eyebrows arched heavily over his eyes.

Abruptly he pulled his gaze away and leaned forward to start the engine. The accumulated snow on the windshield was brushed aside with a flip of the wiper switch. "Isn't that a McDonald's up ahead?"

Shelly squinted to catch a glimpse of the world-famous golden arches through a momentary break in the storm. "Hey, I think it is."

"The exit can't be far, then."

"Do you think we can make it?"

"I think we'd better," he mumbled.

She understood. The car had become their private cocoon, unexpectedly intimate and far too tempting. Under normal circumstances they wouldn't have given each other more than a passing glance. What was happening now was magical, and far more exhilarating than the real life that seemed very far away right now.

With the wipers beating furiously against the window, Slade inched the car toward the exit, which proved to be less than a half mile away.

Slowly they crawled down the side road that paralleled the freeway. With some difficulty he was able to find a place to park in the restaurant lot. Shelly sighed with relief. This was the worst storm she could remember. Wrapping her coat securely around her, she reached for her purse.

"You ready?" she blurted out, opening her door.

"Anytime."

Hurriedly he joined her, tightly grasping her elbow as they stepped together toward the entrance. Pausing just inside the door to stamp the snow from their shoes, they glanced up to note that several other travelers were stranded there, as well.

They ordered hamburgers and coffee, and sat down by the window.

"How long do you think we'll be here?" she asked, not really expecting an answer. She needed reassurance more than anything. This Christmas holiday hadn't started out on the right foot. But of one thing she was confident: their plane hadn't left Portland yet.

"Your guess is as good as mine."

"I'll say two hours, then," she murmured, taking a bite of her burger.

"Why two hours?"

"I don't know. It sounds reasonable. If I thought it would be longer than that I might start to panic. But, if worse comes to worst, I can think of less desirable places to spend Christmas. At least we won't starve."

He muttered something unintelligible under his breath and continued eating. When he finished, he excused himself and returned to the car for his briefcase.

She bought two more cups of coffee and propped her feet on the seat opposite her. Taking the latest issue of *Mad* from her purse, she was absorbed in the magazine by the time he returned. Her gaze dared him to comment on her reading material. Her love of *Mad* was a long-standing joke between her and her father. He even read each issue himself so he could tease her about the contents. Since moving, she'd fallen behind by several issues and wanted to be prepared when she saw her dad again. She didn't expect Slade to understand her tastes.

He gave her little more than a glance before reclaiming his seat and briskly opening the *Wall Street Journal*.

Their reading choices said a lot about them, she realized. Rarely had two people been less alike. A lump grew in her throat. She liked Slade. He was the type of man she would willingly give up *Mad* for.

An hour later she contentedly set the magazine aside and reached in her purse for the romance novel she kept tucked away. It wasn't often that she was so at ease with a man. She didn't feel the overwhelming urge to keep a conversation going or fill the silence with chatter. They were comfortable together.

Without a word she went to the counter and bought a large order of fries and placed it in the middle of the table. Now and then, her eyes never leaving the printed page, she blindly reached for a fry. Once her groping hand bumped another, and her startled gaze collided with Slade's.

"Sorry," he muttered.

"Don't be. They're for us both."

"They get to be addictive, don't they?"

"Sort of like reading the *Wall Street Journal?*"

"I wondered if you'd comment on that."

She laughed. "I was expecting you to mention *my* choice."

"*Mad* is exactly what I'd expect from you." He said it in such a way that she couldn't possibly be offended.

"At least we agree on one thing."

He raised his thick brows in question.

"The fries."

"Right." Lifting one, he held it out for her.

She leaned toward him and captured the fry in her mouth. The gesture was oddly intimate, and her smile faded as her gaze met his. It was happening again. That heart-pounding, room-fading-away, shallow-breathing syndrome. Obviously this…feeling…had something to do with the weather. Maybe she could blame it on the season of love and goodwill toward all mankind. Apparently she was overly endowed with benevolence this Christmas. Given the sensations she was already experiencing, heaven only knew what would happen if she spied some mistletoe.

Slade raked his hand through his well-groomed hair, mussing it. Quickly he diverted his gaze out the window. "It looks like it might be letting up a little."

"Yes, it does," she agreed without so much as checking the weather. The French fries seemed to demand her full attention.

"I suppose we should think about heading out."

"I suppose." A glance at her watch confirmed that it was well into the afternoon. "I'm sorry about your appointment."

He looked at her blankly for a moment. "Oh, that. I knew when we left that there was little likelihood I'd be able to make it in time today. Luckily I've already made arrangements to meet tomorrow morning."

"It's been an enjoyable break."

"Very," he agreed.

"Do you think we'll have any more problems?"

"We could, but there are enough businesses along the way that we don't need to worry about getting stranded."

"In other words, we could hit every fast-food spot between here and Seattle."

He responded with a soft chuckle. "Right."

"Well, in that case, bring on the French fries."

By the time they were back on the freeway, Shelly saw that the storm had indeed lessened, though it was far from over. And when the radio issued a weather update that called for more snow, Slade groaned.

"You could always spend Christmas with me and Dad," she offered, broaching the subject carefully. "We'd like to have you. Honest."

He tossed her a disbelieving glare. "You don't mean that."

"Of course I do."

"But I'm a stranger."

"I've shared French fries with you. It's been a long time since I've been that intimate with a man. In fact, it would be best if you didn't mention it to my dad. He might be inclined to reach for his shotgun."

It took a minute for Slade to understand the implication. "A shotgun wedding?"

"I *am* getting on in years. Dad would like to see me married off and producing grandchildren. My brothers have been lax in that department." For the moment she'd forgotten about Margaret. When she remembered, she felt her exhilaration rush out of her with all the force of a deflating balloon. "Don't worry," she was quick to add. "All you need to do is tell Dad about your fiancée and he'll let you off the hook." Somehow she managed to keep her voice cheerful.

"It's a good thing I didn't take a bite of your hamburger."

"Are you kidding? That would have put me directly into your last will and testament."

"I was afraid of that," he said, laughing good-naturedly.

Once again she noticed how rich and deep the sound

of his laughter was. It had the most overwhelming effect on her. She discovered that, when he laughed, nothing could keep her spirits down.

Their progress was hampered by the still-swirling snow, and finally their forward movement became little more than a crawl. She didn't mind. They chatted, joked and sang along with the radio. She discovered that she enjoyed his wit. Although a bit dry, under that gruff, serious exterior lay an interesting man with a warm but subtle sense of humor. Given any other set of circumstances, she would have loved to get to know Slade Garner better.

"What'd you buy your dad for Christmas?"

The question came so unexpectedly that it took her a moment to realize that he was speaking to her.

"Are you concerned that I have soup in my bag?"

He scowled, momentarily puzzled. "Ah, to go with the bread. No, I was just curious."

"First I got him a box of his favorite chocolate-covered cherries."

"I should have known it'd be food."

"That's not all," she countered a bit testily. "We exchange the normal father-daughter gifts. You know. Things like stirrup irons, bridles and horse blankets. That's what Dad got me last Christmas."

He cleared his throat. "Just the usual items every father buys his daughter. What about this year?"

"Since Sampson and I aren't even living in the same state, I imagine he'll resort to the old standbys, like towels and sheets for my apartment." She was half hoping that, at the mention of her place in San Francisco, Slade would turn the conversation in that direction and ask her something about herself. He didn't, and she was hard-pressed to hide her disappointment.

"What about you?" she asked into the silence.

"Me?" His gaze flickered momentarily from the road.

"What did you buy your family?"

He gave her an uncomfortable look. "Well, actually, I didn't. It seemed simpler this year just to send them money."

"I see." She knew that was perfectly acceptable in some cases, but it sounded so cold and uncaring for a son to resort to a gift of money. Undoubtedly, once he and Margaret were married, they would shop together for something appropriate.

"I wish now that I hadn't. I think my parents would have enjoyed fresh sourdough bread and chocolate-covered cherries." He hesitated for an instant. "I'm not as confident about the stirrups and horse blankets, however."

As they neared Tacoma, Shelly was surprised at how heavy the traffic had gotten. The closer they came to Maple Valley, the more anxious she became.

"My exit isn't far," she told him, growing impatient. "Good grief, you would expect people to stay off the roads in weather like this."

"Exactly," he agreed without hesitation.

It wasn't until she heard the soft timbre of his chuckle that she realized he was teasing her. "You know what I mean."

He didn't answer as he edged the car ahead. Already the night was pitch-dark. Snow continued to fall with astonishing vigor. She wondered when it would stop. She was concerned about Slade driving alone from Maple Valley to Seattle.

"Maybe I should phone my dad," she suggested, momentarily forgetting that her cell was dead.

"Why?"

"That way he could come and pick me up, and you wouldn't—"

"I agreed to deliver you to Maple Creek, and I intend to do exactly that."

"Maple Valley," she corrected.

"Wherever. A deal is a deal. Right?"

A rush of pleasure assaulted her vulnerable heart. Slade wasn't any more eager to put an end to their adventure than she was.

"It's the next exit," she informed him, giving him the directions to the ten-acre spread on the outskirts of town. Taking out a pen and paper, she drew a detailed map for him so he wouldn't get lost on the return trip to the freeway. Under the cover of night, there was little to distinguish one road from another, and he could easily become confused.

Sitting straighter, she excitedly pointed to her left. "Turn here."

Apparently in preparation for his departure for the airport, her father had plowed the snow from the long driveway.

The headlights cut into the night, revealing the long, sprawling ranch house that had been Shelly's childhood home. A tall figure appeared at the window, and almost immediately the front door opened.

Slade had barely put the car into Park when Shelly threw open the door.

"Shortcake!"

"Dad." Disregarding the snow and wind, she flew into his arms.

"You little... Why didn't you tell me you were coming by car?"

"We rented it." Remembering Slade, she looped an arm around her father's waist. "Dad, I'd like you to meet Slade Garner."

Her father stepped forward. "Don Griffin," he said, and extended his hand. "So you're Shelly's surprise. Welcome to our home. I'd say it was about time my daughter brought a young man home for her father to meet."

Four

Slade extended his hand to Shelly's father and grinned. "I believe you've got me confused with sourdough bread."

"Sourdough bread?"

"Dad, Slade and I met this morning on the plane." Shelly's cheeks brightened in a self-conscious pink flush.

"When it looked like the flight wasn't going to make it to Seattle, we rented the car," Slade explained further.

A curious glint darkened Don Griffin's deep blue eyes as he glanced briefly from his daughter to Slade and ran a hand through is thick thatch of dark hair. "It's a good thing you did. The last time I phoned the airline, I learned your plane still hadn't left Portland."

"Slade has an important meeting first thing tomorrow." Her eyes were telling him that she was ready to make the break. She could say goodbye and wish him every happiness. Their time together had been too short for any regrets. Hadn't it?

"There's no need for us to stand out here in the cold

discussing your itinerary," her father inserted and motioned toward the warm lights of the house.

Slade hesitated. "I should be getting into Seattle."

"Come in for some coffee first," her father invited.

"Shelly?" Slade sought her approval. The unasked question in his eyes pinned her gaze.

"I wish you would." *Fool!* her mind cried out. It would be better to sever the relationship quickly, sharply and without delay, before he had the opportunity to touch her tender heart. But her heart refused to listen to her mind.

"For that matter," her father continued, seemingly oblivious to the undercurrents between Slade and Shelly, "stay for dinner."

"I couldn't. Really." Slade made a show of glancing at his wristwatch.

"We insist," Shelly said quickly. "After hauling this bread from here to kingdom come, the least I can offer you is a share of it."

To her astonishment Slade grinned, his dark eyes crinkling at the edges. The smile was both spontaneous and personal—a reminder of the joke between them. "All right," he agreed.

"That settles it, then." Don grinned and moved to the rear of the car while Slade extracted Shelly's suitcase and the huge tote bag. "What's all this?"

"Presents," she said.

"For me?"

"Well, who else would I be bringing gifts for?"

"A man. It's time you started thinking about a husband."

"Dad!" If her cheeks had been bright pink previously, now the color deepened into fire-engine red. In order to minimize further embarrassment, she returned to the car and rescued the bread. Her father carried the gifts inside, while Slade brought up the rear with her carry-on.

The house contained all the warmth and welcome that she always associated with home. She paused in just inside the open doorway, her gaze skimming over the crackling fireplace and the large array of family photos that decorated the mantel. Ol' Dan, their thirteen-year-old Labrador, slept on the braided rug and did little more than raise his head when Don and Slade entered the house. But on seeing Shelly, the elderly dog got slowly to his feet and with difficulty ambled to her side, tail wagging. She set the bread aside and fell to her knees.

"How's my loyal mangy mutt?" she asked, affectionately ruffling his ears and hugging him. "You keeping Dad company these days?"

"Yeah, but he's doing a poor job of it," her father complained loudly. "Ol' Dan still can't play a decent game of chess."

"Do *you* play?" Slade asked her father as his gaze scanned the living room for a board.

"Forty years or more. What about you?"

"Now and again."

"Could I interest you in a match?"

Slade was already unbuttoning his overcoat. "I'd enjoy that, sir."

"Call me Don, everyone does."

"Right, Don."

Within a minute the chessboard was out and set up on the coffee table, while the two men sat opposite each other on matching ottomans.

Suspecting that the contest could last a while, she

checked the prime rib roasting in the oven and added large potatoes, wrapping each in aluminum foil. The refrigerator contained a fresh green salad and her favorite cherry pie from the local bakery. There were also some carrots in the vegetable drawer; she snatched a couple and put them in her pocket.

After grabbing her denim jacket with its thick wool padding from the peg on the back porch and slipping into her cowboy boots, she made her way out to the barn.

The scent of hay and horses greeted her, and she paused, taking in the rich, earthy odors. "Howdy, Sampson," she said, greeting her favorite horse first.

The sleek black horse whinnied a welcome as she approached the stall, then accepted the proffered carrot without pause.

"Have you missed me, boy?"

Pokey, an Appaloosa mare, stuck her head out of her stall, seeking a treat, too. Laughing, Shelly pulled another carrot from her pocket. Midnight, her father's horse and Sampson's sire, stamped his foot, and she made her way down to his stall.

After stroking his sleek neck, she took out the brushes and returned to Sampson. "I suppose Dad's letting you get fat and lazy now that I'm not around to work you." She glided a brush down his muscled flank. "All right, I'll admit it. Living in San Francisco has made *me* fat and lazy, too. I haven't gained any weight, but I feel flabby. I suppose I could take up jogging, but it's foggy and rainy and—"

"Shelly?"

Slade was standing just inside the barn door, looking a bit uneasy. "Do you always carry on conversations with your horse?"

"Sure. I've talked out many a frustration with Sampson. Isn't that right, boy?"

Slade gave a startled blink when the horse answered with a loud snort and a toss of his head, as if agreeing with her.

"Come in and meet my favorite male," she invited, opening the stall door.

Hands buried deep in his pockets, Slade shook his head. "No, thanks."

"You don't like horses?"

"Not exactly."

Having lived all her life around animals, she had trouble understanding his reticence. "Why not?"

"The last time I was this close to a horse was when I was ten and at summer camp."

"Sampson won't bite you."

"It's not his mouth I'm worried about."

"He's harmless."

"So is flying."

Surprised, Shelly dropped her hand from Sampson's hindquarters.

Slade strolled over to the stall, a grin lifting the edges of his mouth. "From the look on your face when we landed, one would assume that your will alone was holding up the plane."

"It was!"

He chuckled and tentatively reached out to rub Sampson's ebony forehead.

She went back to grooming the horse. "Is your chess match over already?"

"I should have warned your father. I was on the university chess team."

Now it was her turn to look amused. She paused in midstroke. "Did you wound Dad's ego?"

"I might have, but he's regrouping now. I came out here because I wanted to have a look at the famous Sampson before I headed for Seattle."

"Sampson's honored to make your acquaintance." *I am, too,* her heart echoed.

Slade took a step in retreat. "I guess I'll get back to the house. No doubt your dad's got the board set for a rematch."

"Be gentle with him," she called out, trying to hide a saucy grin. Her father wasn't an amateur when it came to the game. He'd been a member of the local chess club for years, and she wondered just what his strategy was tonight. Donald Griffin seldom lost at any game.

An hour later she stamped the snow from her boots and entered the kitchen through the back door. She shed the thick coat and hung it back on its peg, then went to check the roast and the baked potatoes. Both were done to perfection, and she turned off the oven.

Seeing that her father and Slade were absorbed in their game, she stepped up behind her father and slipped her arms around his neck, resting her chin on the top of his head.

"Dinner's ready," she murmured, not wanting to break his concentration.

"In a minute," he grumbled.

Slade moved his bishop, leaving his hand on the piece for a couple of seconds. Seemingly pleased, he released the piece and relaxed. As though sensing her gaze on him, he lifted his incredibly dark eyes, which locked with hers. They stared at each other for long, uninterrupted moments. She felt her heart lurch as she basked in the warmth of his look. She wanted to hold on to this moment, forget San Francisco, Margaret, the snowstorm. It felt paramount that she capture this magic with both hands and hold on to it forever.

"It's your move." Don's words cut into the stillness.

"Pardon?" Abruptly Slade dropped his eyes to the chessboard.

"It's your move," her father repeated.

"Of course." Slade studied the board and moved a pawn.

Don scowled. "I hadn't counted on your doing that."

"Hey, you two, didn't you hear me? Dinner's ready." She was shocked at how normal and unaffected her voice sounded.

Slade got to his feet. "Shall we consider it a draw, then?"

"I guess we better, but I demand a rematch someday."

Shelly's throat constricted. There wouldn't be another day for her and Slade. They were two strangers who had briefly touched each other's lives. Ships passing in the night and all the other clichés she had never expected would happen to her. But somehow she had the feeling that she would never be the same again. Surely she wouldn't be so swift to judge another man. Slade had taught her that, and she would always be grateful.

The three of them chatted easily during dinner, and Shelly learned things about Slade that she hadn't thought to ask. He was a salesman, specializing in intricate software programs, and was meeting with a Seattle-based company, hoping to agree on the first steps of a possible distribution agreement. It was little wonder that he'd considered his meeting so important. It was. And although he hadn't mentioned it specifically, she was acutely aware that if his meeting was successful, he would be that much closer to achieving his financial and professional goals—and that much closer to marrying coldly practical Margaret.

Shelly was clearing the dishes from the table when Slade set his napkin aside and rose. "I don't remember when I've enjoyed a meal more, especially the sourdough bread."

"A man gets the feel of a kitchen sooner or later," Don said with a crusty chuckle. "It took me a whole year to learn how to turn on the oven."

"That's the truth," she added, sharing a smile with her father. "He thought it was easier to use the microwave. The problem was, he couldn't quite get the hang of that, either. Everything came out the texture of beef jerky."

"We survived," her father grumbled, affectionately looping an arm around Shelly's waist. The first eighteen months after her mother's death had been the most difficult for the family, but life went on, and almost against their wills they'd adjusted.

Slade paused in the living room to stare out the window. "I can't remember it ever snowing this much in the Pacific Northwest."

"Rarely," Don agreed. "It's been three winters since we've had any snow at all. I'll admit this is a pleasant surprise."

"How long will it be before the snowplows are out?"

"Snow*plow*, you mean?" Don said with a gruff laugh. "King County is lucky if they have more than a handful. There isn't that much call for them." He walked to the picture window and held back the draperies with one hand. "You know, it might not be a bad idea if you stayed the night and left first thing in the morning."

Slade hesitated. "I don't know. If I miss this meeting, it'll mean having to wait over the Christmas holiday to reschedule."

"You'll have a better chance of making it safely to Seattle in the morning. The roads tonight are going to be treacherous."

Slade slowly expelled his breath. "I have the distinct feeling you may be right. Without any streetlights, Lord knows where I'd end up."

"I believe you'd be wise to delay your drive. Besides, that will give us time for another game."

Slade's gaze shifted to Shelly and softened. "Right," he concurred.

The two men were up until well past midnight, engrossed in one chess match after another. After watching a few games, Shelly decided to say good-night and go to bed.

Half an hour later Shelly lay in her bed in her darkened room, dreading the approach of morning. In some ways it would have been easier if Slade had left immediately after dropping her off. And in other ways it was far better that he'd stayed.

She fell asleep with the bright red numbers of the clock insidiously counting down the minutes to six o'clock when Slade would be leaving. There was nothing she could do to hold back time.

Before even being aware that she'd fallen asleep, she

was startled into wakefulness by the discordant drone of the alarm.

Tossing aside the covers, she automatically reached for the thick housecoat she kept at her father's. Pausing only long enough to run a comb through her hair and brush her teeth, she rushed into the living room.

Slade was already dressed and holding a cup of coffee. "I guess it's time to say goodbye."

Five

Shelly ran a hand over her weary eyes and blinked. "You're right," she murmured, forcing a smile. "The time has come."

"Shelly—"

"Listen—"

"You first," Slade said, and gestured toward her with his open hand.

Dropping her gaze, she shrugged one shoulder. "It's nothing, really. I just wanted to wish you and Margaret every happiness."

His gaze softened, and she wondered if he knew what it had cost her to murmur those few words. She did wish him happiness, but she was convinced that he wouldn't find it with a cold fish like Margaret. Forcefully she directed her gaze across the room. For all her good intentions, she was doing it again—judging someone else. And she hadn't even met Margaret.

When she turned back his eyes delved into hers. "Thank you."

"You wanted to say something?" she prompted softly.

He hesitated. "Be happy, Shelly."

A knot formed in her throat as she nodded. He was telling her goodbye, *really* goodbye. He wouldn't see her again, because it would be too dangerous for them both. Their lives were already plotted, their courses set. And whatever it was that they'd shared so briefly, it wasn't meant to be anything more than a passing fancy.

The front door opened and her father entered, brushing the snow from his pant legs. A burst of frigid air accompanied him, and she shivered.

"As far as I can see you shouldn't have a problem," Don said to Slade. "We've got maybe seven to ten inches of snow, but there're plenty of tire tracks on the road. Just follow those."

Unable to listen anymore, she headed into the kitchen and poured herself a cup of hot black coffee. Clasping the mug with both hands, she braced her hip against the counter and closed her eyes. Whatever Slade and her father were saying to each other didn't matter to her. She was safer in the kitchen, where she wouldn't be forced to watch him leave. The only sound that registered in her mind was the clicking of the front door opening and closing.

Slade had left. He was gone from the house. Gone from her life. Gone forever. She refused to mope. He'd touched her heart, and she should be glad. For a long time she'd begun to wonder if there was something physically wrong with her because she couldn't respond to a man. Slade hadn't so much as kissed her, but she'd experienced a closeness to him that she hadn't felt with all the men she'd dated in San Francisco. Without even realizing it, he had granted her the priceless gift of expectancy. If he was capable of stirring her restless heart, then so would another.

Humming softly, she set a skillet on the burner and laid thick slices of bacon across it. This was the day before Christmas, and it promised to be a full one. She couldn't be sad or filled with regrets when she was surrounded by everything she held dear.

The door opened again, and her father called cheerfully, "Well, he's off."

"Good." She hoped her tone didn't give away her feelings.

"He's an interesting man. I wouldn't mind having someone like him for a son-in-law." He entered the kitchen and reached for the coffeepot.

"He's engaged."

He sighed, and there was a hint of censure in his voice when he spoke. "That figures. The good ones always seem to be spoken for."

"It doesn't matter. We're about as different as any two people can be."

"That's not always bad, you know. Couples often complement each other that way. Your mother was the shy one, whereas I was far more outgoing. Our lives would have been havoc if we'd had identical personalities."

Silently Shelly agreed, but to admit as much would reveal more than she wanted to. "I suppose," she murmured softly, and turned over the sizzling slices of bacon.

A few minutes later she was sliding the eggs easily from the hot grease onto plates when there was a loud pounding on the front door.

Her gaze rose instantly and met her father's.

"Slade," they said simultaneously.

Her father rushed to answer the door, and a breathless Slade stumbled into the house. She turned off the stove and hurried out to meet him.

"Are you all right?" Her voice was laced with concern. Heart pounding, she looked him over for any obvious signs of injury.

"I'm fine. I'm just out of breath. That was quite a hike."

"How far'd you get?" Don asked.

"A mile at the most. I was gathering speed to make it to the top of an incline when the wheels skidded on a patch of ice. The car, unfortunately, is in a ditch."

"What about your meeting?" Now that she'd determined that he was unscathed, her first concern was the appointment that he considered so important to his future.

"I don't know."

"Dad and I could take you into town," she offered.

"No. If I couldn't make it, you won't be able to, either."

"But you said this meeting is vital."

"It's not important enough to risk your getting hurt."

"Not to mention my truck has been acting up, so I took it in for servicing," her father said, then smiled. "But there's always the tractor."

"Dad! You'll be lucky if the old engine so much as coughs. You haven't used that antique in years." As far as she knew, it was collecting dust in the back of the barn.

"It's worth a try," her father argued, looking to Slade. "At least we can pull your car out of the ditch."

"I'll contact the county road department and find out how long it'll be before the plows come this way," Shelly said. She didn't hold much hope for the tractor, but if she could convince the county how important it was to clear the roads near their place, Slade might be able to make his meeting somehow.

Two hours later, Shelly was dressed in dark cords and a thick cable-knit sweater the color of winter wheat as she paced the living room carpet. Every few minutes she paused to glance out the large front window for signs of either her father or Slade. Through some miracle they'd managed to fire up the tractor, but how much they could accomplish with the old machine was pure conjecture. If they were able to rescue Slade's car from the ditch, then there was always the possibility of towing it up the incline so he could try again to make it into the city.

The sound of a car pulling into the driveway captured her attention, and she rushed onto the front porch just as Slade was easing the Taurus to a stop. He climbed out of the vehicle.

"I called the county. The road crew will try to make it out this way before nightfall," she told him, rubbing her palms together to ward off the chill. "I'm sorry, Slade, it's the best they could do."

"Don't worry." His gaze caressed her. "It's not your fault."

"But I can't help feeling that it is," she said, following him into the house. "I was the one who insisted you bring me here."

"Shelly." He cupped her shoulder with a warm hand. "Stop blaming yourself. I'll contact Walt Bauer, the man I was planning to see. He'll understand. It's possible he didn't make it to the office, either."

Granting him the privacy he needed to make his

call, she donned her coat and walked to the end of the driveway to see if she could locate her father. Only a couple of minutes passed before she saw him proudly steering the tractor, his back and head held regally, like a benevolent king surveying all he owned.

Laughing, she waved.

He pulled to a stop alongside her. "What's so funny?"

"I can't believe you, sitting on top of a 1948 Harvester like you own the world."

"Don't be silly, serf," he teased.

"We've got a bit of a problem, you know." She realized she shouldn't feel guilty about Slade, but she did.

"If you mean Slade, we talked about this unexpected delay. It might not be as bad as it looks. To his way of thinking, it's best not to appear overeager with this business anyway. A delay may be just the thing to get the other company thinking."

It would be just like Slade to say something like that, she thought. "Maybe."

"At any rate, it won't do him any good to stew about it now. He's stuck with us until the snowplows clear the roads. No one's going to make it to the freeway unless they have a four-wheel drive. It's impossible out there."

"But, Dad, I feel terrible."

"Don't. If Slade's not concerned, then you shouldn't be. Besides, I've got a job for you two."

Shelly didn't like the sound of that. "What?"

"We aren't going to be able to go out and buy a Christmas tree."

She hadn't thought of that. "We'll survive without one." But Christmas wouldn't be the same.

"There's no need to. Not when we've got a good ten

acres of fir and pine. I want the two of you to go out and chop one down like we used to do in the good old days."

It didn't take much to realize her father's game. He was looking for excuses to get her together with Slade.

"What's this, an extra Christmas present?" she teased.

"Nonsense. Being out in the cold would only irritate my rheumatism."

"What rheumatism?"

"The one in my old bones."

She hesitated. "What did Slade have to say about this?"

"He's agreeable."

"He is?"

"Think about it, Shortcake. He's stuck here. He wants to make the best of the situation."

It wasn't until they were back at the house and Slade had changed into borrowed jeans and a flannel shirt, along with a pair of heavy boots, that she truly believed he'd fallen in with her father's scheme.

"You don't have to do this, you know," she told him on the way to the barn.

"Did you think I was going to let you traipse into the woods alone?"

"I could."

"No doubt, but there isn't any reason why you *should*. Not when I'm here."

She brought out the old sled from a storage room in the rear of the barn, wiping away the thin layer of dust with her gloves.

He located a saw, and she eyed him warily.

"What's wrong now?"

"The saw."

"What's the matter with it?" He tested the sharpness by carefully running his thumb over the jagged teeth and raised questioning eyes to her.

"Nothing. If we use that rusty old thing, we shouldn't have any trouble bringing home a good-sized rhododendron."

"I wasn't planning to chop down a California redwood."

"But I want something a bit larger than a poinsettia." She grabbed an axe and headed for the door.

He paused, then followed her out of the barn. "Are you always this difficult to get along with?"

Dragging the sled along behind her in the snow, she turned and said, "There's nothing wrong with me. It's you."

"Right," he growled.

Shelly realized that she was acting like a shrew, but her behavior was a defense mechanism against the attraction she felt for Slade. If he was irritated with her, it would be easier for her to control her own feelings for him.

"If my presence is such an annoyance to you, I can walk into town."

"Don't be silly."

"She crabs at me about cutting down rhododendrons and *I'm* silly?" He appeared to be speaking to the sky.

Plowing through the snow, Shelly refused to look back. She started determinedly up a small incline toward the woods. "I just want you to know I can do this on my own."

He laid his hand on her shoulder, stopping her in her tracks. "Shelly, listen to me, would you?"

She hesitated, her gaze falling on the long line of trees ahead. "What now?"

"I like the prospect of finding a Christmas tree with you, but if you find my company so unpleasant, I'll go back to the house."

"That's not it," she murmured, feeling ridiculous. "I have fun when I'm with you."

"Then why are we arguing?"

Against her will she smiled. "I don't know," she admitted.

"Friends?" He offered her his gloved hand.

She clasped it in her own and nodded wordlessly at him.

"Now that we've got that out of the way, just how big a tree were you thinking of?"

"*Big.*"

"Obviously. But remember, it's got to fit inside the house, so that sixty-foot fir straight ahead is out."

"But the top six feet isn't," she teased.

Chuckling, Slade draped his arm across her shoulder. "Yes, it is."

They were still within sight of the house. "Don't worry. I don't want to cut down something obvious."

"How do you mean?"

"In years to come, I don't want to look out the back window and see a hole in the landscape."

"Don't be ridiculous. You've got a whole forest back here."

"I want to go a bit deeper into the woods."

"Listen, Shortcake, I'm not Lewis and Clark."

Shelly paused. "What did you call me?"

"Shortcake. It fits."

"How's that?"

His gaze roamed over her, his eyes narrowing as he studied her full mouth. It took every ounce of control, but she managed not to moisten her lips. A tingling sensation attacked her stomach, and she lowered her gaze. The hesitation lasted no longer than a heartbeat.

His breath hissed through his teeth before he asked, "How about this tree?" He pointed to a small fir that barely reached his waist.

She couldn't keep from laughing. "It should be illegal to cut down anything that small."

"Do you have a better suggestion?"

"Yes."

"What?"

"That tree over there." She marched ahead, pointing out a seven-foot pine.

"You're being ridiculous. We wouldn't be able to get that one through the front door."

"Of course we'd need to trim it."

"Like in half," he mocked.

She refused to be dissuaded. "Don't be a spoilsport."

"Forget it. This tree would be a nice compromise." He indicated another small tree that was only slightly bigger than the first one he'd chosen.

Without hesitating, she reached down and packed a thick ball of snow. "I'm not willing to compromise my beliefs."

He turned to her, exasperation written all over his features, and she let him have it with the snowball. The accuracy of her toss astonished her, and she cried out with a mixture of surprise and delight when the snowball slammed against his chest, spraying snow in his face.

His reaction was so speedy that she had no time to

run before he was only inches away. "Slade, I'm sorry," she said, taking a giant step backward. "I don't know what came over me. I didn't mean to hit you. Actually, I was aiming at that bush behind you. Honest."

For every step she retreated, he advanced, packing a snowball between his gloved hands.

"Slade, you wouldn't," she implored him, arms wide in surrender.

"Yes, I would."

"No!" she cried, and turned, running for all she was worth. He overtook her almost immediately, grabbing her shoulder and turning her to face him. She stumbled, and they went crashing together to the snow-covered ground.

His heavy body pressed her deeper into the snow. "Are you all right?" he asked urgently, fear and concern evident in the tone of his voice as he tenderly pushed the hair from her face.

"Yes," she murmured, breathless. But her lack of air couldn't be attributed to the fall. Having Slade this close, his warm breath fanning her face, was responsible for that. Even through their thick coats she could feel the pounding rhythm of his heart echoing hers.

"Shelly." He ground out her name like a man driven to the brink of insanity. Slowly he slanted his mouth over hers, claiming her lips in a kiss that rocked the very core of her being. In seconds they were both panting and nearly breathless.

Her arms locked around his neck, and she arched against him, wanting the kiss to go on and on.

"Shelly…" he said again as his hands closed around her wrists, pulling free of her embrace. He sat up with his back to her. All she could see was the uneven rise and fall of his shoulders as he dragged in air.

"Don't worry," she breathed in a voice so weak that it trembled. "I won't tell Margaret."

Six

"That shouldn't have happened," Slade said at last.

"I suppose you want an apology," Shelly responded, standing and brushing the snow from her pants. In spite of her efforts to appear normal, her hands trembled and her pulse continued to hammer away madly. From the beginning she'd known that his kiss would have this effect on her, and she cursed her traitorous heart.

He stared, clearly shocked that she would suggest such a thing. "*I* should be the one to apologize to *you*."

"Why? Because you kissed me?"

"And because I'm engaged."

"I know." Her voice rose several decibels. "What's in a kiss, anyway? It wasn't a big deal. Right?" *Liar,* her heart accused, continuing to beat erratically. It had been the sweetest, most wonderful kiss of her life. One that would haunt her forever.

"It won't happen again," he said without looking at her. He rose and held himself stiffly, staying a good two feet away from her. His facade slipped tightly into place, locking his expression right before her eyes. She was reminded of the man she'd first seen on the plane—

that polished, impeccable businessman who looked at the world with undisguised indifference.

"As I said, it wasn't a big deal."

"Right," he answered. Her dismissive attitude toward his kiss didn't appear to please him. He stalked in the direction of the trees and stopped at the one he'd offered as a compromise. Without soliciting her opinion, he began sawing away at its narrow trunk.

Within minutes the tree toppled to the ground, stirring up the snow. She walked over, prepared to help him load the small fir onto the sled, but he wouldn't let her.

"I'll do it," he muttered gruffly.

Offended, she folded her arms and stepped back, feeling awkward. She knew she would feel better if they could discuss the kiss openly and honestly.

"I knew it was going to happen." She'd been wanting him to kiss her all morning, in fact.

"What?" he barked, heading in the direction of the house, tugging the sled and Christmas tree behind him.

"The kiss," she called after him. "And if I was honest, I'd also admit that I wanted it to happen. I was even hoping it would."

"If you don't mind, I'd rather not talk about it."

He was making her angrier every time he opened his mouth. "I said *if* I was being honest, but since neither of us is, then apparently you're right to suggest we drop the issue entirely."

This time he ignored her, taking long strides and forcing her into a clumsy jog behind him. The north wind whipped her scarf across her mouth, and she tucked it more securely around her neck. Then she turned and walked backward, so the bitter wind stopped buffeting her face.

Unexpectedly her boot hit a small rock hidden under the snow, and she momentarily lost her balance. Flinging her arms out in an effort to catch herself, she went tumbling down the hill, somersaulting head over heels until she lay spread-eagled at the base of the slope.

Slade raced after her, falling to his knees at her side, his eyes clouded with emotion. "Do you have to make a game out of everything?"

What was he talking about? She'd nearly killed herself, and he was accusing her of acrobatics in the snow. She struggled to give him a sassy comeback, but the wind had been knocked from her lungs and she discovered that she couldn't speak.

"Are you all right?" He looked genuinely concerned.

"I don't know," she whispered tightly. Getting the appropriate amount of oxygen to her lungs seemed to require all her energy.

"Don't move."

"I couldn't if I wanted to."

"Where does it hurt?"

"'Where doesn't it?' would be a more fitting question." Then, giving the lie to her previous answer, she levered herself up on one elbow and wiggled her legs. "I do this now and then so I can appreciate how good it feels to breathe," she muttered sarcastically.

"I said don't move," Slade barked. "You could've seriously injured something."

"I did," she admitted. "My pride." She got slowly to her feet, then bowed mockingly before him and said, "Stay tuned for my next trick when I'll single-handedly leap tall buildings and alter the course of the mighty Columbia River."

"You're not funny."

"There goes my career in comedy, then."

"Here." He tucked a hand under her elbow. "Let me help you back to the house."

"This may come as a shock to you, but I'm perfectly capable of walking on my own."

"Nothing you do anymore could shock me."

"That sounds amazingly like a challenge."

His indifference visibly melted away as he stared down at her with warm, vulnerable eyes. "Trust me, it isn't." He claimed her hand, lacing his fingers with hers. "Come on, your father's probably getting worried."

Shelly sincerely doubted it. What Slade was really saying was that things would be safer for them both back at the house. Temptation could more easily be kept at bay with someone else present.

He let go of her hand and placed his palm at the small of her back, and they continued their short sojourn across the snowy landscape.

The house looked amazingly still and dark as they approached. Only a whisper of smoke drifted into the clear sky from the chimney, as though the fire had been allowed to die. She had expected to hear Andy Williams crooning from the stereo and perhaps smell the lingering scent of freshly popped popcorn.

Instead, they were greeted by an empty, almost eerie silence.

While Slade leaned the tree against the side of the house, she ventured inside. A note propped against the sugar bowl in the middle of the kitchen table commanded her attention. She walked into the room and picked it up.

Sick horse at the Adlers' place. Ted W came for
me and will bring me home. Call if you need me.
Love,
Dad.

She swallowed tightly, clenching the paper in her
hand as the back door shut.

"Dad got called out to a neighbor's. Sick horse," she
announced without turning around. "Would you like a
cup of coffee? The pot's full, although it doesn't look
too fresh. Dad must have put it on before he left. He
knew how cold we'd be when we got back." She realized she was babbling and immediately stopped. Without waiting for his response, she reached for two mugs.

"Coffee sounds fine." His voice was heavy with
dread. The same dread she felt pressing against her
heart. Her father was the buffer they needed, and now
he was gone.

She heard Slade drag out a kitchen chair, and she
placed the mug in front of him. Her thick lashes fanned
downward as she avoided his gaze.

Reluctantly she pulled out the chair opposite his and
joined him at the table. "I suppose we should put up
the tree."

He paused, then said, "We could."

From all the enthusiasm he displayed, they could
have been discussing income taxes. Her heart ached,
and she felt embarrassed for having made the suggestion. No doubt Margaret had her tree flocked and decorated without ever involving Slade.

Her hands tightened around the mug, the heat burning the sensitive skin of her palms.

"Well?" he prompted.

"I think I'll wait until Dad's back. We—every year since Mom died, we've done it together. It's a fun time." The walls of the kitchen seemed to be closing in on them. With every breath she drew, she became more aware of the man sitting across from her. They'd tried to pretend, but the kiss had changed everything. The taste of him lingered on her lips, and unconsciously she ran her tongue over them, wanting to recapture that sensation before it disappeared forever.

His eyes followed her movement, and he abruptly stood and marched across the kitchen to place his half-full mug in the sink.

"I'll see to the fire," he offered, hastily leaving the room.

"Thank you."

After emptying her own mug in the sink, she joined him, standing in the archway between the kitchen and living room.

She watched as he placed a small log in the red coals, and in moments flames were sizzling over the dry bark. Soon the fire crackled and hissed, hungry flames attacking the fresh supply of wood. Ol' Dan got slowly off the couch where he'd been sleeping and lay down in front of the fire with a comfortable sigh.

"I wonder what's happening with the road crew," Slade said.

"They could be here anytime."

They turned simultaneously toward the phone and collided. She felt the full impact of the unexpected contact, and her breath caught somewhere between her lungs and her throat, but not from pain.

"Shelly." His arms went around her faster than a shooting star. "Did I hurt you?"

One hand was trapped against his broad chest, while the other hung loosely at her side. "I'm fine," she managed, her voice as unsteady as his. Still, he didn't release her.

Savoring his nearness and warmth, she closed her eyes and pressed her head to his chest, listening to the beat of his heart beneath her ear.

Slade went utterly still, and then his arms tightened around her and he groaned her name.

Could anything that felt this wonderful, this good, be wrong? Shelly knew the answer, and her head buzzed with a warning. Even though her eyes were closed, she could see flashing red lights. Slade had held and kissed her only once, and he had instantly regretted it. He'd even refused to talk about it, closing himself off from her. This couldn't end well.

Yet all the logical arguments melted away like snow in a spring thaw when she was in his arms. His lips moved to her hair, and he breathed in deeply, as though to capture her scent.

"Shelly," he pleaded, his voice husky with emotion. "Tell me to stop."

The words wouldn't form. She knew that she should break away and save them both the agony of guilt. But she couldn't.

"I want you to hold me," she whispered. "Just hold me."

His arms tightened even further, anchoring her against him, and his lips nuzzled her ear, shooting tingles of pleasure down her spine. From her ear he found her cheek, her hair. For an eternity he hesitated.

The phone rang and they broke apart with a suddenness that made her lose her balance. Slade's hand on her shoulder steadied her. Brushing the hair from her face, she drew a steadying breath and picked up the phone.

"Hello." Her voice was barely above a whisper.

"Shelly? Are you all right? You don't sound like yourself."

"Oh, hi, Dad." She glanced up guiltily at Slade. His returning look was heavy with his own unhappiness. He brushed a hand through his hair and walked to the picture window, and she returned her attention to the call. "We got the tree."

"That's good." Her father paused. "Are you sure everything's fine?"

"Of course I'm sure," she answered, somewhat defensively. "How are things at the Adlers'?"

"Not good. I may be here awhile. I'm sorry to be away from you, but Slade's there to keep you company."

"How…long will you be?"

"A couple of hours, three at the most. You and Slade will be all right, won't you?"

But her father didn't sound any more convinced than she felt when she replied, "Oh, sure."

She replaced the receiver. Without the call as a buffer, the air in the room seemed to vibrate with Slade's presence. He turned around and met her gaze. "I've got to get to Seattle. Bauer said he's going to be at the office late anyway, finishing up some things so he can enjoy Christmas without work hanging over his head. I've really got to get there."

What he was really saying was that he had to get away from her. "I know," she told him. "But how?"

"How'd your dad get to that sick horse?"

"The Adlers' neighbor, Ted Wilkens, has a pickup with a plow blade. He came for Dad."

"Would it be possible for him to take me into Seattle?"

Shelly hadn't thought of that. "I'm not sure. I'll call."

"Although…it's Christmas Eve." He sounded hesitant, so different from the man she'd overheard on the phone yesterday, the man who hadn't cared about setting up a meeting for Christmas Eve.

"They're good people," she said, reaching for the phone. Slade paced nearby while she talked to Connie Wilkens.

"Well?" He studied her expectantly as she hung up the phone.

"Ted's out helping someone else, but Connie thinks he'll be back before dark. She suggested that we head their way, and by the time we arrive, Ted should be home."

"You're sure he won't mind?"

"Positive. Ted and Connie are always happy to help out their friends."

"They really are good people—like you and your dad," he murmured softly.

She laced her fingers together in front of her. "We're neighbors, although they're a good four miles from here. And friends." She scooted down in front of Ol' Dan and petted him in long, soothing strokes. "I told Connie that we'd start out soon."

Slade's brow furrowed as her words sank in. "But how? The tractor?"

"I couldn't run that thing if my life depended on it."

"Shelly, we can't trek that distance on foot."

"I wasn't thinking of walking."

"What other way is there?"

A smile graced her soft features until it touched her eyes, which sparkled with mischief. "We can always take the horses."

Seven

"You have to be kidding!" Slade gave her a look of pure disbelief.

"No," Shelly insisted, swallowing a laugh. "It's the only possible way I know to get there. We can go up through the woods, where the snow isn't as deep."

Rubbing a hand over his eyes, Slade stalked to the far side of the room, made an abrupt about-face and returned to his former position. "I don't know. You seem to view life as one big adventure after another. I'm not used to…"

"Pokey's as gentle as a lamb," she murmured coaxingly.

"Pokey?"

"Unless you'd rather ride Midnight."

"Good grief, no. Pokey sounds more my speed."

Doing her best to hold back a devilish grin, she led the way into the kitchen.

"What are you doing now?"

"Making us a thermos of hot chocolate."

"Why?"

"I thought we'd stop and have a picnic along the way."

"You're doing it again," he murmured, but she noticed that an indulgent smile lurked just behind his intense dark eyes. He was a man who needed a little fun in his life, and she was determined to provide it. If she was only allowed to touch his life briefly, then she wanted to bring laughter and sunshine with her. Margaret would have him forever. But these few hours were hers, and she was determined to make the most of them.

"It'll be fun," she declared enthusiastically.

"No doubt Custer said the same thing to his men," he grumbled as they put their coats and boots back on, and he followed her out to the barn.

"Cynic," she teased, holding the barn door for him.

Reluctantly he preceded her inside.

"How do you feel about a lazy stroll in the snow, Pokey?" she asked as she reached the Appaloosa's stall and petted the horse's nose. "I know Sampson's ready anytime."

"Don't let her kid you, Pokey," Slade added from behind her. "Good grief, now you've got *me* doing it."

"Doing what?"

"Talking to the animals."

"Animals often share human characteristics," she said. "It's only natural for people to express their feelings to the animals that share their lives."

"In which case we're in trouble. Pokey is going to have a lot to say about how I feel when I climb on her back."

"You'll be fine."

"Sure, but will Pokey?"

"You both will. Now stop worrying."

When Shelly brought out the tack, Slade just stared at her, hands buried deep in his pockets, but then he stepped up and did what he could to help her saddle the two horses. Mostly he circled her awkwardly, looking doubtful.

When she'd finished, she led the horses out of the barn. Holding on to both sets of reins, she motioned for him to mount first. "Do you need any help?" she asked. He looked so different from the staid executive she'd met in Portland that she had trouble remembering that he really was the same person. The man facing her now was clearly out of his element, nothing like the unflappable man on the airplane.

"I don't think so," he said, reaching for the saddle and trying to follow Shelly's directions. Without much difficulty he swung himself onto Pokey's back. The horse barely stirred.

Looking pleased with himself, he smiled down at Shelly. "I suppose you told her to be gentle with me."

"I did," she teased in return. Double-checking the cinch, she asked, "Do you need me to adjust the stirrups or anything?"

"No." He shifted his weight slightly and accepted the reins she handed him. "I'm ready anytime you are."

She mounted with an ease that spoke of years in the saddle. "It's going to be a cold ride until we get under the cover of the trees. Follow me."

"Anywhere."

She was sure she must have misheard him. "What did you say?" she asked, twisting around in the saddle.

"Nothing." But he was grinning, and she found him so devastatingly appealing that it demanded all her willpower to turn around and lead the way.

They quickly reached the path that took them through the woods. Gusts of swift wind blew the snow from the trees. The swirling flakes were nearly as bad as the storm had been. Even Pokey protested at having to be outside.

"Shelly," Slade said, edging the Appaloosa to Sampson's side. "This may not have been the most brilliant idea. Maybe we should head back."

"Don't be ridiculous."

"I don't want you catching cold on my account."

"I'm as snug as a bug in a rug," she said, using one of her father's favorite expressions.

"Liar," he purred softly.

"I want you to have something to remember me by." She realized she must sound like some lovesick romantic. He would be gone soon, and she had to accept that she probably would never see him again.

"Like what? Frostbite?"

She laughed. The musical sound was carried by the wind and seemed to echo in the trees around them. "How can you complain? This is wonderful. Riding along like this makes me want to sing."

He grumbled something unintelligible under his breath.

"What are you complaining about now?"

"Who says I'm complaining?"

She grinned, her head bobbing slightly with the gentle sway of Sampson's gait. "I'm beginning to know you."

"All right, if you insist on knowing, I happen to be humming. My enthusiasm for this venture doesn't compel me to burst into song. But I'm doing the best I can."

Holding an unexpectedly contented feeling to her

heart, she tried not to think about what would happen when they reached the Wilkens place. She was prepared to smile at him and bid him farewell, freely sending him out of her life. But that would have been easier before he'd held her in his arms and she'd experienced the gentle persuasion of his kiss. So very much easier.

Together, their horses side by side, they ambled along, not speaking but singing Christmas songs one after the other until they were breathless and giddy. Their voices blended magically in two-part harmony. More than once they shared a lingering gaze. But Shelly felt her high spirits evaporating as they neared the landmark that marked the half-way point of their journey.

"My backside is ready for a break," Slade announced unexpectedly.

"You aren't nearly as anxious to scoff at my picnic idea now, are you?" she returned.

"Not when I'm discovering on what part of their anatomy cowboys get calluses." A grin curved his sensuous mouth.

They paused in a small clearing, looping the horses' reins around the trunk of a nearby fir tree.

While she took the hot chocolate and some homemade cookies from her saddlebags, he exercised his stiff legs, walking around as though he were on stilts.

"We'll have to share the cup," she announced, holding out the plastic top of the thermos. She stood between the two horses, munching on a large oatmeal cookie.

Slade lifted the cup to his lips and hesitated as their eyes met. He paused, slowly lowering the cup without breaking eye contact.

Her breath came in shallow gasps. "Is something wrong?" she asked with difficulty.

"You're lovely."

"Sure." She forced a laugh. "My nose looks like a maraschino cherry and—"

"Don't joke, Shelly. I mean it." His voice was gruff, almost harsh.

"Then thank you."

He removed his glove and placed his warm hand on her cold face, cupping her cheek. The moment was almost unbearably tender, and she swallowed the surging emotion that clogged her throat. It would be the easiest thing in the world to walk into his arms, lose herself in his kiss and love him the way he deserved to be loved.

As if reading her thoughts, Sampson shifted, bumping her back and delivering her into Slade's arms. He dropped the hot chocolate and hauled her against him like a man in desperate need.

"I told myself this wouldn't happen again," he whispered against her hair. "Every time I hold you, it becomes harder to let you go."

Her heart gave a small leap of pleasure at his words. She didn't want him to let her go. Not ever. Everything felt right between them. Too right and too good.

How long he held her, Shelly didn't know. Far longer than was necessary and not nearly long enough. Each second seemed to stretch, sustaining her tender heart for the moment when she would have to bid him farewell.

Not until they broke apart did she notice that it was snowing again. Huge crystalline flakes filled the sky with their icy purity.

"What should we do?" he asked, looking doubtful.

Her first instinct was to suggest that they return to the house, but she hesitated. The thought of their inevitable goodbye became more difficult to bear every minute.

"We're going back," he said, answering his own question.

"Why?"

"I'm not leaving you and your father to deal with the horses. It's bad enough that I dragged you this far." Placing his foot in the stirrup, he reached for the saddle and remounted. "Come on, before this snow gets any worse."

"But we can make it to the Wilkens place."

"Not now." He raised his eyes skyward and scowled. "It's already getting dark."

Grumbling, she repacked her saddlebags, tugged Sampson's reins free of the tree trunk and lifted her body onto his back with the agile grace of a ballerina.

The house was in sight when Slade finally spoke again. "Once we get back, I need to contact Margaret. She'll be waiting. I told her I'd call Christmas Eve."

Shelly's heart constricted at the mention of the other woman's name. Until now, unless she'd asked about Margaret, Slade hadn't volunteered any information about his fiancée. Now he had freely thrust her between them.

"She's a good woman," he said when Shelly stayed silent.

She didn't know who he was trying to convince. "I didn't think you'd love a woman who wasn't."

"I've known Margaret a lot of years."

"Of course you have." And he'd only known *her* a few days. She understood what he was saying. It was almost as if he were apologizing because Margaret had

prior claim to his loyalties and his heart. He didn't need
to. She'd accepted that from the beginning.

When they left the cover of the woods, she spoke,
managing to keep her voice level and unemotional.
"You'll never get a cell signal way out here, not in this
weather. You go in and use the phone," she said, surprised that her voice could remain so even. "I'll take
care of the horses so you can make your call in private,
and I'll call the Wilkenses when I'm done."

"I won't talk long."

"Don't cut the conversation short on my account."

He wiped his forearm across his brow. The movement brought her attention to the confusion in his eyes.
"I won't."

By then they were at the barn, where she dismounted
slowly, lowering both booted feet to the ground. He did
the same, but she avoided his gaze as she opened the
barn door and led the horses through. The wind followed her inside the dimly lit building. The cold nipped
at her heels.

With a heavy heart she lifted the saddle from Pokey's back before she noticed Slade's dark form blocking
the doorway. Her hands tightened around the smooth
leather. "Is there a problem?"

"No."

After cross-tying Pokey in the aisle, Shelly turned
back to Slade, only to find that he'd left.

Taking extra time with the horses, she put off entering the house as long as possible. Removing the gloves
from her hands one finger at a time, she walked in the
back door to discover Slade sitting in the living room
staring blindly into the roaring fire. She walked quickly
to the phone and called the Wilkenses. Connie was glad

to hear from her and admitted that after a full day driving neighbors around in the snow, Ted was exhausted.

"I don't know about you," she called out cheerfully after hanging up the phone, "but I'm starved." The tip of her tongue burned with questions that pride refused to let her ask. She was dying to know what Slade had said to Margaret, if anything, about his current circumstances. "How about popcorn with lots of melted butter?"

He joined her, a smile lurking at the edges of his full mouth. His eyes were laughing, revealing his thoughts. He really did have wonderful eyes, and for a moment Shelly couldn't look away.

"I was thinking of something more like a triple-decker sandwich," he admitted.

"You know what your problem is, Garner?" It was obvious he didn't, so she took it upon herself to tell him. "No imagination."

"Because I prefer something meatier than popcorn?"

She pretended not to hear him— easy to do with her head buried in the open refrigerator. Without comment she brought out a variety of fixings and placed them on the tabletop.

She peeled off a slice of deli ham, tore it in two and gave Slade half. "How about a compromise?"

He looked dubious, as if he were sure she was about to suggest a popcorn sandwich. "I don't know…"

"How about if you bring in the tree while I fix us something to eat?"

"That's an offer I can't refuse."

Singing softly as she worked, Shelly concocted a meal neither of them was likely to forget. Sandwiches piled high with three different kinds of meat, sliced dill pickles and juicy green olives. In addition, she set out Christmas cookies and thick slices of fudge that she found sitting around the kitchen.

Slade set the tree in the holder, dragged it through the front door and stood it in the corner. "The snow's stopped," he told her when she carried in their meal.

"That's encouraging. I was beginning to think we'd be forced to stay until the spring thaw." Of course, she wouldn't have minded, and her smile was wistful.

Sitting Indian-style in front of the fireplace, their backs resting against the sofa, they dug into the sandwiches. But she found herself giving most of hers to Ol' Dan, having discovered that she had little appetite. Never had she been more aware of a man. They were so close that, when she lowered her sandwich to the plate, her upper arm brushed against his. But neither one of them made any effort to move, and she found that the contact, although impersonal, was soothing. She paused, trying to capture this moment of peacefulness.

"This has been a good day," he murmured, his gaze following hers as he stared out the living room window.

"It's certainly been crazy."

Without replying immediately, he reached for her hand, entwining their fingers. "I don't know when I've enjoyed a day more." His dark gaze flickered over her and rested on her mouth. Abruptly he glanced away, his attention on the piano at the far side of the room. "Do you play?"

She sighed expressively. "A little. Dad claimed that my playing was what kept the mice out of the house."

He raised one dark brow with a touch of amusement. "That bad?"

"See for yourself." She rose and walked to the piano, lifted the lid of the bench seat and extracted some Christmas music.

When she pressed her fingers to the keys, the discordant notes were enough to make her wince, and cause Ol' Dan to lift his chin and cock his head curiously. He howled once.

"I told you I wasn't any good," she said with another dramatic sigh. Staring at the music, she squinted and sadly shook her head.

Slade joined her. Standing directly behind her, he laid his hands on her shoulders, leaning over to study the music.

"I think I may have found the problem," she stated seriously. Dimples formed in her cheeks as she tried not to smile. Turning the sheet music right side up, she leaned forward to study the notes a second time and tried again. This time a sweet melody flowed through the house.

Chuckling, Slade tightened his hands around her shoulders and spontaneously lowered his mouth to her cheek. "Have I told you how much fun you are?"

"No, but I'll accept that as a compliment."

"Good, because it was meant as one."

She continued to play, hitting a wrong note every once in a while and going back to repeat the bar until she got it right. Soon his rich voice blended with the melody. Her soprano tones mixed smoothly with his, although her playing faltered now and again.

Neither of them heard the front door open. "Merry Christmas Eve," Don announced.

Shelly froze with her hands above the keys and

turned to look at him. "Welcome home. How's the Adlers' horse?"

Her father wiped a weary hand over his face. "She'll make it."

"What about you?" He was clearly exhausted. His pants were caked with mud and grit.

"Give me half an hour and I'll let you know."

"I can make you a sandwich if you're hungry."

"All I want right now is a hot shower." He paused to scratch Ol' Dan's ears. "Keep playing. You two sound good together."

"I thought we were scattering the mice to the barn," Slade teased.

Don scratched the side of his head with his index finger. "Say that again?"

"He's talking about my piano playing," she reminded her father.

"Oh, that. I don't suppose you play?"

"As a matter of fact, I do," Slade admitted.

"You do?" Shelly was stunned. "Why didn't you say something earlier? Here." She slid off the bench. "Trade places."

He claimed her position and ran his large, masculine hands over the keys with a familiarity that caused her heart to flutter. His fingers moved over the keys with reverence. Stroking, enticing the instrument, until the music practically had the room swaying. She felt tears gather in the corner of her eyes. Slade didn't play the piano; he made love to it.

When he'd finished, he rested his hands in his lap and slowly expelled his breath.

She sank into an easy chair. "Why didn't you tell me you could play like that?"

A smile brightened his eyes. "You didn't ask."

Even her father was awestruck and, for the first time in years, at a complete loss for words.

"You could play professionally. You're magnificent." Her soft voice cracked with the potency of her feelings.

"I briefly toyed with the idea at one time."

"Why didn't—"

"I play for enjoyment now." The light dimmed in his eyes, and the sharp edge of his words seemed to say that the decision hadn't come easy. And it clearly was not one he was willing to discuss, even with her.

"Will you play something else?" her father asked, his shower apparently on hold.

Judging by the look he shot her father, Slade appeared to regret admitting that he played the piano. She could tell that music was his real love, and he'd abandoned it. Coming this close again was probably pure torture for him. "Another time, perhaps."

Except that there wouldn't be another time, not for them. "Please," she whispered, rising to stand behind him, then placing her hands on his shoulders in a silent plea.

He covered her hand with his as he looked up into her imploring gaze. "All right, Shelly. For you."

For half an hour he played with such intensity that his shoulders sagged with exhaustion when he'd finished.

"God has given you a rare gift," her father said, his voice husky with appreciation. He glanced down at his mud-caked clothes. "Now, if you'll excuse me, I'll go take that shower before I start attracting flies."

As her father left the room, she moved to Slade's side, sitting on the bench beside him. Unable to find the words to express herself, she simply traced the sculptured line of his jaw as tears blurred her vision. The tightness in her chest made her breathing shallow and difficult.

He lifted a hand and stopped her, then brought her fingers to his lips and gently kissed her palm. She bit her bottom lip to hold back all the emotion stored in her heart.

A lone tear escaped and trickled down her pale cheek. Slade gently brushed it aside, his finger cool against her heated skin. He bent down and found her mouth with his. She realized that, without speaking a word, he was thanking her. With her, he'd allowed his facade to crumble. He'd opened his heart and revealed the deep, sensitive man inside. He was free now, with nothing more to hide.

Wrapping her arms around him, she kissed him in return, telling him in the only way she could how much she appreciated the gift of seeing his true self.

"Merry Christmas, Shortcake," her father greeted her on the tail end of a yawn.

Shelly stood in front of the picture window, cupping her coffee mug. Her gaze rested on the sunrise as it blanketed the morning with the bright hues of another day. She tried to force a smile when she turned to her father, but it refused to come. She felt chilled and empty inside.

"Where's Slade?" he asked.

"The snowplows came during the night," she whispered through the pain. "He's gone."

Eight

"Gone? Without saying goodbye?" A look of disbelief filled her father's eyes.

"He left a note." She withdrew it from her pocket and handed it to him. The message was only a few lines. He thanked them for their hospitality, and wished her and her father much happiness. And then said goodbye. Without regrets. Without second thoughts. Without looking back.

Her father looked up from the note and narrowed his eyes as he studied her. "Are you okay?"

"I'm fine."

He slowly shook his head. "I've never seen you look at a man the way you looked at Slade. You really liked him, didn't you?"

I love him! her heart cried. "He's a wonderful man. I only hope Margaret and that computer firm realize how lucky they are."

"They don't, you know," he whispered, slipping an arm around her shoulders and hugging her close. She offered him a feeble smile in return. "He might come back."

She knew differently. "No." He'd made his choice. His future had been charted and defined as precisely as a road map. Slade Garner was a man of character and strength. He wouldn't abandon Margaret and all that was important to him for a two-day acquaintance and a few stolen kisses. He'd shared his deepest desires and secrets with her, opened his heart and trusted her. She shouldn't wish for more. But she did. She wanted Slade.

Christmas Day passed in a blur. Her brothers and their families were there, and somehow she managed to smile and talk and eat, with no one but her father any the wiser about her real feelings. She flew back to San Francisco the following afternoon, still numb, still aching, but holding her head up high and proud.

Her tiny apartment in the Garden District, although colorful and cheerfully decorated, did little to boost her drooping spirits.

Setting her suitcase on the polished hardwood floor, she kicked off her shoes and reached for the phone.

"Hi, Dad. I'm home." Taking the telephone with her, she sank into the overstuffed chair.

"How was the flight?"

"Went without a hitch."

"Just the way you like it." He chuckled, then grew serious. "I don't suppose...?"

"No, Dad." She knew what he was asking. He had thought that Slade would be in San Francisco waiting for her. She knew better. Slade wouldn't want to think of her. Already he'd banished any thought of her to the furthest corner of his mind. Perhaps what they'd shared was an embarrassment to him now.

She spoke to her father for a few minutes longer, then

claimed exhaustion and said goodbye. After she hung up she sat with the receiver cradled in her lap, staring blindly at the wallpaper.

Starting the next day she worked hard at putting her life back on an even keel. She went to work each day and did her utmost to forget the man who had touched her so profoundly.

Her one resolution for the New Year was simple: Find a man. For the first time since moving to San Francisco, she was lonely. Oh, she had friends and plenty of things to do, but nothing to take away the ache in her soul.

Two days before New Year's Eve, she stepped off the bus and on impulse bought flowers from a vendor on the street corner, then headed inside her building.

The elderly woman who lived across the hall opened her door as Shelly approached. "Good afternoon, Mrs. Lester," she said, pulling a red carnation from the bouquet and handing it to her neighbor.

"Now, isn't that a coincidence." Mrs. Lester chuckled. "I've got flowers for you."

Shelly's heart went still.

"The delivery boy asked me to give them to you." She stepped back inside, then stepped out and handed Shelly a narrow white box. "Roses, I suspect."

"Roses?" Shelly felt the blood drain from her face. She couldn't get inside her apartment fast enough. Closing the door with her foot, she walked across the room and set the box on a table. Inside she discovered a dozen of the most perfect roses she'd ever imagined. Each bud was identical to the others, their color brilliant.

Although she went through the box twice, she found no card. It was foolish to think Slade had sent them. Surely he wouldn't be so cruel as to say goodbye, only to invade her life again. Besides, he'd claimed roses were stupidly expensive, and she couldn't argue with that. They were, especially this time of year.

She was still puzzling over who could have sent them when the doorbell rang. She opened the door, and a deliveryman handed her a second long narrow box, identical to the first.

"Sign here." He offered her his pen.

Shelly scribbled her name across the bottom of the delivery order, then carried the second box to the kitchen table and opened it. Another dozen red roses, and again there was no card.

No sooner had she arranged all twenty-four flowers in her one and only tall vase when the doorbell chimed again. It was a deliveryman from another flower shop with another dozen roses.

"Are you sure you have the right address?" she asked.

"Shelly Griffin?" He read off her street address and apartment number, and raised expectant eyes to her.

"That's me," she conceded.

"Sign here."

She did. And for a third time discovered—with no surprise whatsoever at this point—that there was no card.

Without another vase to hold them, she emptied her tall jar of dill pickles into a bowl, rinsed out the jar and used that. With the first roses already brightening her living room, she left these to grace the kitchen.

Whoever was sending her so many flowers was either very rich or else extremely foolish, she thought.

Hands pressed against her hips, she surveyed the small apartment and couldn't decide if it resembled a flower shop or a funeral parlor.

When the doorbell chimed again, she sighed expressively. "Not again," she groaned aloud, turning the dead bolt and opening the door.

But instead of opening it to yet another delivery, she came face-to-face with Slade. He was so tall, so incredibly good-looking, that her breath became trapped in her lungs.

"Slade."

"Hello, Shelly." His eyes delved into hers, smiling and warm. "Can I come in?"

"Of…of course." Flustered, she stepped aside.

"Do you realize you only have on one shoe?"

"Why are you here?" she demanded. With her hands behind her back, she leaned against the closed front door, desperately wanting to believe everything she dared not even think about.

"I've missed you."

She closed her eyes to the tenderness in his voice. Words had never sounded sweeter. "Did you reschedule your meeting?" When he nodded, she asked, "How did it go?"

"Fine. Better than I expected."

"That's nice." She studied him, still unsure.

"I got a hefty bonus, but I may have offended a few friends."

"How did you do that?"

"They were hoping I'd accept a promotion."

"And you aren't?" A promotion sounded like something Margaret would love.

"No, I resigned this afternoon."

"Resigned? What did…Margaret have to say about that?"

"Well—" He took a step closer, stopping just short

of her but near enough to reach out and touch her if he wanted to. "—Margaret and I aren't exactly on speaking terms."

"Oh?" Her voice went incredibly weak.

"She didn't take kindly to some of my recent decisions."

I'll just bet, Shelly mused. "And what are those decisions...the most recent ones?"

"I decided to postpone the wedding."

She couldn't fault his fiancée for being upset about that. "Well, I can't say that I blame her. When—when's the new date?"

"Never."

"Never?" She swallowed tightly. "Why not?"

"Why not?" He smiled. "Because Margaret doesn't haul sourdough bread on an airplane or look forward to getting a horse blanket for Christmas or laugh at every opportunity or do any of the things that make life fun."

Speechless, she stared at him, love shining from her eyes.

"Nor does she believe I'll ever make a decent living as a pianist," he continued. "Hell, I'm nearly thirty now. It could be too late."

"But...?"

"But—" He smiled and reached for her, bringing her into the loving circle of his arms. "—I'm going to give it one whopper of a try. I'm no prize, Shelly Griffin. I don't have a job, and I'm not even sure the conservatory will renew the offer they made me once upon a time, but for the first time in too many years, I've got a dream."

"Oh, Slade," she whispered and pressed her face to

his broad chest. "I would consider it the greatest honor of my life to be a part of that dream."

"You couldn't help but be," he whispered, lifting her mouth to his. "You're the one who gave it to me."

* * * * *

SHEILA ROBERTS

Cass Wilkes, owner of the Gingerbread Haus bakery in Icicle Falls, was looking forward to her daughter Danielle's holiday wedding. But every B and B is full, and it looks as if Danielle's father, his trophy wife and their yappy little dog will be staying with Cass.

Her friend Charlene Albach has just seen the ghost of Christmas past: her ex-husband, Richard, who ran off a year ago with the hostess from *her* restaurant. Now the hostess is history and he wants to kiss and make up. Hide the mistletoe!

Then there's Ella O'Brien, who's newly divorced but still living with her ex—and still fighting as though they were married. The love is gone. Isn't it?

But Christmas has a way of working its magic. Merry Ex-mas, ladies!

Available wherever books are sold.

MSR1392

REQUEST YOUR FREE BOOKS!

2 FREE NOVELS
FROM THE ROMANCE COLLECTION
PLUS 2 FREE GIFTS!

YES! Please send me 2 FREE novels from the Romance Collection and my 2 FREE gifts (gifts are worth about $10). After receiving them, if I don't wish to receive any more books, I can return the shipping statement marked "cancel." If I don't cancel, I will receive 4 brand-new novels every month and be billed just $5.99 per book in the U.S. or $6.49 per book in Canada. That's a saving of at least 25% off the cover price. It's quite a bargain! Shipping and handling is just 50¢ per book in the U.S. and 75¢ per book in Canada.* I understand that accepting the 2 free books and gifts places me under no obligation to buy anything. I can always return a shipment and cancel at any time. Even if I never buy another book, the two free books and gifts are mine to keep forever.

194/394 MDN FELQ

Name	(PLEASE PRINT)

Address		Apt. #

City	State/Prov.	Zip/Postal Code

Signature (if under 18, a parent or guardian must sign)

Mail to the **Reader Service:**
IN U.S.A.: P.O. Box 1867, Buffalo, NY 14240-1867
IN CANADA: P.O. Box 609, Fort Erie, Ontario L2A 5X3

Not valid for current subscribers to the Romance Collection
or the Romance/Suspense Collection.

Want to try two free books from another line?
Call 1-800-873-8635 or visit www.ReaderService.com.

* Terms and prices subject to change without notice. Prices do not include applicable taxes. Sales tax applicable in N.Y. Canadian residents will be charged applicable taxes. Offer not valid in Quebec. This offer is limited to one order per household. All orders subject to credit approval. Credit or debit balances in a customer's account(s) may be offset by any other outstanding balance owed by or to the customer. Please allow 4 to 6 weeks for delivery. Offer available while quantities last.

Your Privacy—The Reader Service is committed to protecting your privacy. Our Privacy Policy is available online at www.ReaderService.com or upon request from the Reader Service.

We make a portion of our mailing list available to reputable third parties that offer products we believe may interest you. If you prefer that we not exchange your name with third parties, or if you wish to clarify or modify your communication preferences, please visit us at www.ReaderService.com/consumerschoice or write to us at Reader Service Preference Service, P.O. Box 9062, Buffalo, NY 14269. Include your complete name and address.

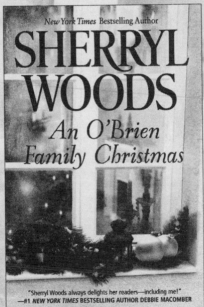

DEBBIE MACOMBER

(limited quantities available)

TOTAL AMOUNT $ _____
POSTAGE & HANDLING $ _____
($1.00 for 1 book, 50¢ for each additional)
APPLICABLE TAXES* $ _____
TOTAL PAYABLE $ _____

(check or money order—please do not send cash)

To order, complete this form and send it, along with a check or money order for the total above, payable to Harlequin MIRA, to: **In the U.S.:** 3010 Walden Avenue, P.O. Box 9077, Buffalo, NY 14269-9077; **In Canada:** P.O. Box 636, Fort Erie, Ontario, L2A 5X3.

Name: _____
Address: _____ City: _____
State/Prov.: _____ Zip/Postal Code: _____
Account Number (if applicable): _____
075 CSAS

*New York residents remit applicable sales taxes.
*Canadian residents remit applicable GST and provincial taxes.

H HARLEQUIN® MIRA®
www.Harlequin.com

MDM1112BL